She followed so close that when he stopped, she walked right into him.

Tom righted her, his hands clasping her arms and automatically pulling her toward him. Heather looked up expectantly, and before he could stop himself—not that he wanted to—his lips were on hers.

Her lips were soft and warm, pliant and giving at the same time. He wanted her closer, but that wasn't even possible. Her arms wound around his neck. In the car, she'd smelled like strawberries. Right now, though, she smelled like the outdoors, crisp October leaves with maybe a hint of rain.

Yes, rain had a scent, and it made him feel more alive than he had in years.

Dear Reader,

Have you ever caught a glimpse of someone ahead of you, sucked in your breath, got all excited and hurried over to say hi only to discover you'd made a mistake. LOL, I have. I've shouted greetings only to get the "who are you?" stare.

They say everyone has a doppelgänger. I just love that word. I heard it first in a movie. It took me two weeks to learn how to spell it (I'm so glad spell-check will put that little thing over the *a*), and it's really, really hard to work into conversations.

Lately, my misidentifications have to do with my dad. He was a WWII vet who passed away over a decade ago. But often I go into a restaurant and there's an eightyish balding man, wearing baggy jeans and a plaid shirt— sometimes suspenders—and even though the face isn't my dad's, it's all I can do not to go over, fall to my knees, touch his face and tell him how much I miss him.

In *The Woman Most Wanted*, Chief Tom Riley sees a woman he thinks he recognizes, one wanted by the police, and one he has a special interest in. Except it's a case of mistaken identity. Though it takes him a while to figure out the truth, in his heart, he knows from the beginning that, indeed, Heather Graves was wanted. By him. Forever.

And in this case, it takes an entire book to get over a first impression because, boy, did he blow their first meeting.

Ain't romance grand?

Thank you so much for reading Harlequin Heartwarming books! If you'd like to know more about me, please visit www.pamelatracy.com. You can also get to know most of the authors at heartwarmingauthors.blogspot.com.

Pamela

HEARTWARMING

The Woman Most Wanted

———

USA TODAY Bestselling Author

Pamela Tracy

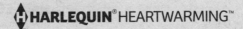 **H HARLEQUIN®** HEARTWARMING™

Recycling programs
for this product may
not exist in your area.

ISBN-13: 978-0-373-36862-4

The Woman Most Wanted

Copyright © 2017 by Pamela Tracy Osback

This edition published by arrangement with Harlequin Books S.A.

For questions and comments about the quality of this book, please contact us at CustomerService@Harlequin.com.

® and TM are trademarks of Harlequin Enterprises Limited or its corporate affiliates. Trademarks indicated with ® are registered in the United States Patent and Trademark Office, the Canadian Intellectual Property Office and in other countries.

Printed in U.S.A.

Pamela Tracy is a *USA TODAY* bestselling author who lives with her husband (the inspiration for most of her heroes) and son (the interference for most of her writing time). Since 1999, she has published more than twenty-five books and sold more than a million copies. She's a RITA® Award finalist and a winner of the American Christian Fiction Writers' Book of the Year Award.

Books by Pamela Tracy

Harlequin Heartwarming

Holding Out for a Hero

The Missing Twin

Love Inspired

The Rancher's Daughters

Finally a Hero
Second Chance Christmas
Arizona Homecoming

Daddy for Keeps
Once Upon a Cowboy
Once Upon a Christmas

Love Inspired Suspense

The Price of Redemption
Broken Lullaby
Fugitive Family
Clandestine Cover-Up

To Daniel Crawford, who looks like me, or maybe I look like him—doesn't matter, we look like each other. Except I'm shorter and wider. Next time I see you we'll do "rock, paper, scissors" to see who's cuter.

I love you, baby brother!

CHAPTER ONE

TRAFFIC ALWAYS MADE Police Chief Tom Riley want to jump out of his SUV and redirect vehicles until every lane ran smoothly. Sitting still, waiting longer than he deemed necessary for his turn to exit, annoyed him. He didn't like it, didn't want it and even his badge could do nothing about it.

Truthfully, his little town of Sarasota Falls seldom required a vehicle to suffer through one rotation from the traffic light. Today, however, was Founder's Day and Tom was idling in front of Sweet Sarasota, the town's bakery, far enough back to know it would take two turns before he got to hang a left.

He had something to do, it was police-related, and he was half-tempted to engage the siren.

The town's hundredth year. Mayor Rick Goodman had gone overboard with marketing the event, at least in Tom's opinion, and for the last few days the town experienced a boon as family, friends and past residents made their way back, all to celebrate.

Tom hadn't participated in the pumpkin-toss competition and he hadn't played horseshoes, although he'd wanted to, but he had ridden the celebration train this morning—as security.

Rah, rah. It had gone a mile down the tracks, turned and ended abruptly.

Tom had also worked late last evening and had personally driven five inebriated people home from the Hoot & Holler. None had been in a police car before. All except him had found it a joyous occasion. They'd even tried to tip him. Then, he'd also changed a flat, found a lost kid and received a proposal of marriage.

He hadn't minded the flat. He hadn't minded finding the lost kid, who'd just taken off with a family member who'd been more than surprised because she insisted she'd informed the family of who was going where and when. But Tom had been somewhat taken aback by the marriage proposal, which came from a woman more than forty years his senior. She'd been at the front-desk area at ten last night, holding a bag of the town's finest chocolate chip cookies and wanting to thank the police for the good job they were doing.

He'd honestly told her it was the best offer he'd had all day, but, unfortunately, he wasn't looking for the next Mrs. Riley. What he didn't tell her was that his heart still had a hole in the center from the ex–Mrs. Riley.

Eighty-three-year-old Helen Williams had slipped her phone number in his hand and said should he ever make it to Arizona to give her a call.

He had a gut feeling she'd been at the Hoot & Holler, too. He'd taken a cookie and thanked her. Then, he'd followed her out the door, grateful, and watched her walk one block to a small motel.

He'd finished up his paperwork and gone home, and now at four the next afternoon, he was back on duty. Man, he'd be glad when Founder's Day festivities ended. He much preferred tourists to people he shared a history with.

At least a dozen had asked about his ex-wife.

Two hadn't known about Max's death. He'd given them the condensed version. Partner killed in the line of duty; when they buried Max, Tom buried himself in work. The next thing he knew his house was empty and his wife gone.

Everyone agreed it was bad.

Didn't matter. Tom finally got the green light, turned left and twenty minutes later was on the outskirts of town, where houses were few and traffic nonexistent. Most of the people who lived out here just liked open spaces. Some, however, lived in the middle of nowhere so they'd not be observed.

Case in point: Richard Welborn, who'd been arrested not quite a year ago and had taken off before his court date, leaving his mother alone in a rental house she could barely afford. She claimed she didn't know where Richie was. But Tom knew she got checks from Richie.

Welborn needed to own up to his responsibility for driving drunk and putting an elderly woman in the hospital. She'd been through months of physical therapy and now almost a year of pain.

Tom drove by the Welborn house a few times a month, even though Richie's mother shot him dirty looks and the sight of the house brought back memories he'd prefer to keep at bay.

He willed Welborn to show up so he could

arrest him and never have to drive to this particular address again.

This time, being out on bond wouldn't be an option.

To Tom's annoyance, even this fairly remote section of Sarasota Falls had traffic.

The woman in the white Chevy ahead of him had Arizona plates. Maybe a relative of Helen Williams? Even from behind he could tell the driver was under thirty, with long blond hair. Something niggled at his subconscious, but Helen—who'd been friends with Tom's grandmother—didn't have children, so that guess seemed unlikely. Tom gave his head a shake. During the past few days, with so many out-of-towners, he'd paid close attention, driven by the motels and through neighborhoods, keeping his town safe.

Little Miss Sunshine blocked his way and needed to either speed up or pull over. He had more things to do before he could head home, and thanks to an unexpected speeding ticket he'd given out as he headed this way, he was now running behind.

He might get even further behind because something about the woman in the car tugged at his memory: might be the hair color, the shape of her head, or a gut feeling. Something.

He needed to pull this woman over.

Problem was, she wasn't doing anything wrong.

Tags up to date: check. Speed limit observed: check. Tom looked at the time on his dashboard. Not even five. The Hoot & Holler didn't get rowdy until about ten or eleven most nights, so she probably hadn't just left. Then again, Founder's Day changed everything. His officers, all ten of them, had been working overtime.

He wondered if he was on a fool's errand. Tom didn't for a moment believe Welborn might return to his last address, but in the name of good police work, the importance of paperwork and the promise he'd made to a victim, Tom intended to do his job.

His turn was still a far distance ahead. He checked the lane next to him, glanced in his rearview mirror and started to edge over for the pass as the center line had gone from solid to striped. He wanted to see the driver.

Simultaneously, the white Chevy increased its speed so he could no longer safely pass. He was in no mood for this. The driver continued to be a pain.

Problem was, he couldn't decide what to do. Technically, she had the right of way. At first, she'd been going so slow that he figured she was looking for a turnoff. Now, she was slowing down and speeding up. Usually, this indicated someone under the influence. Since she hadn't started this type of maneuver until she'd seen him, he was willing to hold off. Something was up with her.

He sped up more, thinking to get ahead of her.

He started to flip on his siren, but decided that was overkill, and he always tried to put rational thought before reaction.

Once the opportunity arose, he went for the pass, slowing to look at her as he was beside her.

She looked back.

And he almost lost control of the SUV as the image from a police wanted poster stared at him from the driver's seat.

Rachel Ramsey in the flesh!

It only took a second to catch his breath. He loosened his death grip on the steering wheel and activated the siren with one hand while motioning for her to pull over with the other.

Her blue eyes widened in innocent surprise.

Innocent? Not a chance. He'd been hunting her from the moment his partner, Max, had been shot in cold blood during a convenience-store robbery right in Sarasota Falls.

She'd been the passenger, not the driver, back then. Her boyfriend, Jeremy Salinas, was a punk kid who'd been sent to Sarasota Falls to live with his aunt. The idea had been that maybe a small town would be good for him.

That hadn't quite worked out.

Rachel hadn't pulled the trigger, but according to the witness, she'd been the distraction.

Every bit as guilty.

Watching Rachel's every move—no way was she escaping this time—he radioed in a 10-29 so his men would know where he was and what he was doing, then, not even giving her an inch, he motioned for her to pull over.

If she tried to lose him, he'd use his car as a weapon.

He cared that much.

She carefully coasted to a stop on the shoulder, apparently pretending to be nothing other than a law-abiding citizen.

How could Rachel seem this safe or look even remotely carefree? Obviously, she didn't recognize him. Well, he'd enjoy nothing more than shoving a photo of his partner in her face. He'd make sure it was an eight-by-twelve complete with Max's wife and kids. He intended to tattoo their likenesses on Rachel's brain. He wanted to remind her of what she'd destroyed. She hadn't just killed a cop, she'd helped erase a husband, son, brother…

HEATHER GRAVES didn't feel at home in Sarasota Falls, New Mexico, and doubted she ever would. Already she missed her job working as a dental assistant in Phoenix.

She'd been safe there.

She wasn't so sure she was safe here.

Friday, two full weeks ago, had been her last day of work. She'd spent the next few days packing up her parents' house—she'd let it go too long, even paying rent on a home with no occupants—keeping only what had memories for her, like a train clock that had a different whistle for every hour. No matter where they lived, she'd grown up with the sound.

When she'd finished, she gave the house keys to the rental company and her own apartment key to her best friend, Sabrina. Sabrina thought Heather was foolish. Heather figured Sabrina was right.

Heather had been in Sarasota Falls ever since, renting a room at Bianca's Bed-and-Breakfast, a quaint older house that came with a happy, somewhat mothering proprietress.

Yes, she was foolish, but she also liked to think of herself as brave. According to the lawyer who'd reviewed her parents' will with her, she now owned a farmhouse in this town, one with the same tenant for the last twenty-five years.

Her parents had acquired the farm and acres around it when she was a little over one year old. Yet, to her memory, neither they nor she had ever stepped foot in Sarasota Falls. The lawyer had provided the name of the local company that handled collecting the rent as well as maintaining its upkeep. Apart from her parents' basic details, the leasing office wasn't much help.

Heather kept trying every avenue, though, because she had a lot of questions and knew of very few people who might have the answers.

She'd also gone out to the farmhouse and knocked on the door. No one answered. It looked empty; it felt unloved. It didn't look like the type of house her city-loving parents would invest in. There was too much land, the location was too remote.

Bill and Melanie Graves had gone up in a helicopter to tour the Pacific coastline to celebrate their 27th wedding anniversary. She and her dad had planned it. Mom had said it was her dream. Dad's dream, too, then.

Thirty minutes later, a sudden electrical storm had hit. No one on board survived.

In the space of minutes, she'd lost the only people who loved her, who applauded her, who thought she was the best thing that had ever happened. Period.

Everything was passed down to her: their belongings, both their cars and their secrets.

It was the secrets that had inspired the move, not the rental house. She might have been able to wrap her mind around them having property she didn't know about. *Might* being the operative word. She'd have still investigated and tried to figure out why.

But soon after visiting the lawyer's office, armed with their death certificates, she'd gone to her parents' bank to close their account and was asked if she was aware that her parents also had a safe-deposit box.

No, she hadn't been aware.

The steel drawer was long, hard and half-full. It contained the deed to the property in Sarasota Falls, her dad's discharge papers as well as a bible, two birth certificates, a marriage license and two old drivers' licenses.

She doubted the cop, who'd suddenly appeared behind her, would take her angst over family issues as a good excuse for her meandering style of driving. Surely, though, he had better things to do than pull her over for a warning.

She couldn't shake the memory of standing in the bank's vault, the safe-deposit box open in front of her, and finding the identification: the photos on the drivers' licenses were of her parents.

The photos, not the names.

CHAPTER TWO

THE COUNTRYSIDE HEATHER was driving past was stunning—it was mostly grazing land, and a few small homes with long driveways nestled between trees with their leaves still green but turning yellow, orange and brown as the October weather took control. She tried to focus on the giant pines because what wasn't stunning was the cop who was beside her, staring. His siren was screeching and he was frantically motioning to the side of the road.

"You've got to be kidding," she murmured as she pulled over. She hadn't been speeding that much. Her tags were current and her cell phone was in her purse, not plastered against her ear or in her hands while she texted.

Rolling down her window, Heather waited while the cop did his thing. Boy, he looked stoic sitting back there in his chief-of-police SUV. The siren hadn't been enough for this officer, as his rapid do-or-die gestures actually had Heather considering her gas pedal and showing him what speeding really looked like.

That would have been a mistake.

What was taking him so long? She wanted to drive by the rental property, see if she could meet the tenant and visit a local farm that advertised a country store, a petting zoo and more. Then she would return to Bianca's Bed-and-Breakfast, enjoy a hot bath and relax. Maybe even visit with Bianca a bit and discreetly ask about her parents.

This cop—or chief of police, as his vehicle indicated—was slow. Although Heather knew she should stay in the car, this wasn't Phoenix, it was Sarasota Falls, so she pushed open the door. In a flash, the cop was out of his vehicle and striding toward her. He made it to her car in seconds, kicked her door shut before she could step out and looked through her open window.

Okay, time to get worried.

She swallowed, trying to push back the fear threatening to surface. "What's the problem, Officer?" She twisted, trying to get a good look at the man who stood next to her car.

"Put both hands on the steering wheel."

"What?"

"Both hands on the steering wheel. Now."

"But—but, why? What's going on?"

"Don't. Make. Me. Repeat. Myself."

She put her hands on the steering wheel while the fear came, roiled in her stomach. This cop had an agenda and for some reason she was it.

Not where she wanted to be. Somehow, she had to make him realize he'd made a mistake, a serious mistake. "Look," she sputtered, "I have to tell you, you're really scaring me. I have my driver's license and proof of insurance. Write me the ticket if you have to, but stop acting like this."

In the distance came a siren, its sound gradually getting louder. Then came another and still another. In the blink of an eye, three squad cars—their wheels screeching—surrounded her vehicle.

Clearly, they thought she was public enemy number one instead of a random speeder. Two other cars slowly drove by, one a family and the other a lone female. From the expressions on their faces, they offered no pity, only curiosity and accusation.

"Open your door slowly and keep your hands where I can see them at all times." The cop's voice didn't sound any friendlier now that he had backup.

"I will open the door. I don't have a weapon." Her teeth started to chatter, even though it wasn't cold. Her mind, ever logical, grasped at any possible reason for the cop's behavior.

She heard more doors opening, the sound of voices, all coming her way, and her fear escalated.

Apparently, she wasn't moving fast enough. He jerked open the door for her, and she threw her purse out, not caring where it landed. "I can do it!"

But he had control of the door and was partially in the way. Instead of a graceful exit, she spilled awkwardly from the car—maybe what he intended. Her knees hit the road first. Her jeans offered little protection. Her palms hit hot, rough pavement, and bits of rocks pressed against tender skin. Her purse was right in front of her. She started to reach for it.

Simultaneously, she heard the chief of police drawing his gun and his steely warning. "Keep your hands where I can see them at all times."

Her purse stayed where it was, and the cop pushed her closer to the hot pavement while yanking her hands behind her back and handcuffing her. Another cop—this one younger, a kid really, but looking just as stoic—went for her purse, while another read her rights to her. Oddly, all she wanted to do was talk, tell them the truth—that she'd done nothing. Instead, her throat closed and she swallowed.

"Do you understand?" the cop snapped.

She swallowed again and managed to answer. "I understand my rights, yes, but I don't understand why you're doing this to me."

"Tom, she wasn't going for a gun," the cop who'd picked up her purse said. He looked no-nonsense and had a military haircut. "At least there's not one among her things, and her license says Heather Marie Graves."

"Considering who she hangs around with, getting a fake ID is as easy as ordering a pizza," the chief replied.

She lost her breath… Her parents had fake ID. Is that who he'd meant? She'd thought maybe they had been in witness protection, but surely her parents' identification would have been destroyed. They wouldn't have been so careless as to keep it. No way could her parents have been involved in something criminal, not a chance.

"Tom, her vehicle's clean," said an officer.

Clean? Of course it was clean. She'd washed it just yesterday. Tom? His name was Tom? Okay, maybe it fit him. Tom was the kind of name that belonged to a guy grilling steaks in the backyard, keeping an eye on the neighborhood, right? A good cop? Make that chief of police. Well, this one might look like a serve-and-protect type, but he acted a little too much like a fight-to-the-death title contender.

Tom straightened, a line of sweat dotting his forehead.

"Sir, I haven't done anything wrong," Heather protested, no longer looking at him but now focusing on the ground at her feet because she was afraid to look up, especially at the gun being aimed at her. "I'm a dental assistant. I just moved to Sarasota Falls, and I'm trying to find work. And, of course, I don't have a gun."

In one of the police cars, the radio crackled. An officer she couldn't see yelled, "The plates are registered to Heather Graves, age twenty-seven, of Phoenix, Arizona."

"I didn't want to get a New Mexico license until I was sure I could find a job here," Heather offered.

"Why did you come back here?" Tom snapped.

"I've never been here before, not that I remember." Maybe she'd been born here, maybe some woman she'd passed in town today had carried Heather in her womb, but other than that, until her parents' death, Sarasota Falls hadn't existed.

"Right." None too gently he hauled her to her feet and turned her to face her car. With her hands cuffed behind her, she couldn't rub at her sore knees or even brush away the dust and dirt of the roadway clinging to her clothes. A female officer stepped forward and quickly patted her down.

"Nothing," the female told the others.

"I told you. I'm a dental assistant. I don't need a gun. What's go—"

They weren't listening to her. Instead, the woman cop frowned at Tom. "You're going to have to fill out a report for drawing your weapon, Chief Riley."

"You saw everything, right?"

Heather noted the slight trembling of the chief's hand.

The one still holding the gun.

"Her purse. When she went for it, I thought…"

He looked at Heather and his expression shut down, unreadable. Silently, he stepped back.

"You'll be all right taking her in?" the cop who'd read her rights asked.

The chief nodded.

"Let's roll," the female officer said.

Her mind screamed protests that her mouth didn't utter. She was so numb that she blindly allowed the chief to escort her into the back seat of the SUV, no questions asked.

She witnessed the female officer attach an orange sticker to the back window of her car.

She could consider it impounded.

All this was for real.

Chief Riley climbed behind the steering wheel and quickly radioed in a code she didn't know and then reported both the current time and the mileage on his vehicle.

She couldn't breathe, couldn't swallow, couldn't believe this was happening.

"Ex-excuse me," she said softly. Chief Riley glanced in his rearview mirror.

Anger came off of him in waves. Wait. Innocent until proven guilty, right? The cops were the good guys, right?

What if they weren't cops?

Yeah, right, only Heather Graves could have

such a ridiculous thought after one SUV and three squad cars surrounded her little hatchback.

"I—I…" Words fought to form but didn't leave her throat in even the semblance of a sentence.

Come to think of it, every time she had a nightmare, she lost the power of speech.

Since this was the biggest nightmare of all, she'd most likely lose a lot more before the ordeal was finished.

FINALLY.

Tom was almost afraid to take his eyes away from the rearview mirror. She might disappear. She'd done it before, leaving the Sarasota Falls Police Department frustrated and amazed.

He'd taken it the hardest. The chief of police back then had finally taken him aside and said, "If you intend to keep your job, focus on what you can change and leave what you can't for another day. Otherwise, you won't get anything done."

Good advice. If he'd taken it, he might still be married. Instead, he'd spent hours driving the back roads, stopping by Rachel Ramsey's friends' houses.

They were all convinced of her innocence. Not him. He continued to drive, even though he knew it was a long shot.

"I haven't done anything wrong," she protested again, eyes wide open, with a little shimmer. Too bad. Tears really didn't work on him anymore. Still, she continued to amaze him. He'd expected her to be mad, resist arrest, pretend surprise. The only thing she'd done was cooperate and try to get his attention.

She had that, all right.

He thought back to when he'd been a rookie and picked up Rachel multiple times. Early on for shoplifting and once for truancy. Tom still remembered trying later to explain to her mother that Rachel just needed guidance. The advice had fallen on deaf ears.

Still, he'd often helped Rachel return what she'd stolen.

As a young cop, only a year on the force, he'd been appalled that Rachel Ramsey was raising herself and that he knew little about how to help her. Her mother was negligent, not abusive. Social services had visited twice, both times because Tom had personally phoned. Their report was the house was livable and there was food in the fridge. Rachel had no bruises or complaints. Apparently, those were the core expectations for parenthood.

He'd actually escorted the social worker once and had realized that Rachel was stealing only what she needed: clothes that fit and school supplies.

It was still stealing.

She was dressed pretty fancy now. Her shirt was pale pink with glittery buttons. Her jeans were fitted, without tears, and he recalled her white tennis shoes looked brand-new. She wore a pearl necklace and tiny earrings, too. The phone he'd confiscated was top-of-the-line.

She'd obviously done all right for herself and had upgraded from a house that was in the middle of nowhere and a delinquent mother.

He should have arrested Rachel when he'd had the chance back then. Played hardball with the shoplifting and truancy offenses. Maybe a stint in juvie would have done her good. But he'd known a few kids who'd gone to juvie and only learned how to be better criminals. So, even during his third year on the force, he'd continued to take Rachel home, talk to her mother about providing support and drive away.

Looking in the rearview mirror, at Rachel

Ramsey, he tried to see the girl she'd been. It was there. Buried. Her blond hair was still long and wavy. She should have dyed it, curled it, or something. Her cheekbones were still high and her mouth was still lined with a shade of red lipstick that most women didn't dare wear—not in his experience. His ex-wife sure couldn't.

Her blue eyes were the giveaway.

After almost a decade, Rachel Ramsey had changed very little, apart from her circumstances. Tom Riley, however, had changed a lot.

"Truly," she said, clearing her throat, "you've made a mistake. I did speed up and was probably over the limit. I admit it. Give me a ticket, but I've done nothing else wrong."

He could think of only one word in reply. "Nothing?"

His tone must have had some effect because she sat back, twisting a bit as the handcuffs restricted movement, and stared at him. Boy, she had fake confusion nailed.

What had she been thinking by coming back to Sarasota Falls? He had a million other questions to ask, but not before every word could be recorded. No chance would he mess up this case, because of his close connection to it. He longed to knock on Max's widow's door and say, "Sylvia, we got her. And, I'll make sure she leads me to Jeremy Salinas. Justice will be served."

In the back, Rachel settled and stared out the window. She was pale, and her teeth worrying her bottom lip. She had aged a bit. There were a few lines by her eyes. He'd have called them laugh lines on anyone else.

Not her.

Nothing to laugh about.

And today he was going to do something he should have done more than ten years ago—see that she was put away for a long, long time.

If he'd done that when she was fifteen, she might not have met Jeremy Salinas, wouldn't have participated in a convenience store robbery and wouldn't have helped lure a police officer to his death.

Chief Tom Riley could only blame himself that she'd been free to roam the streets ever since.

He wouldn't make that mistake again.

CHAPTER THREE

FOR THE FIRST TIME since he'd joined the force, paperwork was a blessing. Tom stared at the computer screen and coughed wryly as Heather Graves's picture revealed a background check so squeaky clean it had to be fake.

Until recently, Heather had been working in Phoenix, Arizona, as a dental hygienist in a small practice, just as she'd said. Before that, she'd been at the state university.

Now the same woman sat in a Sarasota Falls jail cell, a prime suspect involved in a homicide.

His fist clenched and he suppressed the urge to hit the table hard. He didn't need for his team to see how angry he was.

It made sense that Rachel would change her name, but he'd never have guessed she'd have the ability to create a false history that gave her a college degree and also enabled her to immediately find work. Had she really done all this?

With a quick phone call he learned that the dentist in Phoenix would hire her back in a heartbeat and that as far as the dentist knew, family matters had inspired the move. She'd been a model employee, left her personal business at home and gave two weeks' notice before quitting. And, no, the dentist hadn't met a boyfriend.

Maybe she'd been smart enough to shed Jeremy Salinas a while ago.

Tom hadn't been able to shed the memory of what the man had done. He opened a file on his computer, staring at the likeness of Rachel Ramsey.

There had to be a flaw in the cover she'd created for herself, and he'd find it.

He took the time to study her academic history at Arizona State University. A few taps on the computer keys had her photo. Student IDs weren't supposed to be all that good. Rachel's, make that Heather's, was. This photo was from her senior year. He found the first three years' of student ID photos online, too.

Every one of them showed a smiling coed. Blond hair, so shiny and glossy it seemed to glow. Heart-shaped face. Lips red even without lipstick.

It was Rachel's face all right, but it didn't make sense. The timing of it didn't work. No way could Rachel be here, in high school, dating Jeremy Salinas and living under an alternate name and actually graduating with honors.

It defied logic. Still, Tom's years in law enforcement showed him time and time again that improbability was a condition best investigated.

Still, a tiny thread of doubt pulled at his consciousness. Could he have made a mistake? Could Rachel have a doppelgänger? Or, could this Heather, who looked so very much like Rachel, be a relative? He'd called her Rachel, and she hadn't even flinched. He'd marveled at her control.

More than a decade on the force. He was seldom wrong, and he especially didn't want to be this time.

He enlarged Heather's student ID photo, looking at the area on her face, just above the left lip, where there was a red birthmark. Then, he brought up his photo of Rachel, taken a half dozen years ago, and enlarged it.

Same red birthmark, same size and shape.

What were the odds? He searched for statistics of family members having the same marks and found it was rare but possible.

So, right now, he could have Rachel Ramsey in a cell or he could have a complete innocent.

He pushed back his chair, stood and looked across the busy room. His officers were on the phone, writing reports, scanning the computers.

There was something else, though. A tension in the air as well as a few furtive glances in the direction of his office.

They knew the story, knew how close he'd been to his partner, and worried about him.

Maybe this nightmare was about to come to an end, maybe Tom would finally go to bed at night knowing he'd done his job.

Caught the accomplice of Max's killer.

"Looks like her," Lieutenant Lucas Stilwater said. "Only older." Lucas—near retirement age—was one of a few officers left who'd worked with Tom's previous partner. The rest were new, hired within the last three to five years. Good cops, every one of them. Sometimes, listening to their banter, he wanted…

Wanted to go back in time.

For the first few months after Max's death, when Tom had looked across the busy room, by habit he'd still been looking for Max. The room hadn't pulsed with activity then. Instead, it was like someone had turned down the volume, changed the scene to slow motion. For a long time, Tom felt as if he didn't belong, that he was role-playing. Then, when the chief retired, Tom had been approached by the mayor, Rick Goodman.

The pluses: Tom was a captain, Tom had a master's in criminal justice and the people of Sarasota Falls knew and trusted him.

The minuses: Tom's whole life was his job, so much so that his wife had left him.

In the end, Tom hadn't turned his back on his job, nor had it turned its back on him. He'd found that being chief gave him a renewed sense of purpose—just not in his late partner's case.

Until today.

There were still things to do, he reminded himself. Unless Tom missed his guess, Heather Graves was either a crime stamped "solved" or a new door opening on an old case that had troubled him through to his soul.

He headed for the cell, thinking he'd personally escort Rachel to booking, but she wasn't there. For a moment, he felt fear. Immedi-

ately, his phone beeped as if someone knew
he needed an answer. He glanced at the caller
ID. Captain Daniel Anderson, in records, was
always quick to deliver information. He was
someone Tom could rely on and, in fact, he
called the man a friend.

"Give me good news," Tom barked.

Daniel didn't react at all, just stated, "She
has no criminal record."

CHAPTER FOUR

HEATHER HAD ANSWERED every question she'd been asked, but the police hadn't known to ask about her parents' real names, Raymond Tillsbury and Sarah Tillsbury, née Lewis. They'd accepted her history because everything checked out. Of course it did. Her life story hadn't changed until recently.

She thought about telling them the truth, but the chief was already so certain she was guilty of a crime. What if her mother and father had done something awful? What if that was why they'd changed their names and moved to Phoenix? If that was correct, Heather wasn't sure she wanted to know the truth.

But really, Melanie Graves a crook? Her dad a killer? They were the kindest people she'd ever known. They'd loved her, she loved them, but... *No, no, no.*

"Ma'am, if you'll just give me a minute." The booking officer had led her from her cell to sitting across from him at his desk. Then, he stood and walked over to the chief, who was looking at her and clearly wasn't happy.

She continued wiping at the black residue on her fingers. They'd taken her fingerprints digitally, but then used ink and paper, saying something about an international component.

This Rachel Ramsey person must be in a lot of trouble if they thought she'd fled the country. Heather almost looked forward to her release—and she truly thought she'd be out soon—so she could go research exactly what Rachel had done.

And what she looked like.

Possibly, Heather would find a link between Rachel and her parents. Focusing on the two police officers, she wished she'd felt some sort of connection to them that would allow her to trust them. If she shared every detail about what she'd discovered, would they fill in some of the missing pieces? She wasn't sure.

Closing her eyes, she willed herself away from the police station and imagined her apartment in Phoenix. She'd left the lawyer's office in such a daze; she didn't even remember driving home. But she'd spent the whole of that evening perched at her kitchen table, laptop in front of her, and she'd researched Raymond Tillsbury, not Bill Graves.

He'd said he was raised by a mostly absent father; she assumed that was still true. But her grandfather's real name had been Terrance Tillsbury. She found three obituaries, and two mentioned children. There was no other history for him. Her father, Raymond Tillsbury, had a bit more presence. She found his military record, complete with a few photos. He'd honestly shared his accurate United States Army history. He'd been a hero. That wasn't a surprise. He'd been her hero.

She'd kept at it for hours before finally finding his name tagged on a Christmas photo posted by someone on Facebook. The photo was thirty years old and from a company party. She cut and pasted, enlarged and then decided it indeed was a picture of a much younger version of her dad. Going back to the original post, she wrote down the information shared. It was from a work party for the employees of Little's Grocery Store in Sarasota Falls, New Mexico.

So, she now owned a home there, and her father had once had a job there. Since her father's real name was Raymond Tillsbury, did that mean she was Heather Tillsbury?

Heather Tillsbury. She said the name out loud, feeling a little queasy, as if she'd lost her parents for a second time.

Of her mother—real name, Sarah Lewis—she'd found too many hits to investigate, so she narrowed her search to Arizona and then to New Mexico. Still too many. So she narrowed her search to Sarasota Falls. There was a family named Lewis there, but no mention of a Sarah. Google provided a few photos but they meant nothing and might've not even really been Lewises. She wanted to find them, ask them questions.

According to the photo she'd found online, the house her parents had been renting out in Sarasota Falls was a white clapboard farmhouse in need of a little tender, loving care and with a lot of land.

Since she'd seen it, she knew it needed a lot of tender, loving care.

Another police officer had joined the two standing at the door. They were having a meeting. No one looked happy.

"Lawyer?" she said. They all turned toward

her. "I want a lawyer. Or, at the very least, my phone call."

"We'll see to it," the officer who'd taken her fingerprints promised, but he didn't move from the impromptu gathering. Her back was getting stiff, and she was cold. She also wanted a drink of water.

Maybe something stronger.

Sitting back, she was almost glad when the chair creaked loud enough to disturb the officers. Still, they didn't move.

She sighed and sat back. Looking out the big window, she watched as a few cars drove by, followed by a firetruck, complete with streamers. No doubt it had been featured at the Founder's Day celebration.

Why had her parents left and why didn't they talk about their hometown, family, or friends. The way she figured it, this was the town where she could have been raised. Instead, from the time she was one until she turned sixteen, she and her parents had moved from one town to another, about every three years. Her dad claimed his military background had put the wanderlust in him. Her mother said it was the need to explore that drove him.

At sixteen, her mother's diabetes meant it

was wise to stay in one place and with one doctor. Or maybe, Heather now mused, they'd decided they were safe.

Maybe their feeling safe had something to do with Sarasota Falls. Maybe not. Maybe she was silly to come here. There were way too many *maybes*. But in her heart, she knew there was a piece missing from her life: her roots.

Roots were so important to her, she'd started putting in job applications from the moment she'd arrived in town. No luck yet, but people had seemed encouraging.

Earlier today, she wandered around the Founder's Day celebration trying to get a better lay of the land. Once the crowds got to her, she decided to take a drive. The countryside was so different from the metropolis of Phoenix.

Sarasota Falls: thirty-two thousand. Phoenix: four million and climbing.

She wondered who her parents had been friends with, and if they'd missed this place.

How they'd thought it would somehow remain a secret.

Why she was crazy enough to think that moving here, even temporarily, was a good idea.

She shook off the doldrums. Moving had been a brave and wondrous thing.

Right.

She'd just have to keep telling herself that.

"She's hiding something," Captain Daniel Anderson said.

"Tell me something I don't know." Tom glared at Heather, willing her to glare back, annoyed when she didn't.

Daniel cleared his throat and said the words Tom didn't want to hear. "She's hiding something but it isn't that she's Rachel Ramsey. I can tell you what you already suspect, which is that everything points to a case of mistaken identity. This lady is shorter than Rachel and—"

"Shorter? You've got to be kidding me. We've had her in custody not even an hour and you can already tell—"

"I've studied Rachel's photos, almost as often as you, especially the ones from the convenience store," Daniel said calmly. "Plus, I watched the surveillance video a hundred times.

"She was wearing heels during the robbery! Keep talking to her," Tom ordered before heading to his office to study the photos, even the ones that would tick him off. He switched out Heather's photos to compare to what they had of Rachel.

Heather Graves might indeed be legitimate and just happened to look like Rachel Ramsey.

Right down to a red birthmark!

The most recent photo they had of Rachel, save the surveillance video, was her driver's license. A head shot, which while nice, didn't tell them all that much, except that Daniel was correct. The woman he'd hauled in was shorter than the height listed on Rachel's license But, everything else was spot-on.

Rachel Ramsey, girlfriend of Jeremy Salinas. Guilty of robbing the convenience store—at gunpoint—and taking off. Max hadn't been looking for them on that hot, muggy August day. He'd been responding to a call on the other side of town. Somehow, they'd crossed paths. The final radio check-in from Max gave a license plate number and reported that he'd hit the siren to warn the vehicle ahead of him—someone driving erratically, dangerously—to pull over.

Jeremy Salinas and Rachel Ramsey.

Guilty of murdering a cop.

Max hadn't even been aware that the car they were driving was stolen.

Tom should have been with him that day, and would have, if his court appearance hadn't taken twice as long as necessary.

The only witness to the shooting, a frightened high school senior who'd skipped school that day and had been trying to keep a low profile heading home, said that the car Salinas was driving spun out of control and hit a telephone pole. Max had parked next to it and jumped out. Then the passenger side door had flung open from the impact, and Rachel had fallen from the car, on her stomach, acting hurt.

Max, doing what he did best, bent down to help her up. The moment he'd made sure Rachel was all right and was straightening, the boyfriend fired his weapon into Max's heart.

Max's blood was on Rachel's hands in more ways than one.

"Hard to believe she's been living under an assumed identity and has been so successful." Lucas was back and staring over Tom's shoulder at the mug shots—left side, front, right side—of Heather's face on screen. How she managed to keep her expression both shocked and innocent-looking was pretty amazing. Maybe she'd worn the same expression the day she pretended to be hurt.

She was that good of an actress.

But making herself shorter? a little voice questioned inside Tom's head.

"I wonder why she didn't try to change her looks more," Lucas remarked.

Tom wondered the same thing.

"Man, I'll bet this is making your day," Lucas added.

"It would make my day if she'd just admit she was Rachel," Tom muttered, knowing it wouldn't happen.

Deputy Oscar Guzman walked over and looked at Heather's photo. "Maybe Rachel Ramsey was the fake name all along— maybe Heather Graves is the real name."

If only it was that easy, but Tom knew Rachel's history like the back of his hand.

"Not a chance. I knew Rachel personally. She is Diane Ramsey's daughter."

Oscar raised an eyebrow. He'd brought Ms. Ramsey in twice for being drunk and disorderly. She'd died of an overdose a year ago.

"Rachel was born to an alcoholic mother and raised by a succession of stepfathers and squatters. She even spent some time in foster care," Tom said, momentarily feeling sorry for the girl, then remembering what she'd done. "She's been in and out of trouble with the law most of her early life. Despite it all, I'd thought she was a decent person, until…" Reminding himself that he was talking to colleagues, he kept his voice even and his words matter-of-fact. "Both Jeremy and Rachel, we figured, disappeared across the border. Maybe we were wrong about Rachel. She—" he looked at the computer screen, hit a button and continued hoping that saying the words would make him believe them "—went to college and became a dental hygienist in Arizona."

No one said, "Yeah, right," but he wondered if anyone besides himself thought it.

Five years. He'd been looking for her for five years. Still, disappearing was nothing compared to the way she'd reinvented herself.

He almost believed her name was Heather.

Almost didn't count.

CHAPTER FIVE

HEATHER GOT THE feeling that while everyone—everyone, that is, except Chief Riley—knew they'd made a mistake, no one wanted to admit it.

No, that wasn't quite right.

No one wanted to be the one to admit it and then try to convince Chief Tom Riley he was wrong.

She didn't get the idea they were afraid of him. More, they were afraid for him.

"I can see why he mistook her for Rachel," one of the cops muttered. The officer standing next to him nodded.

"I'd avoid Tom for the rest of the day," another officer advised.

Heather wished she could avoid him, but he stood in the middle of the fingerprinting room, leaning against a counter and grilling the tall officer who'd taken her prints. "Find something," he ordered.

Luckily, the police officer who'd already introduced himself to her as Daniel didn't even blink. He just shook his head slowly.

Then came a few moments of waiting: the cops waiting for some action, Daniel waiting to be believed, Heather waiting for someone to yell "April Fool's" and Tom waiting for what he would never hear because Heather was not Rachel.

"Find something," Chief Riley repeated, leaning against a counter and staring at her image on the computer. He seemed mesmerized by her likeness.

He was tall; she hadn't noticed that at first. His hair was a slightly curly and as blue-black as the crows that came to her backyard looking for food and making unnecessary noise.

The same color as her father's, actually, but the knowledge didn't encourage a connection of trust.

He looked at her now, but his eyes weren't as piercing as back when they were on the interstate and he'd pulled her over.

Funny how she'd noticed his dark eyes throughout this whole outrageous venture. They'd gone from shock to hate to murderous. Now they were cloudy, as if some door had closed on an emotion so near to the surface he couldn't control it unless he locked it away.

"It's her," he said. "It's Rachel, and we can't let her walk away. We might never find her again."

"Tom, I agree, physically, in looks, you picked up Rachel." This cop, the kid who'd retrieved her purse back on the interstate, was the one speaking.

The cop who'd introduced himself as Officer Guzman said, "You didn't have a warrant, Chief. No other markers, besides the physical resemblance, support your arrest. Electronically, I'm finding no criminal history. Live scan doesn't have her in their system. We can't charge her."

Frantically, Heather tried to think of what to say. Part of her was amazed they were talking so openly in front of her. If the chief of police had made a mistake, why weren't they having this conversation behind closed doors. When she got a lawyer... No, she wouldn't need a lawyer. If she needed a lawyer, she could use this conversation in her defense.

"I—"

They stopped talking and looked at her.

Chief Riley frowned, his steely gaze accusing her, making her feel guilty.

"I was only speeding a little," she squeaked.

The man flinched a bit. Kid Cop managed to portray a hint of compassion—a blink, a slight contortion of his face that was almost a smile—and then he was back concentrating his attention on Tom.

"Look at her," Chief Riley growled. "Unless Rachel Ramsey has a twin we don't know about, that's her. No mistake. There was a witness when Max died. Let's do a lineup. Bring the convenience store clerk in, also. I guarantee he'll confirm it's her. That's enough probable cause."

Kid Cop didn't say anything. When Heather glanced around the room, suddenly the other officers got busy as if there was so much to do in a room without desks, without general everyday conversation, without hope. Finally, an older man, not in uniform, walked over and put his hand on Tom's shoulder. "We'll do an appearance bond for the speeding and see what we can find before the court date. You'll have at least seventy-two hours to prove you're right."

"Seventy-two hours, my foot," Chief Riley

growled again. He was glaring at Kid Cop, who already had a sheepish look on his face. "This isn't a bailable offense, is it?"

Kid Cop shook his head.

"Which means," Tom continued, "with an appearance bond, I don't have enough time to do squat, but it gives her enough time to disappear again."

"I won't," Heather protested, finding her voice. "I'm not guilty of anything, and there's no need for me to disappear."

Tom returned to growling. Kid Cop started to nod, but instead gestured to the man coming through the door.

An elderly man wearing a blue cambric shirt tucked into worn jeans with scuffed brown work boots took one step forward. "I'm Father Joseph McCoy," he said to Heather. "I understand you might need a bit of help."

Though surprised at the clergyman's casual attire, Heather felt relief, pure and welcoming. She opened her mouth, but the words didn't come.

By his stance and the way the cops took him in as one of their own, it was clear he'd been here before. But it wasn't Heather, the room, or the bunch of cops that Joe looked at. It was Chief Riley.

"Who called him?" Tom demanded.

Joe took another step into the room, running a hand through his hair. "Tom, it's good to see you."

They were on a first name basis?

The other cops, spectators really, started to shuffle from the room. Judging by the expressions on their faces, she wasn't the only one feeling relief.

"Miss Bianca called me," Joseph McCoy said. "Someone told her that her boarder had been arrested. Bianca seems to think it's taking a bit too long for you to realize your mistake and release her." He glanced at Heather and smiled; it went all the way to his eyes. There was a sadness there, though, and Heather wondered what had put it there.

One of the cops muttered, "Trust Miss Bianca." He was the first to back out of the room. None of the others focused on her, not really. They were focused on Chief Riley as they exited.

If she'd have been anywhere else, Heather would have laughed out loud. It just figured.

Even though she'd been the one harassed and accused, it was Chief Riley who needed saving.

HE'D ACTUALLY VOUCHED for her! Used the word *innocent* to describe her and claimed that Bianca Flores knew there'd been a mistake.

Tom didn't know how Bianca could be so sure, and Father Joe was no better, siding with a woman who coldheartedly assisted her boyfriend in murder. Tom watched as Father Joe led the woman going by the name of Heather Graves to his old white truck. Her blond hair swayed in the wind. She held herself stiffly, arms folded as if fighting off a chill that didn't exist—at least not in Sarasota Falls, New Mexico, in October. They were going to fetch her car. The tow company had retrieved it, the order hadn't been canceled.

Unlike Tom's arrest.

Staring out the window at their retreating figures, Tom felt somewhat like a little boy watching as someone important disappeared from his life. Years ago, that someone had been his real father—who hadn't been much of a father at all. Tom barely remembered him.

Then, five years ago, it had been Max dying.

Later, it had been his wife, who complained that Tom was married to his job. That it took him three weeks to get around to calling her and suggesting he still loved her and—

She'd hung up, and he really hadn't thought of her again, until this business with Rachel had come up.

Rachel would literally disappear, Tom had no doubt. Heck, maybe this time she'd become a teacher in Miami or a lawyer in Nashville. She was good at reinventing herself.

Joe, well... Joe wouldn't disappear. Since Max's death, Father Joe had faithfully—at least once a month—either stopped by the police station or phoned. He always wanted to take Tom out to breakfast, lunch, or even invite him to some sort of social activity. In Tom's mind, Father Joe was someone to avoid, someone who made Tom worry about choices and how everything came together only to eventually fall apart.

"Really," Oscar Guzman said, "she might not be Rachel."

Tom shook his head at the only man brave enough to come back to the room. Oscar'd only joined the force last year, but he'd been FBI before that and a marine even before that.

He was, besides Daniel, the only officer willing to tell Tom he "might" be wrong who still, in his naïveté, had a wide-eyed optimism about people.

Tom had been that young once.

"How can you say that with such certainty?" he asked. Turning to Daniel, he added, "And, judging by the way you've been banging on the keys of your computer, it's looking like Heather's fingerprints are new to the system."

"No history," Daniel agreed.

"Has anyone contacted the convenience store clerk for identification? I don't care if it starts a media storm. I want it done." Tom hated the way his words sounded—desperate, human, uncertain.

"It's not the media that's kept us from doing more," Daniel said. "It's the evidence, or should I say lack thereof. Nevertheless, I emailed him her photo. Now we're waiting for a response."

"Call him."

"I did." Daniel sounded a bit exasperated. "He didn't answer. Even if he says it's not—"

"You haven't proven Heather is not Rachel." Tom's words weren't an accusation, but were simply a statement of fact.

"And you haven't proven she is." Daniel

looked a little guilty, as if he personally was at fault. But it wasn't Daniel's fault that Rachel had avoided being fingerprinted. She'd gotten lucky, more than once, possibly had gotten lucky again today…except now they did have the woman's, Heather's, fingerprints.

Tom glanced out the window and watched Father Joe shut the passenger side door and walk to the driver's side of his truck. Before opening his door, he looked up and his eyes locked with Tom's.

Father Joe was getting old, soft. And right now, he looked a little distressed. Not a look Tom had seen on Father Joe.

"I wonder why Father Joe is getting involved?" Daniel said.

"I'm going to find out," Tom promised. What Tom wanted to know, more than anything, was why Bianca had called Joe instead of coming herself. She'd never been one to shy away from a sticky situation, and apparently she liked Heather.

One thing Tom couldn't argue, Joe was the kind of preacher who greeted everyone as if they were already friends and wouldn't know a foe if the person outright threatened him. That didn't mean Joe wasn't smart, though.

The friend-rather-than-foe attitude had alleviated more dangerous situations than Tom's badge and gun ever had.

Joe's presence had diffused this one. The other cops went back to work as Joe drove Heather away from the station, and Tom turned to head back to his office.

"Think of it this way," Daniel said. "In my quest to prove she's not Rachel, I just might prove she is. Except for that height thing."

Tom wished he didn't have to listen to logic. He wanted time alone, time to think, time to look into just when Heather Graves arrived in town, where she was working and what friends she'd already made.

"I don't think you're listening to me," Daniel complained.

"I'm listening," Tom murmured, watching as Joe and Heather disappeared into traffic.

Tom started to get irritated but then noticed how intently Daniel studied his computer. "You got something?" Tom finally asked.

"I do," Daniel said. "There's quite a few things to think about when it comes to this case. Let's face it. The resemblance between Rachel and Heather, it's uncanny."

"They have to be related." Tom walked over and stood behind the captain.

Daniel nodded. "That's what we need to investigate." He hit a few more buttons and Heather's photo shrunk to half the page. Then, Daniel arranged the grainy shots of Rachel— the most recent they had, taken at the convenience store the day Max died—next to Heather. After a moment, he shrunk the two photos so they took up a third of the screen. Then, photo after photo appeared in the center box, hundreds, before finally, one froze in place. The woman was blonde, but it looked poorly dyed. Her hair was short and jaggedly cut, but there was something about the turn of the head, the way the older woman's chin jutted out, the somewhat pointy eyebrows.

"This, my friend," Daniel said, as if Tom needed a reminder, "is Rachel Ramsey's mother."

"Was," Tom reminded him.

Diane Ramsey had a fairly extensive rap sheet and Tom had followed her through Sarasota Falls's underbelly, sometimes to arrest her, but most often to keep an eye out for her daughter. Diane had changed her hair color weekly, wore wild clothes, although nothing cosmetic could hide her battle with drugs and alcohol.

Rachel Ramsey had been a pretty girl. It was anyone's guess if she took after her mother.

Daniel worked his magic with the computer, going through dozens of photos of Heather Graves, who had a web presence. The officer enlarged, shrunk, stretched, sharpened. Then, he said, "This one."

"Got it."

"Yes!" And the image of an older woman appeared onscreen, again blonde, but not poorly dyed, this lady had a tired but happy smile on her face.

Finally, satisfied with his findings, Daniel said, "Heather's mother, taken from her driver's license. Now we have Heather's photos and fingerprints, and I'm sure Diane's DNA is still in the system. We should run a comparison."

Tom agreed. "Anything to get us closer to catching a killer."

CHAPTER SIX

A CATHOLIC PRIEST. She was sitting in the passenger seat of a big white truck being driven by a priest. She felt the need to confess but didn't know for what or even how.

"Thank you so much for getting me out of there. Why did you do that? How did you know?" she finally asked.

"Miss Bianca asked me to."

Heather nodded. She'd figured out the owner of the bed-and-breakfast liked to help her guests, but this went a bit beyond common courtesy.

"I want to know everything," Father Joe McCoy said. "What happened?"

"I honestly don't know," Heather admitted. "One minute I was driving, taking a scenic tour, sort of looking for Turner's farm."

"It would be closed. The Turners had a honey booth in the festival."

"That's where I picked up their brochure

with directions to their farm. I was a bit lost. Then, suddenly, I notice a cop behind me— the chief of police, no less—and soon he has his siren on and is motioning me to the side of the road.

"Were you speeding?"

"Maybe a little, which is unusual for me. I slow down for yellow lights."

"As you should," he agreed.

"He thought I was someone named Rachel Ramsey. Do I look a lot like her?"

Father Joe didn't answer but clutched the steering wheel, white-knuckled, reminding her of the way Chief Riley had acted while driving her to the police station.

"Do you know her?"

For a moment, she didn't think he would answer.

"Rachel," he said, turning into Bart's Auto Repair and Towing, "is a young woman born and bred in Sarasota Falls who is a few years younger than you, and who has made a few poor choices." After a moment, he amended, "More than a few."

"I look like her?"

"Yes, quite a bit. But anyone who knows the

two of you, once they got close enough, could tell you apart."

"So, you can tell us apart?"

"Oh, yes," he said. "Quite easily."

"Are we related?"

He didn't so much as hesitate. "No one knows who Rachel's father was. And her mother wasn't born here in Sarasota Falls."

He parked in the lot, choosing a spot by the door, and exited the vehicle. She followed him into a tiny office located next to a large repair shop.

"There is no Bart," Father Joe said, pointing to the sign that read Bart's Auto and Towing. "There is a man named Taylor Jacoby. He bought the business from Bart and didn't bother to change the name." Heather didn't smile. Nothing felt funny, not after the day she'd had.

"I've no doubt," Father Joe continued, "that he's already got your vehicle here. If he tries to charge us, I'll have him call the chief. Since you were brought in by mistake, the city will need to cover the cost."

"How do you know all of this?"

"You're not the first person I've picked up from the jail." He grinned and added, "But I think you're the first who claimed to be innocent who really was."

Funny how good it felt to be believed. The reassurance erased some of the stress. Thank goodness she was no longer at the police station, no longer being questioned. And there were two people in town who believed her: Bianca and Father Joe.

She turned to thank him, but he was over by a candy machine talking to a little boy. Shaking her head at how surreal it was, she headed for the front desk and started the process to get her vehicle. It took all of ten minutes and two phone calls to the chief of police. Keys finally in hand, she went back to find Father Joe. Part of her just wanted human contact, someone to feel safe with. Another part of her wanted someone who would answer her questions. "You hungry?" she asked him.

Joe hesitated a bit, then nodded. "Quite. Have you been to the Station Diner? That's train station, not police station."

"No, but I've driven by it."

"Let's go there. It's a staple around here and should be pretty empty since tonight's big hooray for the Founder's Day celebration is a chili cook-off. Unless you like chili?"

She loved chili but right now didn't feel like being in a crowd. "The diner would be fine."

She followed him away from Bart's. The sun had almost disappeared behind grayish clouds. A slight wind swayed the trees that lined the fairly empty streets. The diner was two blocks from the well-lit high school, where the cook-off was being held. She remembered seeing a flyer for it. Faint lights chased each other in the sky. Heather rolled down her window, took a breath of fresh air—so different than the police station's—and listened to the sound of cheering.

The Station Diner's parking lot had three cars. She pulled into a spot and Father Joe positioned his car next to hers. Together they walked to the heavy wooden door and pushed it open.

She'd gone back in time. A waitress wearing a retro-looking blue uniform, complete with a conductor's hat, guided Heather and Joe to a booth. "Hi, Joe," she greeted.

"Good evening, Maureen. This is Heather Graves. She's new to town, been here less than a week. Maureen's been here almost a year now."

"Nice to meet you," Maureen said.

"Great place," Heather said, looking around at the decor. She could well imagine that at one time this area had been where passengers waited for their trains, but the benches had been replaced with tables and booths. The window where tickets would have been sold now featured a cook dressed in white rather than an agent dressed in black with a cool hat. The walls and shelves had railroad paraphernalia. The only things out of place were the animal heads fastened right above the restroom signs and over the chalkboard menu.

Joe settled in and handed Heather a menu from behind the napkin holder.

"Are you going to eat?" Heather asked when he didn't take a menu for himself.

"I've got their selection memorized."

It took Heather a few minutes to order. Then, after taking a long drink of water, she said, "I got the idea from listening to the officers that Rachel was responsible for someone's death. Is that true?"

Joe's lips went together, his brow furrowed and his nostrils flared a little.

Heather almost wished she hadn't asked. But she'd just spent the last few hours being interrogated and falsely accused. She'd never forget the way the cell walls seemed to close in on her.

"I'll check online and find out on my own," Heather said. "I'm sure the story's there."

"Many stories about what happened that day are online," Joe agreed. "And much of what you read will be factual. But it's what's not said that makes a difference."

It made her think about her parents, how close her father had kept to the truth, and how her trying to figure out what their secrets were had led her here.

His phone pinged then, and with an apologetic look, he answered. She didn't hear much, just "Oh, I was hoping for better news" and "Not entirely unexpected" and "I'm so sorry you have to deal with this loss. I'll be right there." His expression changed from concern to distress to pure sorrow.

She recognized the sorrow as she'd worn the expression quite a bit since her parents' accident.

Nodding the whole time, Father Joe paused, listened and then said, "Someday that young man will realize exactly what he's done, and he'll have to live with it."

When he ended the call, he said, "Lucille

Calloway just passed away. She was in a car accident last year and never got her full strength back. I'm heading over to be with the family."

"What about the young man?"

"Richard Welborn. I'm guessing Chief Riley was heading to the Welborn place to see if Richard had returned. He was driving drunk last Christmas and hit Lucille head-on. She was an amazing lady, in her eighties, and still going strong, at least back then. She went through many months of therapy and never really recovered. Depending on others made her miserable." Father Joe smiled, looking a bit happier. It only lasted a moment before he added, "Richard was an amazing young man. People hereabouts forget that. He moved here with his mother, took care of her. I'm so surprised he was driving drunk. Still, can't get past that he posted bond and disappeared. Never made restitution or apologized. Lucille's family is angry at him although Lucille wasn't."

He stood, looked at the counter and said, "Maureen, I'll take my food to go if you don't mind."

"Already packed. I heard your phone go off and figured you'd be leaving."

Father Joe left, and Maureen put Heather's meal on the table, asked if she needed anything and then walked over to another customer.

Heather had never felt so alone. For a few long seconds she just sat there, trying to get her bearings, and wondered what she should do next. Maybe leave Sarasota Falls? Some secrets were best left buried. Stay? Find out if she had family? Well, she didn't have to decide tonight.

It had been a long time since breakfast. Heather stabbed a piece of chicken-fried steak and brought the fork halfway to her mouth before freezing.

Chief Tom Riley came through the restaurant's front door, and his eyes honed in on hers. He said something to Maureen, and then made his way over to stand in front of her.

"I just lost my appetite," she said, putting her fork down.

"May I sit?" He didn't like asking permission. He wanted to sit, question...yes, even press. Yet, he had to watch his step, do this the right way.

"I really don't feel like company," she said.

"And I won't be good company," he responded. "But, there are a few things I still need to know. This—" he looked around the diner "—is as good a place as any."

She didn't protest, so he sat across from her, so close he could reach out and brush a finger down her cheek if he wanted. He didn't want to, but did struggle to accept that she wasn't Rachel. Everything but his memory of a face proved she wasn't Rachel.

"How old are you?" he asked.

"Twenty-seven," she responded.

"Born?"

"In Phoenix, Arizona."

"I mean what year."

She responded with the year and stared at him. In all the time he'd walked a beat, driven the streets, worked the desk and finally taken the job of chief, he'd never had a suspect so obviously wrong yet so right. He couldn't stop looking at her, but he knew he needed to be professional, go with the idea that she indeed knew nothing.

Gain her trust.

Maureen bought over a cup of coffee, shot Heather a somewhat proprietary look and sweetly said to Tom, "Freshly made. I've already got Cook fixing your regular."

He needed to talk to Maureen. He'd given her a ride home from work a few times when her car didn't start. Seemed she was reading a bit more into the gesture than he'd intended. He should have noticed before.

"Thanks." He took a long drink, closed his eyes and counted to ten. He was too close to this case, could blow it because of the kind of emotion he realized he had with respect to it. Opening his eyes, he said, "I've spent the last couple of hours investigating you, Heather Graves."

She started to sputter her indignation, but he held up a hand, expecting her to stop. Most people would have, but she wasn't most people. Freedom and an hour spent with Father Joe seemed to have loosened her tongue. "You have no right, no—"

He placed a folder on the table, opened it and withdrew two pictures. One, not flattering, was of her just a few hours ago. The other was of a woman, much younger, with darker blond hair, blue eyes, high cheekbones and a wide mouth. All similar to what Heather looked like, except she wore her hair short.

With two fingers, she drew the photos close to her, squinting as she studied both of them side by side. She started eating again, eliminating half her meal and saying nothing. His hamburger arrived and he took a bite, watching her brow furrow and a frown distort her features.

"I see the resemblance," she admitted. "This could have been me when I was a teenager."

"Rachel Ramsey was sixteen when this was taken nine years ago. It was her sophomore year at Sarasota Falls High School."

"I would have been eighteen and finishing up high school. How come you're not showing me her police photo?"

"We don't have one. She was never arrested or charged with anything. She spent a year in foster care, but she was only seven."

"Father Joe said she made a few poor choices. He didn't get the chance to tell me what they were. Why don't you tell me?"

Poor choices? Tom cleared his throat. "Father Joe likes to sugarcoat the truth."

"He seems like a nice man."

"He is, but he tends to get involved in situations that hinder more than help."

"Like mine?"

"No, not really yours. If you've created a false identity, you're out of my league of expertise. Every avenue I explore turns up viable. The man who owns the dental practice in Phoenix says he'd hire you back in a heartbeat. I even managed to call one of the parents who had a little boy in your mother's childcare. She says her son loved you, and she described you perfectly." He put his hamburger down, wishing he was better at showing emotion. "You lost your parents such a short time ago. I cannot even imagine the pain you must be in. I'm sorry."

She blinked, then looked out the window as if the streetlights were the most fascinating thing she'd ever seen. Finally, she said, "You're one hundred percent sure I'm not Rachel Ramsey?"

He wanted to answer with a firm "yes." But he couldn't, so he admitted, "I'm getting there. Sometimes, I'm a bit slow."

"Father Joe said I looked like Rachel, but that he could tell the difference."

"How?" Tom asked, amazed. The only tangible piece of evidence he couldn't seem to wish away was Heather's height, or lack of it.

"Before we could get much further into our

conversation and I could ask him, he got a phone call. Someone passed away."

"Who?"

"Lucille Calloway."

Tom couldn't help the "umph" that escaped his lips. He'd wanted justice for her, just like he'd wanted justice for Max. Now it was too late for either of them.

"Father Joe was telling me about her and Richard Welborn."

Father Joe was a talker; most ministers were. As a matter of fact, Joe had been the minister who'd married Tom and Cathy ten years ago. He took his job seriously.

"I was heading to Welborn's place when I pulled you over," Tom confessed.

"Where's it at?" Heather asked.

"Two-one-six Decator."

She blinked again, looking somewhat taken aback and slightly guilty. Every time he thought he could wrap his mind around her not being Rachel, something spooked him. "You know it?" he asked.

"I drove by it right before you pulled me over." She pushed the photos back to him, her face wary and full of distrust. If he wasn't careful, she'd leave, and he had so much he needed to know. She was poised for flight, too, inching toward the end of the booth.

"Tell me about your parents," he said, quickly, hoping she'd open up.

Instead, she turned and swung both legs to the edge of the booth so she could easily exit, and then she muttered, "Why? Why are my parents important to you? Why don't you tell me about Rachel Ramsey and her poor choices and why you couldn't be bothered to listen to me earlier when you pulled me over? It's innocent until proven guilty in America. You stamped *criminal* across my forehead without giving me the chance to defend myself. I've been scared, humiliated. And I'm annoyed at you."

He'd been the center of attention many times, usually it wasn't at the Station Diner. The place was only half-full, but all of the customers were paying more attention to Heather and her words than to their meals.

"You deserve to be annoyed at me," he said quietly, so no one else could hear, and he hoped she'd lower her voice, too. "I overreacted when I saw you. I thought you were Rachel Ramsey. You look just like her."

"What exactly did she do?"

He hadn't spoken about it in detail for years, not since the psychologist the sheriff sent to Sarasota Falls declared Tom fit for duty. He didn't want to talk about it now.

To his surprise, she leaned closer, looking at him directly in the eyes, and then her expression softened before she settled back in the booth. "Look," she said, "I get that whatever happened all those years ago was somehow personal. I could tell that by how you behaved when you pulled me over. Just give me the basic facts. What can't be disputed. I deserve to know."

He half turned in the booth, held up his cup and said, "Maureen, more coffee."

"Comin' up."

After he'd downed half the fresh cup, he said, "A little over five years ago, my partner was Max Stockard. He was ten years my senior, and when I started on the force, he mentored me. After a few years, he became my partner. More than the academy, Max taught me what policing was."

He stopped. His dad had been a plumber; his mom, a librarian. Both were amazed that he became an officer of the law, proud, but kind of terrified. There were no police officers in the family on either side.

"I never met anyone as brave as he was. He made me want to be a better man, a better cop. Max died…" His voice cracked. He swallowed, quickly, and went on, "In the line of duty. Rachel Ramsey, more or less, caused his death by pretending to be hurt."

"What do you mean?"

"There was a car accident during a chase. She fell out of the passenger side door and lay there, just lay there. Max thought she was hurt. When he hurried to help, her boyfriend shot Max, point-blank."

Heather again seemed like she wanted to leave. "And I look exactly like her?"

"Yes. She disappeared that day and hasn't been heard from since. You're my first lead."

"I'm not a lead. I've never heard of her until today."

"I want to believe you. Really I do. What I'm about to ask will sound a little strange, but hear me out."

She didn't say anything, but drew back, looking like there wasn't a chance she'd help him.

"I want a swab of DNA, to compare against

Rachel's mother's. And I'd appreciate something personal from your mother. Did you keep a hairbrush or—"

"Why?"

"I'm betting you must be related to the Ramseys somehow. For that matter, let's get something from your father, too."

To Heather's credit, she didn't pretend surprise or indignation. "And if I am, what does that prove?"

Tom opened his mouth, tried to say something and shut it again. She was right. What did it prove? It might prove that Heather Graves was related to the Ramseys, but it wouldn't get him any closer to finding Rachel. Unless Heather was a master liar and knew where Rachel was.

His eyes narrowed, but before he could say another word, she said, "No," scooted out of the booth and headed toward the door. He started to follow, but Maureen plopped his bill down.

He wound up paying not only for his hamburger and coffee, but also for her food and Father Joe's.

It had been that kind of day.

CHAPTER SEVEN

SUNDAY WAS TOM'S day off. Didn't keep him from stopping by the office to see if Daniel or anyone else had anything new to report. They did and didn't.

"Lucille Calloway died last night," Oscar Guzman said. "My wife went over this morning and took a meal. The kids are taking it pretty hard even though it was expected."

Lucille could have had a few more years if Richard Welborn hadn't slammed his car into hers.

"I'll find time to go over today," Tom said. "Anything else?"

Oscar grinned and nodded. "My aunt says to tell you that Heather isn't Rachel Ramsey. Seems Bianca noticed the resemblance right away, but, and this is straight from Bianca's lips, Heather is much too short to be mistaken for Rachel."

Tom rolled his eyes. More than anything,

he wished it was the other way around, that Heather was taller than Rachel. Then he could have argued that she'd grown.

But she'd been wearing tennis shoes yesterday—not enough heel. Combine that with his little talk with her last evening, and he knew he needed to be looking at a different scenario. Still, Tom was frustrated that he hadn't gotten around to speaking to Bianca. "You get anything else?"

"Yes. Bianca says that Diane Ramsey had a sister. She wonders if perhaps Heather is some sort of cousin to the family."

Again, this was information Tom knew. "Diane Ramsey had two full sisters that we know of," he replied. "They came for the funeral."

"You talked to them?"

"In detail. Neither were surprised their sister Diane was dead. Both were surprised she'd lived as long as she did. Both said she'd had no business raising a child."

"Rachel was in foster care for a while, right?" Oscar asked. "Any chance she lived with either of her aunts?"

"No—one aunt didn't have children and clearly didn't want any. The other had two boys and said no way did she want Rachel's influence around her sons."

"Rachel was that bad?" Oscar queried, one eyebrow raised.

"No," Tom said. "But Rachel did hang around a rough crowd. Takes a special person to guide a young teen into the 'hows' and 'whys' of choosing better friends."

Oscar didn't shoot back with another question. Unusual for the officer who'd left the fast track of a career with the FBI to protect and serve the small town of Sarasota Falls. Of course, he'd fallen in love with someone here and chosen to be married to her instead of married to his job. Not once had Oscar bemoaned changing his career path. Instead, the man was happy. Tom didn't think he'd ever been that happy.

After a moment, Oscar said, "You know, this is the first time you've ever talked about Rachel Ramsey without snarling."

"I don't snarl."

Oscar only smiled and asked, "But Rachel didn't kill Max, exactly. Right?"

"She didn't pull the trigger. Her boyfriend did."

"How old was Rachel when all this happened?"

"Rachel would have been a teenager, just. She was retained in third grade."

"And back then Heather Graves would have been, what, early twenties?"

"And in college. Heather's twenty-seven now. Rachel should be twenty-five." The same age as Max's youngest son. "Excuse me." Tom stood, feeling sympathetic. He'd felt it last night, too, when he'd made his way from the table at the diner, stopped just on the other side of the cash register and watched Heather hurry to her car.

He needed to get close to her, but he didn't know how.

HEATHER HAD NEVER been one to have vivid dreams, but since her parents' death, she'd had more than her share. Last night's had been a combination. The beginning had made her keep her eyes closed tight with her fist in her mouth to keep from crying.

Her mom and dad had been in her dreams, doing what they did best. Mom was in the living room sterilizing and putting away toys, finding items that had been left behind by

the children she cared for, and doing it all
to the music of Pink Floyd. Heather used to
dance with her mother. Her father was outside
mowing the lawn, making sure the sprinklers
worked, and adding more tools to his shed.
Man, he'd loved those tools. The thought of
someone using her dad's things hadn't bothered her until now, as she was finally starting
to accept that the secrets her parents had kept
weren't just about their identities, but hers, as
well.

She opened one eye. The clock face read
six. Way too early to get up, so she lay there
in the half sleep that usually meant she'd have
a headache when she finally did crawl out of
bed. So, obviously, she'd have to crawl out of
bed and take charge of today, make decisions,
do something.

When she'd arrived in town, she'd thought
about taking it slow, observing, but after last
night, Heather was more than curious. She
had two options: the first was to go to the
house, but it was a rental and she didn't want
to bother the people living there. Plus, her attempt to check it out yesterday had ended in
disaster. Even now, she could feel the hard ce-

ment under her body as the police officer hand-cuffed her and...

She forced herself to stop thinking about yesterday. The memory would only slow her down, and she had things to do.

Her second option was to drop by Little's Grocery Store. A long shot, yes, but worth her time. Besides, she needed a few healthy snacks. What Bianca provided would put more curve on Heather's thighs than she wanted or needed. After a shower, she chose a pair of white jeans and a bright pink button-down shirt, along with white tennis shoes with pink laces, as she was a girly-girl. Then, she fixed her face and did her hair before she was ready to greet the day.

She stood at the top of the stairs, listening. Right now, there wasn't a single sound. Sundays, people probably slept in. Heather, however, didn't think Bianca the sleep-in type.

She took two steps, then a loud creak came from the third and she paused. Nope, it wouldn't be easy to make a silent getaway. Last night, she'd pleaded exhaustion when she'd come through the front door, and Bianca had been respectful.

Of course, Bianca had also spent the whole

day working and enjoying the Founder's Day celebration. Then, judging by what Heather had seen, Bianca spent the rest of the evening decorating the bed-and-breakfast for Halloween. Noting all the fake spiders crawling over the walls, the cobwebs in the trees and the witch on a broomstick stuck to the chimney, Bianca had had a busy night, too.

This morning, though, Bianca—all smiles— lingered at the bottom of the stairs, obviously wanting to know what had happened.

"Sit down," Bianca cheerfully ordered when Heather made it to the bottom step. Heather hesitated and thought about pleading no appetite, but then the aroma of cinnamon rolls swirled under her nose and she lost all resolve.

A tall glass of milk cemented their new friendship.

"Chief Riley doesn't usually let his emotions rule," Bianca said a little too casually. "What exactly happened yesterday?"

"He pulled me over thinking I was someone else," Heather said, thinking to herself that what the chief of police had engaged in yesterday had little to do with emotion and more to do with tunnel vision. "Do you think I look like this Rachel Ramsey?"

"Quite a bit, but not a dead ringer," Bianca admitted. "I can see why Tom pulled you over. Without hearing your voice, seeing the way you walk, your mannerisms, well, he did what he thought he had to do."

So, it was her voice, her walk, her mannerisms that Bianca claimed set Heather apart from Rachel.

Their identical looks were still an issue and "dead ringer" was a spot-on description.

Lots of what-ifs filtered through her imagination. In the end, she thought, she really, really, really doubted her dad had ever had a relationship with the likes of Diane Ramsey, but Heather was here to investigate and who knew what avenues she'd need to follow.

"What exactly was Rachel wanted for?"

It took Bianca a moment to answer. "Worst case scenario, first degree murder. Though, there's a chance it will be accessory to a crime."

First degree… It didn't get much worse than that.

"Can you tell me a bit about the family?"

"Well, the Ramseys aren't—weren't—natives," Bianca continued. "Diane just showed up one day in a burgundy-and-black Studebaker, in such bad shape that it puffed dark clouds into the air. Old Albert Turner was the chief then, so he chased her down and cited her."

"You remember like it was yesterday."

"Hard to forget. Diane's antics guaranteed we'd all remember when she turned up in town."

"What kind of antics?"

"Getting drunk at a Founder's Day celebration." Bianca laughed and held up her hand before Heather could counter with "lots of people get drunk" and said, "Let's just say she couldn't sing and no one appreciated the burlesque show."

"Oh."

"The town's barbershop quartet were performing. She stood right on top of a big speaker and interrupted them. She was louder without a microphone. Albert Turner had to haul her down. It made the paper. From then on, I'd say she made the paper about four or five times a year. I always felt like she had something to prove."

"Are any Ramseys still in the area?"

"No, not that I'm aware of. I don't know if Diane and Rachel's father were married when they had her, or if they ever got divorced or what. She and Rachel just stayed."

"In the house over on State Route 4?"

"Yes, how did you know?"

"Chief Riley said something about it." Changing the subject by holding up a cinnamon roll, Heather asked, "You make these?"

"No, I buy them from Shelley Guzman. She has a bakery in town."

Heather'd been in Sweet Sarasota yesterday. She'd picked up a free Founder's Day muffin— it actually had a plastic school toothpicked into its frosting in celebration of the deaf school that used to be the mainstay of the town. Then she'd purchased three chocolate chip cookies that had smelled only slightly better than the cinnamon roll she was currently eating.

"You met her husband last night. He works for Tom." Bianca once again was casual. "He's a cop."

Guzman. He'd been the big guy who'd challenged the chief of police. "So," Heather continued, "what kind of girl was Rachel?"

"I," Bianca said, somewhat sadly, "didn't know her very well. I don't have any kids of my own. They didn't attend church nor did she play with my nephews when they were in town."

"So all you really know about is Diane?"

Bianca nodded. "And she died just over a year ago."

It wasn't the first time Heather heard this. "How?"

"Hard living is what most of the town thinks."

"Was she young? Old?"

"Why, I guess she couldn't be that old. Younger than me. I never gave it much thought. She looked sixtyish, at least she did last time I saw her at the grocery store." Bianca sat back. "Rachel would have been midtwenties, close to your age, which is why Tom must have gotten so flustered. I imagine Diane was fifty or so when she died."

"Rachel didn't come back for the funeral?"

"Most of the town thinks either Rachel has no clue her mother passed away, that Rachel didn't care enough to come back, or that possibly Rachel herself has died. I hope she's okay. I hope she ran away from here and found a whole better world. Met somebody who cared for her. She certainly was making some of the same mistakes her mother did. Father Joe had us all praying for her."

"Thank you for sending Father Joe to get me. How did you know I was in jail?"

Bianca laughed. "The phone started ringing. By the third call, I knew it was serious. As for Father Joe, I know just about everyone, and I knew he'd have the easiest time pulling you out of there. In just an hour I'll be listening to Father Joe's sermon. You should come with me."

Heather was tempted. She wanted to talk to Father Joe, but even more, she wanted to visit with the members of the church and ask questions.

Problem was, after yesterday, she was afraid to start.

AN HOUR LATER, Heather paid for her small supply of groceries. She'd spoken to the man working behind the meat counter. He looked old enough to have been employed at Little's for almost thirty years but claimed only five years. She'd talked to the current security guard on duty, and he'd spouted something about privacy laws and paperwork. She'd gone to the manager, who told her the name of the man who owned Little's and said to contact his secretary.

Then she'd chosen the cashier, who looked closest to her father's age. Trina Gillespie had been employed by Little's for over thirty years and thought the name Raymond Tillsbury sounded familiar, but claimed she'd couldn't remember anything else.

Heather even showed a photo from her cell-phone to Trina, but before Trina could say more than "um," the security guard came over and gave Heather a warning look.

Sunday was not the day to call a corporate office, so Heather added the phone number to her contacts and headed back to the bed-and-breakfast.

She had research to do.

HEATHER'S PHONE RANG at nine o'clock the next morning. She almost didn't answer it. She'd paced her room most of the night, unable to sleep and feeling slightly sorry if anyone happened to be in the room under hers. These old Victorians creaked and moaned. Even with the morning sun coming through the window, she felt like she'd just gotten to bed. She wasn't sure whether to blame it on the time spent in jail, the time spent sitting across from Chief Riley, or spending most of yesterday visiting Little's Grocery Store and later reading online about the whole Ramsey family.

Poor choices had indeed been a sugar-coated phrase. And Bianca was right. Rachel Ramsey's mother had made worse choices than the daughter. Heather couldn't even imagine growing up in such desperate circumstances.

"Miss Graves?" a voice queried once Heather answered her phone.

"Yes."

"This is Tessa down at Sarasota Dental. You came in last Thursday and dropped off a ré-sumé."

Heather sat up in bed, fatigue gone. She'd liked the originality of Sarasota Dental's building. It looked like it was straight from a cartoon— it was a purposely crooked lit-tle clapboard house, painted sky-blue, with giant eyelashes over the top-floor windows and white teeth surrounding the front door. A giant toothbrush served as the mailbox, and a tree in the front—which had a face with an open mouth and one twisted limb, acting like an arm—was flossing.

She half expected the limb to move, but it

hadn't. Clearly children were a big part of their clientele. Who knows, maybe the decor made a few adults feel a little calmer, too.

"Yes, that was me," she said.

"Could you come in this afternoon and meet with Dr. Goodman? We might have a temporary position if you're interested."

"What time?" Heather would be there in five minutes, wearing her pajamas and brandishing a toothbrush with a floss lasso if it meant she got the job.

"Would two work?"

Five hours to kill.

"I'll be there." Heather hit the disconnect button and swung her feet over the edge of the bed. Temporary might be perfect. It would give her something to do, yet allow her to change her mind about staying in Sarasota Falls if things didn't work out.

She wanted to find family, but was now fearful about the kind of family she might find. Before she stood up, she directed Siri to call Father Joe. He'd not answered when she called yesterday, but then it had been Sunday, and as a minister, Sunday was his busy day.

He failed to answer this morning also. He

knew things about her family; she was sure. Maybe things he didn't want to share.

Heather showered and then straightened up the room. It was pretty but a little old-fashioned. Maybe that was what Bianca was going for. The room was painted in dark, vibrant reds and browns. The floor was wood with a huge flower-patterned rug covering most of it. The two chairs in the room were worn but comfortable.

The walls were covered with landscape paintings. There were a few photographs, mostly of the town. Heather recognized a much younger Bianca in a few of them.

Heather's parents' house had been much like Heather's. They'd had nothing antique, and the family photos were only of the immediate family: Bill, Melanie and Heather Graves.

Heather was blond-haired with blue eyes and light skin. Her mother had red hair, freckles and even lighter skin. Her father was black-haired and green-eyed. They'd never talked about the past, they'd never answered her questions about family—she'd known from the time she was nine that they were alone. She just hadn't known they were alone because of so many secrets.

This move was her attempt to solve them, find out who she was. Resembling Rachel Ramsey might not be what she'd figured on, but it was the first card she'd drawn. She just hoped it didn't lead to Colonel Mustard standing over her brandishing a bloody candlestick.

Instead of worrying about it, she settled down on the chair with a romantic suspense novel, kicked her feet up on the bed and got lost in the kind of life she dreamed about but didn't have.

That is, until she'd left the lawyer's office and then found the safe-deposit box and moved here.

At one thirty, she tried Father Joe again. No answer. Then she got in her car and headed to Sarasota Dental, arriving five minutes before her interview.

Dr. Goodman turned out to be James Goodman. He paused and stared at her, then said, "You genuinely do look like the Ramsey girl."

Heather wasn't sure how to answer. She wanted the job, but she didn't want to ruminate over how she resembled a killer, and she certainly hoped he hadn't called her here just to do a comparison.

"In Phoenix, I worked for a small practice," she said. "You can call—"

"I already did. They said they had to hire two hygienists to take your place, and to send you back if things didn't work out here. So, it says on your résumé that you went to work for them right after college. Your first job?"

"It was my first full-time job outside of working for my mother. She did childcare in our home, so I've been around children quite a bit."

"We primarily see children, but a few of my patients aren't willing to leave home after eighteen. I probably have twenty or so adult patients who insist I take care of their teeth."

For another few minutes, they exchanged pleasantries as well as their views on work ethics. She admired the photos on his office walls: a rock star who'd needed a filling when passing through town, a wife and two sons and also one of him and the mayor, who turned out to be his brother. He admired her résumé.

Finally, he leaned forward and asked, "So, if you don't mind my asking, what brought you here?"

If it wasn't for what she'd already experienced, she'd have glibly said, "I'm looking for family." That response, however, no longer felt safe.

"I've friends in the area and was looking to downsize." She met his gaze, thinking how much life had changed in the last few months and how she'd never felt vulnerable before.

Problem was, if she went back home now, she'd always wonder.

"I'm a great believer in downsizing," Dr. Goodman said. "Everywhere except my practice. So, my assistant, Maya, who has been with me twenty-five years, wants to spend the winter with her daughter in New Hampshire. Seems she's about to become a grandmother. When you dropped off your application, she saw a way to make it happen. She, however, intends to return come April. I've only got a temporary position for a few months."

"I'm good with that." Heather smiled.

"My concern," Dr. Goodman said, "is you'll not be happy working as the office administrator. You're a hygienist, and I've already got one. You might grow bored and find another job, one that isn't temporary, and I'll be without my regular assistant and without you."

"There's always that concern," Heather said. She wasn't willing to promise she'd stay if a

better opportunity arose. Then again, a few
months' commitment meant if the family she
found didn't want her—or worse, she didn't
want them—she could head back to Phoenix
with no regrets.

"Then I'd better make it worth your while."
He offered her a salary higher than the one
she'd walked away from at her previous job.
Hmm, how could she say no? Why would she
want to? After shaking his hand, she went up
front to fill out the necessary forms, promised
to return the next day for training and walked
out employed.

Back at the B and B, Bianca was checking in
a guest and Father Joe wasn't taking Heather's
calls, so she had no one to celebrate with. Her
best friend, Sabrina, back in Phoenix, would
only gripe that taking this job meant Heather
really wasn't coming back.

She decided to try Turner's farm again.
She'd been around there Saturday when she'd
been so rudely interrupted by a rogue cop with
a vendetta that somehow involved her.

She pushed away that fear.

She was here to find family. That Rachel
Ramsey happened to look like her was pure
happenstance.

Didn't mean a thing.

She hoped.

Yeah, right.

MAX STOCKARD'S WIDOW, Sylvia, lived with their two children just a couple of blocks behind Main Street. She made jewelry and, during the Founder's Day celebration, had manned what looked to be a successful booth.

"Hey, Sylvia," Tom shouted while also knocking on the screen door that was unlocked no matter how many times he'd warned her to keep it locked, and waited. He was tempted to just enter, like he'd done for so many years.

Instead, he knocked louder.

"Hey, Tom." Sylvia finally came to the door. She wiped her hands on an apron, then pushed her glasses up along the bridge of her nose.

"I'd thought I'd stop by and fill you in on something unusual that happened having to do with…Max's case."

"I've been expecting you. I heard you stopped someone on suspicion, but everyone says you've made a mistake. That's not the Tom I know."

"I'm pretty sure I made a mistake," he admitted and not for the first time, "but hopefully it will lead to something. Let me fill you in."

She nodded, leading him to the kitchen, where he sat at his usual spot and accepted a fresh cup of coffee.

"I was heading over to Richard Welborn's place," Tom said, "wanting to nose around a bit and see if he'd come back."

"He's not coming back."

"You never know."

He and Max always debated the stupidity of some criminals. Sylvia had a different outlook. She also believed in rehabilitation.

Her dad was serving time for fraud, so she had reason to hope.

"The woman," Tom continued, "one Heather Graves, looks exactly like Rachel Ramsey, down to the red birthmark above her left lip."

Sylvia raised an eyebrow. Now he had her attention. Thirty minutes later, after fixing her garbage disposal and tightening the nozzle on her back sprinkler, he left. For five years, he'd taken care of the little things around the house for Sylvia, things Max would have done.

Sometimes he missed being a husband.

He radioed in the time and his destinations, and took off. As he left the downtown area, he thought about getting over loss. Max's death had broken his spirit, but it was Tom's wife leaving him that had broken his heart.

He tried to shake away the memories, and focus on the job ahead of him. He needed to check on the possibility of Richard Welborn's return as well as meet up with Ms. Graves and prod at her history a bit more.

Heather Graves might have shared her story, but he was pretty sure she'd left out whole chapters.

CHAPTER EIGHT

AFTER A FORTY-FIVE-MINUTE drive, twenty minutes longer than it needed to be because she'd made a detour and driven by the house she owned, Heather pulled into a gravel parking lot and stepped out in front of a small store decorated with bees and that smelled like cinnamon. Although the open sign was stuck in the window, no one was inside when she entered.

She walked up and down the aisles, noting that the bee decor from outside dominated inside, too. Turner's farm had twelve different flavors of honey, as well as honey candy, honeycombs and even whipped honey, which was perfect for spreading across a peanut butter sandwich, or so the label on the package advised.

The smell of the place made her hungry.

Heading back outside, she peered out at the fields that stretched as far as she could see. There were two barns, at least five little houses and one big one. The wind picked up, sending tall grass swaying. Along with the faint swishing, voices carried. She looked to her left and saw a big man on a tractor leaning down talking to another man.

Chief Tom Riley.

His voice was strong, clear and all business. "You sure you haven't seen Richard Welborn? I drove past his house this morning, and there were tire tracks in the driveway. If I remember, his mother has her groceries delivered on Friday."

"I haven't seen anyone heading up that road. Maybe with the Founder's Day celebration, they changed her delivery date."

Heather let out a sharp exhale, wondering if the tire tracks might have been hers. She'd even gotten out and knocked on the door and even peeked in a few windows because she'd noted a light on in the back.

"Could be." The chief of police didn't appear convinced.

The old man shrugged and remarked, "You'd think he'd worry about his mother, come back and check on her every once in a while. She won't answer the door when the wife and I head over. Gloria's convinced she's not eating enough. Most unfriendly neighbors we've ever had. At least the Ramseys, daughter anyway, would stop and buy some honey every once in a while."

"He's too smart to come by," the chief said. "If he goes to jail, and believe me, he would, then he won't be able to earn enough money to pay the rent."

The older man shook his head. "She's staying by herself and managing. Most people get by when they have to."

Heather figured the man on the tractor had to be Turner. He was white-haired, with a beard like Santa, and wore a loose oversize shirt and brown pants. He slowly stepped down from the tractor, wiped his brow and moved forward. He was even older than she'd first figured.

"It sure amazes me that he didn't just take his mother with him when he dropped off the face of the earth."

"Maybe she wouldn't go."

"I'd love to go inside that property again, go through his things, see if he left any clues behind."

"Use the warrant. Never mind Richard's mother threatening harassment. If it makes you feel better, find out who he's paying the rent to." The old man pivoted to lean against the tractor, breathing heavily and looking tired. "Then you can get their permission."

"Even that's a mystery," Tom said. "The leasing company sends the payments to a forwarding company in Delaware, of all places. They forward it to whoever owns the house. They have no idea who the owner is."

"Used to be a lot harder to hide," the old man said. He took two steps, stopped and rested, and then took a few more. She wanted to hurry to him, take his arm, help him to the house.

Chief Riley didn't attempt to offer help or sympathy.

Heather took out her cell phone and checked the time—not quite four thirty.

"He really wasn't a bad neighbor. Sure, he'd race down the road a hundred miles an hour, take that curve and scare Gloria. We've got schoolkids around our place all the time. But boys will be boys."

Chief Riley shook his head. "Twenty-eight is hardly a boy. What I really wanted and can no longer offer was some kind of closure for Lucille Calloway. That's what I wanted, Albert."

Albert, Heather thought. It suited the old

gentleman. Albert Turner was the kind of name that belonged to someone old and wise, someone who'd been around a while, and whom you might go to for advice or just to bounce ideas off of. Like Chief Riley was doing now.

Albert put a hand on Chief Riley's shoulder. "You can still offer it to her children. Next time you want to check out the place, I'll go with you if you want me to. I know how hard it is for you, seeing that house."

Feeling slightly guilty about eavesdropping, Heather took a step back. This was a private conversation, but why would it hurt Chief Riley to see the house? Her house?

"No, I'm good. I can do whatever it takes to find him, even search the house again. I shouldn't let it bother me that it's where the Ramseys lived. It's just a house. And honestly, Albert, I think he's been around. Those tire tracks are recent. And Richard's mother doesn't have a car, not that I know of."

The Ramseys? Rachel Ramsey? She'd lived in Heather's house. Someone was living there? It looked so empty, sad.

"Could be some kids drove their car in the driveway or maybe even an out-of-towner," Albert suggested.

Heather frowned. She hadn't noticed anything unusual or out of place.

"Talk with the leasing company again. That's all you can do. It's a nice place that's had a run of bad luck." Albert shook his head. "I remember how nice it was forty years ago when the VanBoggenses lived there. Been through a few owners since then and most of the renters have been brutal."

Riley nodded.

"Sure is funny," the big man said, "that the woman you say looks just like Rachel came back about the time you think someone's been nosing around the old place."

"Quite the coincidence," Chief Riley agreed.

Heather took a step back, her heel getting caught in the sidewalk, and down she went. As far as falls went, it wasn't her worst, but it was her loudest. Chief Riley got to her first with Albert catching up a full minute later.

"You all right?" She was surprised Chief Riley had the decency to ask. She quickly stood and brushed herself off, wishing she could disappear.

"I'm fine, just a little clumsy."

"You weren't kidding." Albert stepped back, rested a hand against the wall of the store and

gave her a once-over. "She's the spitting image
of Rachel Ramsey. I'd have pulled her over,
too."

Twice in the same day, but last week when
she'd been dropping off résumés, shopping in
the grocery store and buying books at a used
bookstore, no one had noticed the resemblance.

Or had they?

The clerk at the bookstore had stared hard
at her and said, "Oh, my." Heather figured the
woman had been surprised by someone actually buying ten books, all romance. Then, too,
the first time she'd gone into the grocery, the
clerk had dropped Heather's change and fum-
bled on the floor for it, looking up at Heather
once or twice as if afraid. The only reason
Heather remembered was because a quarter
had gone into a crevice under the counter and
couldn't be retrieved. She'd told the clerk to
keep it. Instead, without a word, the clerk had
protested, "No, no, it's yours," and pulled another one from the register.

"Heather Graves," Heather said, sticking out
her hand for Albert to shake.

He took it, but instead of shaking it, he
turned it over and looked at her palm and then
reached for her other hand, gently touching the

small scratches she'd just earned. "We'll need to get this cleaned up."

Chief Riley frowned down at her palms. "They don't look that bad."

"Come on up to the house." Albert ignored Chief Riley. "The wife will want to meet you."

Heather wasn't sure she wanted to meet the wife, especially if the woman made a comment about the resemblance.

"My wife's name is Gloria. Half the reason we put in the store and opened the farm up to visitors is because she loves company. She'd never forgive me if I don't bring you up to meet her." He reached inside the store's door, turned the open sign to Closed and stepped out again, silently walking toward the big house as if knowing they'd follow.

"I don't—" Heather began.

Chief Riley stepped to her side and out of the corner of his mouth said, "It won't hurt you. Come to the house."

"Fine," she muttered, frowning at him but then turning a smile on Albert, who didn't notice because he was concentrating hard on just making it to the house. Now she knew why Chief Riley hadn't offered a hand. Albert was proud and determined. He wasn't the type to quit or take help if he could do something on his own. For every step he took, she and Chief Riley had to wait for the count of ten before taking one. Chief Riley stayed by Heather as if afraid she'd bolt. As much as she wanted to tell off Chief Riley, she got caught up enjoying the path to the house. It circled around the side of the store to the back and was surrounded by lush greenery. Tall trees made an archway. A swing was to her left and a fountain was to her right. An old garage, complete with an ancient, rusty red truck, was a short distance from the house.

And the beehives were next to the truck.

"My wife does the bees," Albert said. He'd stopped and turned, as if he anticipated questions and had suddenly decided to spare the time.

Or maybe this was a good excuse to catch his breath.

"I've never seen hives before."

"Get Gloria to give you a tour. She'll tell you all about thriving colonies, storing pollen and good comb-building. Me, I like the honey but I got stung once, twice, maybe a dozen times." He shuddered. "Now I don't want any part of it."

"Don't believe him," Chief Riley said. "Any time Gloria needs something, he's out there helping."

"I'd much rather be working the land." He smiled.

Heather looked around again. It was even prettier than the brochure touted.

Though, the brochure also didn't say, "Expect to run into the chief of police during your visit."

HE WONDERED HOW much she'd heard. At this point, he wasn't sure it mattered anymore. It seemed they were after a lot of the same answers.

When they came to the big farmhouse, Albert slowly used the ramp while Tom and Heather used the stairs. Albert held open the back door, which led right into the kitchen, and waited until they passed.

"You bring someone for supper?" Gloria called. "I've enough on the stove for everyone."

"Two someones," Albert said easily.

"Oh, I don't need to eat." Heather started to turn, but he took her by the elbow and guided her into the room. He wondered why she was intent on leaving, unless she just plain didn't want to be near him.

Hc wasn't crazy about being near her, either. She smelled like sweet summer citrus with just a hint of honey. And really, who wore bright red jeans with a white-and-neon-yellow-striped top and white tennis shoes with bright pink laces? She did, he supposed, and he couldn't stop a grin.

"Wife always makes plenty," Albert said. "You won't leave hungry."

"Who is the second somebody?" Gloria Turner moved her wheelchair through the wide door frame—one that Tom and Albert had spent a whole Saturday widening—and stopped.

"I don't believe I've met you," she said to Heather.

"Ma'am," Heather said. "I'm Heather Graves, and I really like your store. All the honey options as well as the crafts are lovely."

"Hard work, actually. But I have a lot of fun putting it all together. I should have been out there, but the phone rang and then, well, never mind. I'm Gloria Turner, and I take it you've met Albert."

"I have," Heather said. "He even told me about your hives."

"He thinks they're silly." Gloria shot Albert a sly grin, which he returned, suddenly looking twenty years younger.

Heather quickly said, "I'd love to take a closer look sometime."

Albert whistled. "Do it at your own risk. You weren't even able to walk by the store without getting hurt. I'd hate to see what a bee would do to you. Mother, you might want to take a look at her palms."

"They're fine. Really. Just a few scrapes."

"Let me see," Gloria said.

Tom watched as Heather showed Gloria the slightly scratched-up palms, and then they went down the hallway to the bathroom so Gloria could do some mothering, leaving him alone with Albert.

"What do you think?" Tom asked. "I so believed she was Rachel, but Rachel didn't have these mannerisms. And she didn't have the same eyes. This girl's blue eyes make me feel guilty for arresting her. You ever felt like that? Even when you know you did everything right?"

"Not a cop alive who didn't feel guilt when

they made a mistake. Most cops, though, don't attribute the feeling to a pair of blue eyes. They attribute it to cold, hard facts."

"I don't have any cold, hard facts, at least none that I trust," Tom retorted. "And don't tell me I rely too much on technology and that when you were chief of police, gut instinct proved you right more often than not."

"Then I won't tell you, seeing as you already know it."

Tom was tempted to stick out his tongue. Albert was right. Shock had him pulling Heather over, and from almost the very first moment, gut instinct and common sense had been at war.

Heather had led him down a path he'd never expected to take. One that reminded him of Rachel's beginnings and how she'd come to be at Jeremy Salinas's side that day.

What his gut instincts weren't helping with was how Heather figured into the equation: how and why she'd turned up in Sarasota Falls and what he should do about that.

CHAPTER NINE

ALBERT AND TOM went into the living room, while Heather took a seat at the kitchen table and watched Gloria maneuver. The kitchen was designed for the wheelchair, with low counters and plenty of wide space. Still, the woman didn't seem to move the wheelchair at all; she moved herself. For about ten minutes, Heather sat silently, wondering if she should excuse herself.

"I should—" she began.

"Just give me a minute." With that Gloria put a lid on a big black pot and then swirled around.

"It's a nice surprise to have Tom bring a female friend."

"He didn't bring me," Heather said quickly, correcting her. "I wanted to see your place and was in the gift shop. He just happened to be out back talking to your husband."

"He comes by about twice a week." Gloria

leaned close. "He pretends he's looking for advice, but really he does it because he's lonely."

The chief of police lonely? Hah! He was too busy pulling over innocent people. "He doesn't act lonely."

Gloria tsked. "When you're an officer of the law, you learn to compartmentalize anything that's going on outside the job. Me? I was married to the chief of police. Gives me great insight. Plus, I've known Tom since he was a toddler. He's a good guy. Albert likes when Tom stops by. Breaks the monotony."

"Albert must be plenty busy around here with the store and farming and stuff," Heather observed.

"The store's mostly mine and pretty much runs itself except when we have school visits or on holidays. Our two sons do the farming. Albert just crawls on the tractor every once in a while for old time's sake."

"From when he was a farmer," Heather mused.

"Er, well, more like from when he was a teenager. The farming gene skipped him. He was chief of police here in Sarasota Falls for more than thirty years. Sometimes he wishes he hadn't retired."

Everything was so interwoven in this town. Heather was about to eat supper with both the ex-chief of police and the current chief of police. The woman who looked like Heather had lived in the home Heather's parents had owned. It was enough to make Heather want to hurry back to Bianca's Bed-and-Breakfast, dive into bed and cover her head until she could sort it all out.

But that would be boring. "So," Heather said, "Chief Riley took over for your husband?"

"Tom took over for the chief that followed Albert. How long you been in Sarasota Falls?"

"About a week."

"What brought you here?" Gloria asked.

It was a question Heather should have expected by now. Well, the only way she'd find her own answers was by making her quest known, but she didn't totally trust Tom. His agenda and hers might not be the same.

"I might have family here, so I thought I'd look."

"Your last name is Graves?"

"Yes. My mother was Melanie and my dad William, but he went by Bill."

"I've lived here all my life," Gloria said.

"Don't remember a Bill and Melanie Graves. You said *was*. They dead?"

Blunt. It took Heather a few seconds to compose herself before talking about her parents' death. Truly, she'd not had to share it too often before now. In Phoenix, only her friend Sabrina and the people from the dental office where Heather worked had come to the funeral. Even Sabrina had remarked about how small the Graves's world was. There'd not been many people for Heather to notify.

"They died months ago in a helicopter accident."

"I'm so sorry. I lost my mother when I was about your age. To this day, I still stop sometimes and wonder about questions I have that only she could answer."

Heather didn't know whether to cry or scream. She doubted Gloria could fathom the kind of questions Heather needed answered. *Who am I? Who were you, really?*

"As I was putting things in order," Heather said, "I came across quite a few hints that they might be from here." For some reason, Heather felt comfortable talking to Gloria. She seemed to inspire trust in people.

"What kind of things?" Gloria prompted.

Heather wasn't quite ready to share that she owned the house down the road, so she tried a different tactic.

"*Hint* was the wrong word. I'm actually sure they spent time here. Maybe right after my dad got out of the military. His first job was here managing the Little's Grocery Store."

"Little was a good one for giving a helping hand to veterans," Gloria mused. "Some just needed a hand up, getting used to civilian life. Then they'd head on, go back home."

"My dad didn't have a home to go back to, that he knew of. He fostered out of the system at eighteen and joined the army because he had no money or real opportunities. It was a good choice for him. He said he'd not planned on marrying until he met my mom."

"And they met here? How?"

Her dad had told the story, mentioning the store's name, but not the town and state. She should have asked. Back then, though, as a little girl, she'd just enjoyed hearing her mom and dad's story, and assumed the store was in Phoenix.

"My dad was working security at Little's, and one night someone tried to steal my mom's purse. He stopped them. She was so shaken up, he drove her home."

"What was your mother's maiden name."

"Smith."

Gloria snorted. "Not sure how much that helps. We do have some Smiths. I can make a few calls if you want, but I don't remember a Melanie Smith. How old was she?"

"She'd have been sixty this year."

"I'm sixty-five. I don't remember a Melanie Smith following me in school, either."

"Is your memory that good?" Heather queried.

"No, but Sarasota Falls was that small fifty years ago."

Heather laughed. "I'm from Phoenix. This town is amazingly small to me now."

"Well," Gloria soothed, "you've only been here less than a week. It will grow on you. Why don't you go in the living room and tell the fellas that supper is ready." She pointed to the doorway and then turned back to the stove. Heather obediently stood and went down a hallway loaded with photos and a few awards. She stopped and looked at them. For Albert, they all had to do with policing. For Gloria, they all had to do with county fairs and bee competitions.

Heather hadn't even known that bees and honey were a country fair event. Her memory of the State Fair in Phoenix was of rides, games and crowds. Her mother hadn't liked crowds, so they'd only gone once.

Heather rounded a corner to the most beautiful living room she'd ever seen. A giant black-and-beige rock fireplace took up one wall. The front window, even bigger than the fireplace, had its curtains drawn and the view was spectacular. The bright orange sun sat low in the sky, highlighting the plateau of clouds forming a narrow shelf below it. The front double doors were open so the porch, complete with rocking chairs and potted plants, could be seen. There was also a grouping of chairs as well as a television set, which was turned on to the news.

Both men listened intently to the journalist. Heather cleared her throat. "Gloria says to tell you supper is ready."

"Good." Albert pushed himself up. "The news is depressing me."

Chief Riley's expression was a mixture of anger and sorrow.

"Son," Albert said, "the only thing you can

do is help make the world a better place, take care of Sarasota Falls. Keep telling yourself that you're part of the solution and putting on that badge becomes a whole lot easier." He left the room and a few seconds later Heather heard Gloria say, "I hope you're hungry."

Chief Riley stood, turned off the television and waited for Heather to lead the way. Quietly she did, thinking about the shrewd advice she'd received from her best friend in Phoenix. "You need to sue," Sabrina had said, yesterday morning when Heather had called her. "It was harassment. False arrest, even."

Sabrina was always a bit of a drama queen.

Truth was, if Chief Riley felt the same heartbreak, about losing his best friend, as Heather felt about losing her parents, then she was willing to cut him some slack.

Come to think of it, Heather couldn't imagine life without her best friend, Sabrina, who thought Heather was rash for packing up and moving a whole state away just to find family that may not exist.

Albert set the pot of chili in the center of the table. Heather sat down next to Gloria and Tom took a seat beside her. The other night, she'd somewhat shared a meal with him, too.

It hadn't gone well and she'd left with an upset stomach. Maybe chili wasn't such a good idea.

"You're smiling," Chief Riley observed.

"Just had a funny thought."

"Care to share?"

Heather grinned. "It's about chili, and I don't know you well enough."

"We'll have to remedy that," Albert said. "I love cracks about chili."

Heather shook her head, very aware she was sitting so close to the current chief of police that their elbows bumped.

Albert bowed his head and was halfway through a prayer before Heather bowed her head, too, and thought, *Get me through this meal without revealing too much.*

After the "Amen," Albert stood, ladled a decent helping of chili into her bowl and then Chief Riley's. The cornbread plate was passed around, and after everyone had the chance to take a few bites, Gloria said, "So, Tom, how's work?"

Tom looked at Heather. "Lately, we've been busy."

"Always something to do when you're short-handed and the chief of police." Gloria's eyes twinkled as she looked from Heather to Tom.

"I'm sure you knew that Heather's here looking for family."

He turned to stare at her. His eyes were unblinking and his expression was a bit accusing. "No, she didn't mention that the times I spoke with her."

"You didn't ask nicely," Heather said.

Albert barked a laugh, and even Gloria smiled. Chief Riley, however, didn't change his expression. Then he asked, "And your family is…?"

"Haven't found them yet."

"Their names were William and Melanie Graves," Gloria said. "What Heather knows is that William, Bill, that is, used to work for Little's Grocery Store."

"There's got to be a connection—" Tom began.

Gloria interrupted, "Did you tell all this to Father Joe?"

"I didn't get a chance to. By the time I realized he was someone who might be able to help, he got called away and—" she gave Chief Riley a look, then changed direction "—and, he hasn't returned my call."

"When did you call him?" Gloria asked.

"Yesterday," Heather admitted. "But really, it was Sunday."

Gloria and Albert exchanged a long look, then Gloria said, "Joe's usually pretty good about getting back to people. But he's dealing with Lucille Calloway's death. They were quite close."

Even as Gloria said the words, her husband was slowly shaking his head.

"Did Joe say anything to you when he picked you up from the police station?" Tom finished the last of his chili, put the spoon down and turned to look her straight in the eyes. "I realize we keep dancing around how much you look like Rachel. Father Joe's been here forever, counseled half the town. He knows secrets that could keep you up half the night."

Tom had everyone's attention, but no one added anything until Gloria snorted. "Joe might know a few secrets, but in Sarasota Falls most secrets are opened just as soon as they're wrapped. If Bill Graves worked at Little's Grocery Store, we'll find someone who knew him."

"We'll?" Albert queried.

"Yes, *we'll*."

Albert nodded, finished the last of his chili

and asked Heather, "You weren't born here, though?"

"No, my birth certificate says Phoenix."

"How old are you?" Albert asked.

"I'm twenty-seven."

"So, we're looking for people who were here possibly thirty years ago." Albert nodded.

"How old was your dad?" Gloria asked.

"He'd just turned seventy-two."

"Quite a bit older."

"Career army. When he retired, he came here, married my mother and moved with her to Phoenix."

"Why did they move?"

"They said it was because I was on the way and he got a good job offer."

"I'll talk with the manager over at Little's," Tom said. "Your dad should be easy to trace, and we'll see who else worked there at the time."

"I agree," Heather said. "He might also be a bit of a dead end if he doesn't have family for me to find."

Gloria didn't hesitate. "But finding out about him will lead to information about your mother, and eventually, maybe more family."

Chief Riley stood, picking up his bowl and

spoon before heading to the sink. "And what do you intend to do if and when you figure out your connection to Sarasota Falls and possibly meet family?"

"I'm not sure," Heather admitted. "I just know that I've always wondered about my family. Call it an itch I need to scratch." She took her last bite of chili, amazed that she'd finished the entire bowl, but definitely feeling its weight in her stomach. At least she hoped it was the chili and not a combination of guilt and worry.

It was now or never. "Are you finally one hundred percent sure I'm not Rachel Ramsey?"

Last time she'd asked, his face had been grim. This time, he looked resigned. "Yes, I'm one hundred percent certain."

"My best friend, Sabrina, said I should sue you for all you put me through Saturday."

"You wouldn't be the first to try."

"I want to go with you when you talk to the store manager. There are a few details I've not shared."

Chief Riley turned, leaned against the sink and folded his arms across his chest. He didn't seem surprised. Both Gloria and Albert leaned back, too, clearly interested.

She hadn't lied, not really, but that didn't keep her from feeling a moment's guilt at what she was about to say.

"My parents were Bill and Melanie Graves. I have tons of documentation to prove it, however, after they died, I found their safe-deposit box, and the identification inside didn't correspond to those names."

Surprisingly, it felt good to tell someone. She wasn't sure if she'd have been able to do it without Gloria sitting there. Chief Riley no longer looked resigned. He looked intrigued.

At her information, not her.

"The photos on the drivers' licenses were my parents, but the names weren't." Heather looked at Gloria. "You said a Melanie Smith wasn't a few years behind you in school. What about a Sarah Lewis?"

"Oh, my," Gloria said. "That's a name I haven't heard in years."

TOM HAD BEEN a cop for more than a decade. He'd once arrested his best friend, he'd chased meth dealers out of town, he'd had to tell Mayor Goodman that his daughter was a serial shoplifter and he'd helped solve a murder that had a year later become a true-crime television special.

Tom hadn't been too impressed by the cop who'd portrayed him: too pretty.

He'd even arrived at his partner's side in time to hear his last words: *tell my wife and children I love them*.

But never before had he been handed so many twists and turns in a case.

"What do you mean that she's a name you haven't heard in a long time? Could she have something to do with Rachel Ramsey? Know where Rachel is, maybe?"

Gloria gave him a dirty look.

Albert said, "Tom, let her talk."

"Sarah Lewis was four years behind me in school." Gloria settled back in her wheelchair, making herself comfortable, and Tom knew they were in for a long story. "Her sister, Debbie, however, was just one year behind me. You know her stepfather, Tom. He's Taylor Jacoby."

"Oh," Heather interjected, "I've met him. Father Joe introduced me when I went to retrieve my car." She shot Tom a look that almost made him squirm. "After someone had it towed."

"Honest mistake," he responded.

"Sarah and Debbie Lewis were raised by Taylor, almost as if they were his. Half the time even the teachers called them by the last name of Jacoby."

"So?" Tom asked. "Sarah and Debbie are Tammi's daughters from a first marriage. I didn't know she'd been married before."

"Yes, her husband died fairly young. The girls were probably three and five when Taylor married their mother."

"Anything unusual about the marriage or their home situation?" Tom asked.

"Nothing unusual except Sarah was really shy. I can remember overhearing one of the teachers say that Sarah never needed to say anything because Debbie said it for her."

A talkative woman named Debbie...

Talkative.

"Debbie Lewis couldn't be Debbie Stilwater? She's not married to my lieutenant, is she?"

Albert was nodding. "We went to their wedding."

"Do you have photos?" Tom asked. "Maybe Heather's mom would be in them. She was in the wedding, right?"

Gloria shook her head. "She'd left home already. She married some guy in the air force and lived overseas. Debbie said she couldn't make it back."

"My dad was in the army, not the air force," Heather said, looking anxious.

"I need to talk to Debbie Stilwater, then."

Tom took out his cell phone and punched a number. After Lucas answered, Tom said, "Your wife still visiting her sister in Tucson?"

"Yes, she'll be home tomorrow. Why?"

"Heather has a few questions for her. I don't want to go into it now, but I'll fill you in later. Let me call you back."

Tom disconnected and turned to Heather. "I can get you her phone number, or you can wait and talk to her in person on Tuesday."

She thought a moment and then said, "I'll wait until tomorrow."

"In the meantime," Gloria offered, "I can send Albert over to my younger sister's. She'll have the yearbooks that have Sarah's photo in them."

Forty-five minutes later, Heather and Tom sat on the living-room couch looking at the high-school yearbook photos of Sarah Lewis.

"It's my mom," Heather breathed.

"We suspected that," Tom responded.

"I know, but seeing her, so young."

"I don't remember her at all," Tom said.

"Well," Albert had said, "she left when you were still in grade school. No reason for her to cross your radar."

"The Jacobys are well respected in town," Tom told Heather. "They never cause trouble. Only time I've had to deal with them is when someone tries to break in to the auto repair shop, or occasionally, I've had to work on nonpayment issues or his dealing with some irate customer. Taylor's always had right on his side."

Heather touched the yearbook that showed Sarah Lewis during her senior year of high school. "Look at the long red hair," she murmured. "She always kept it short while I was growing up. Said it was easier. What a funny half smile. It's as if she had a secret."

"All teenage girls have secrets," Tom said.

Heather gave a half smile very similar to the one in the yearbook. "Apparently, my mother even had secrets early on."

"Gloria's sister said she remembered Sarah," Albert told them. "Said she was the quietest girl in school."

"I wonder why."

"Were you quiet?" Tom asked.

Heather shook her head. "I wasn't the rowdiest, but definitely not the quietest. I had my gang of friends. We held our own." She closed the final yearbook and handed it to Gloria. "Thank you so much for thinking of this. I feel connected to my mother in a way I never expected."

"So what are you going to do next?" Gloria asked.

"I don't know," Heather admitted. "I need to think this through. I can't head over to Taylor Jacoby's place and speak to..." Her voice broke. "Is this Tammi still alive?"

"Oh, yes," Gloria said. "She is very much alive."

"Then she might very well be my grandmother."

Tom didn't know what to do. The urge to comfort Heather had him reaching his arm around her. Wasn't hard since he sat right next to her on the couch. On the other hand, just forty-eight hours ago, he'd been taking her to jail, convinced she'd helped kill his partner. Even as his arm moved to circle her shoulder, he withdrew. Now was not the time.

"As much as I'd love to meet my grandmother," Heather continued, "I can't just knock on their door out of the blue. What if they don't know about me? Worse, what if they don't know about my mother?"

The room fell silent.

"I don't want to be the one to tell them," Heather whispered.

"I'll go with you," Tom said, "and help explain all this."

She stiffened. Not the response he expected.

"I overreacted on Saturday," he told her in a low, sincere voice. "I've been looking for Rachel for years. Seeing you felt like time was going both backward and forward at lightning speed, and I had to act. Had to.

"I wish I were wired different, I wish I didn't make mistakes, but I do. I'm sorry my mistake involved you."

For a moment, he thought it wouldn't be enough. Then, she gave a slight nod. "Okay."

And maybe it was, for now.

The dark evening sky blanketed them when they walked out of the Turner place. He promised that he'd go to Little's Grocery Store and ferret out some information. She agreed that he could go alone, since she'd already struck out there. He also promised he'd talk to Lieutenant Stilwater and then come get her tomorrow night so they could pay a visit to Debbie Stilwater, née Lewis. And last, he'd promised not to do any other questioning without her that was related to the case.

As he drove back to town, Tom couldn't decide if he was looking forward to tomorrow because he'd be one step closer to finding out more about Rachel Ramsey, or because he'd be helping Heather Graves.

Who wasn't Rachel Ramsey.

How could he have thought there was a similarity?

Besides looks.

CHAPTER TEN

Tom entered the station bright and early Tuesday. He was immediately met by Leann Bailey. "The Duponts had a break-in last night. They want you to call."

Tom nodded. "What was taken?"

"Jewelry, a bit of money and small electronics. Oscar went over this morning. He figures the burglar got in through a bathroom window, making it either a small adult or possibly a young person. Whoever it was, and what surprised Oscar most, was that the person didn't leave a mess behind. The Duponts intend to call a home-security company and get a system. Mr. Dupont's disgusted with this town and says it's not safe anymore."

Tom didn't say what he really thought. Mr. Dupont was a fatalist. Truth was, if Mrs. Dupont had any jewelry worth money, they'd have sold it to help with the son's medical bills. As for electronics, he doubted they had much.

Whoever broke in had to be someone new to town or visiting, someone who didn't know the Duponts.

Any other day, his thoughts might have gone to Heather, the only newcomer in town. But the recent Founder's Day celebration meant they'd had many visitors, a lot always stayed on to visit with family and friends. Today, most folks would be leaving. Meaning, last night would have been a good time to commit a crime. Snatch and go.

"I'll stop by. What else?"

Leann smiled. "Mayor Goodman is in your office."

"I don't like—"

"I know, but he came in, went right on in there and sat down. I offered to keep him company in the break room, as well as make him coffee, but he declined. The break room, not the coffee."

Tom knew how much Leann did not appreciate making coffee. The only man in town that Leann wouldn't forcefully remove from Tom's office was the mayor. Rick Goodman had a finger in about every town endeavor. In other words, he had power. Luckily, he usually had good sense. There'd been a few times, though...

Tom hurried down the hall and turned right into his office. "Mayor?"

"Morning, Tom. Thought you'd never get here."

"It's not even eight, and I got called to an accident early this morning."

"The one on Beecher Street?"

"Yes. No one was hurt. But the teenager at the wheel hit a fire hydrant. Could have turned into a mess, but we got the water shut off before any homes were flooded and damaged."

"Sixteen and a driver's license." Mayor Goodman shook his head. "Too many kids lack good sense at sixteen."

Tom leaned forward. "There are plenty of older people in town who don't have good sense. Most of them were at the Hoot & Holler this past weekend. Would you like to read the reports?"

Mayor Goodman declined. "It's the locals. It's the nonlocals I'm worried about. Did you know that besides the Duponts, Sweet Sarasota was broken into yesterday, too?"

This got Tom's attention. Even if he hadn't caught the call, his deputy, whose wife owned the shop, should have told him. He didn't let his face register any of the surprise he felt. "I'm sure," Tom said, "that we'll figure out what's going on."

Mayor Goodman pushed himself up out of the chair.

"Keep me posted," the mayor said. "Seems funny that all of a sudden we're having so many break-ins."

Tom didn't think two was that many, and he wanted to know how the mayor knew about the Duponts so quickly. Sweet Sarasota he wasn't surprised about. The mayor had probably made a morning stop for a doughnut or something. But the Duponts? The small town's grapevine must be working overtime.

Like Tom often did.

"Don't worry," Tom said. "I'm sure we'll either catch the criminal or he'll disappear with the Founder's Day visitors."

The mayor paused by the office door. "He? Does that mean you have an idea who it might be?"

"No, I used 'he' generically."

"Good, because I've been thinking that the Duponts live near Bianca's Bed-and-Breakfast.

Maybe you should stop by there and see who's on her guest list. Then, maybe—"

"You telling me how to do my job?" Tom asked drily.

The mayor blinked. "No, just worried that all my hard work promoting the town this past weekend will be for nothing if suddenly the big story is two break-ins. Businesses made money. If they also lose money, they might not be willing to—"

The mayor's cell phone pinged, interrupting, and he excused himself. Tom watched the man back out of the room and waited until he'd left the station before beckoning in Leann. "You know anything about a robbery at Sweet Sarasota?"

Leann shook her head. "When did it happen? Who called it in?"

"I'll tell you when I know more," Tom promised. He'd take a walk to Sweet Sarasota, buy himself a doughnut and hear what Shelley Guzman had to say.

He checked his email first and found nothing pressing. Leann handed him some paperwork to sign. He read each page, made a few corrections, signed and handed it all back. He then checked the duty roster. He'd planned on this being a sparse week. His officers had picked up a lot of overtime the past week, but maybe Tom should rethink that.

Something was happening in his town. First it was Heather Graves with her mystery to solve and her resemblance to Rachel Ramsey, and then it was the break-ins and the mayor taking more than a passing interest.

On his way out the front door, he told Leann where he was going and then headed for Main Street, just a block and a half away. A few ribbons fluttered in the street gutters, remnants of the Saturday night fireworks spectacular. Bart's Auto Repair was open. Tom made a detour and found Taylor Jacoby standing in front of Jason Bitmore's car.

"Shouldn't mess with a fire hydrant," Taylor said. "They always win. This one's a shame. Gonna take me a month to find a new hood."

"You always manage. I still say you should have set yourself up as a restorer instead of just auto repair."

Taylor made a wry face. "First of all, when I started out, restoring was a hobby not a television reality show. Second of all, only the guys who do it on television make any real money. I had kids to raise."

"Did the Founder's Day celebration put money in your pocket, too? The mayor thinks local businesses really profited."

"It did. But not in a good way. Most of my money came from impounds."

"Your son still gonna take over the business?"

Taylor laughed. "Yes, but I'm not set to retire yet. Got a grandson to help put through college."

It was on the tip of Tom's tongue to ask about the rest of the family, but he'd promised Heather not to do anything without her. The bell over the entrance sounded, and Taylor excused himself, leaving Tom alone with his conflicted thoughts and the teenager's wrecked car.

Looking at Jason's car was depressing. A classic Ford Mustang from the sixties, beautifully restored, and Jason hadn't even had it a year. The kid had mowed lawns, babysat, as well as been the town's resident computer whiz. He'd specialized in helping parents set up controls on their children's electronics. He'd done a few websites, too. All impressive, especially considering that for a while the whole town worried he'd be a juvenile delinquent.

Jason had started shoplifting at twelve and once, a few years ago, had crawled through a doggy door at the mayor's house thinking he'd find some loose cash.

The mayor had caught him and taken him under his wing, and now Jason was a straight A student who'd worked hard to buy his first car. Looked like he'd be doing it all again. This time to fix his vehicle instead of to buy it.

Not as much fun.

Ever a cop, Tom considered Jason's size and the size of the small window in the Duponts' bathroom. No, not a chance. Jason had also grown into a guard on the Sarasota Falls' high school football team.

Deciding not to wait, Tom walked out the bay doors and back to the street, which was getting busier. At least two cars, loaded with luggage, made their way down Main. Likely the last visitors leaving town.

Yes, things were hopping in Sarasota Falls. Behind him, Tom heard the sound of Taylor getting back to work. He liked Taylor. The man had a shock of white hair and the longest fingers Tom had ever seen. Tom's ex-wife said Taylor should have played the piano. Tom thought Taylor resembled the inventor from

Back to the Future, an old movie that appeared on reruns every now and again.

More than like, Tom respected Taylor. He was still working to help the grandkids go to college. No better legacy than that. Sometimes Tom wondered what his legacy would be. His ex-wife hadn't wanted kids. She'd said cops should think twice before having kids. Their line of work was too dangerous. When Tom had reminded her that he was chief of police in Sarasota Falls, New Mexico, population... well, small enough that Tom knew every resident by sight and big enough to be a headache.

That hadn't been enough to convince her. Maybe he should have pushed more, but she'd never been the kind to give in. She'd had goals and a work schedule that rivaled his. She'd started out as a hair stylist. Soon, she'd owned the salon. What he'd liked most about her job was she'd known the ins and outs of almost every family in Sarasota Falls, who was seeing who, publicly or in secret, who was thinking about moving, within city limits or beyond, and on and on.

In other words, town gossip.

He almost laughed. Maybe she'd known about Sarah Lewis. Nah, why would she? And really, he couldn't blame himself for not knowing Taylor had another daughter, Sarah.

Making his way down the road again, Tom thought about all Gloria had shared yesterday. Sarah Lewis, Taylor Jacoby's stepdaughter and Debbie's sister, had left when she was barely twenty.

No surprise that. Most of the kids in Sarasota Falls dreamed of heading for the big city right out of high school.

Tom had never wanted to leave. He'd always loved his hometown, the feel of it, the people, his job.

No, it was others who left: his parents, his wife and, as soon as she solved the mystery of her parents, Heather Graves.

TUESDAY MORNING, HEATHER was so excited about her new job that she woke up at six thirty. Way too early. Worse, she couldn't go back to sleep. She tidied her room, easy since she had so few belongings. Then she got dressed, tucked a book in her purse and headed for what was fast becoming her favorite restaurant: the Station Diner.

The town looked different, empty. The sidewalks still had barricades up from the weekend's festivities. There were a few outdated signs tacked up promoting events. Heather pushed open the diner's door and stepped in. A waitress she didn't recognize motioned her toward a booth in the front. Heather took her seat. From this angle she could see outdoors. None of the businesses were open; lights weren't on. A few cars passed by. The waitress came, took her order and disappeared. Heather pulled out her book and settled back. This was a favorite routine. She'd only managed a page when she heard tires screech outside. She glanced out the window and saw a police car stopped in the middle of the street. The female officer who'd been present during Heather's arrest got out of the vehicle, hunkered down and was looking under a parked car.

Soon, Heather wasn't the only one watching what was going on.

"She really oughta move the car," one person said.

"She's a cop," another argued, "what's going to happen? Is she going to tell herself to pull to the side?"

After a moment, the female officer was flat on her stomach and crawling under the parked car. Then she pulled what looked like a ball of fur toward her.

"A kitten," the waitress breathed as she set Heather's breakfast in front of her.

"A little one," Heather agreed.

"Amazing she saw it. You want anything else?"

"Ketchup, thanks."

Show over, the restaurant's noise returned to old men talking about yesterday and the weather, as well as a few loners all professionally dressed for work and looking at their cell phones.

Heather checked out her purple cotton scrubs and matching top. The clothes were more suited for a hygienist than front desk staff, but they would have to do. Most of what she had to wear was too casual for an office setting.

The diner's door opened and a woman and a boy came in. Heather recognized the waitress. "You sit over there, Billy, and I'll get you some breakfast. Eat quick because it's almost time for school."

The boy, no more than four, obediently took a stool at the counter. Everyone, from the cook to a businessman busily texting, looked up and smiled at him. Most gave a greeting. Maureen, that was the waitress's name, hung her sweater on a peg and disappeared into the back. She came out a moment later with a coffeepot and started making the rounds, ending with Heather.

She smiled and said, "One more refill?"

"Better not," Heather replied. "I'm not sure I want to be this caffeine-driven on my first day of work."

"So, you're here to stay?"

"For a while," Heather admitted.

"It's a good place," Maureen said. "Kinda grows on you."

She walked away before Heather could agree. It had only been a week, but Heather felt like she was friends with Bianca and Albert and Gloria. She also had more than a passing acquaintance with the chief of police.

A while later, Maureen was back, refilling Heather's cup once again. "Your son's really cute," Heather said, "and so well-behaved."

"Yes, that's my Billy. He'll leave for preschool in about an hour. In the meantime, he'll sit and color."

"You have more children? Or is he your only?" Heather asked.

"For now, he's my only." Maureen hesitated, looking like she'd rather be anywhere else. Finally, she said, "Look, the town's talking. They know about Tom arresting you for no good reason. You could get him into trouble. But Tom's a good cop. The best there is. When I came to town, I was dragging baggage that weighed more than I do. He listened to my side of a sad story, and because of him, I'm pretty free of my past. That's not just the kind of cop he is, it's the kind of man he is."

"I'm beginning to believe that," Heather returned, honestly. She'd picked up the other day that this woman had more than a passing interest in the chief. She'd also picked up that he didn't have the same interest in her. Heather did not want to be in the middle.

"Everyone in Sarasota Falls knows the story," Maureen continued, even when Heather put up a hand indicating she should stop. "Rachel Ramsey, apparently, didn't have a chance in life. She didn't have a father. Her mother disappeared for days, leaving that girl to raise herself. When the wrong boy came along, Rachel could only think, 'Finally, someone is paying attention to me.'"

Heather heard the story from both Bianca

and Gloria, and a bit from the chief himself. Still, Heather asked, "Pretty much the whole town thinks this Rachel Ramsey was responsible for Max's death?"

"I wasn't here when it happened," Maureen confided, "but in the diner you hear things. Yup, I'd say the whole town believes Rachel played a part."

"And everyone thinks I look like her."

"I've waited on a hundred customers since Saturday night. They all say the same thing. You look like her, but," Maureen added, "you don't act like her."

"Good, because I can't even imagine luring someone to their death. I'd have never been able to look at myself in the mirror again."

"One thing I've learned is to not assume." Maureen picked up the empty plate and stepped back from the table. "No one's spoken with Rachel since that day. No one knows the whole story."

"But they saw what happened," Heather said softly.

"They saw the external," Maureen responded just as softly. "Not the internal. I married a man who, by looks and how he presented himself, appeared to be a hero. He wasn't. I'd like to hear the truth from Rachel because, quite honestly, I'm prejudiced because of my—

Heather expected the word *love*.

"—respect for Chief Riley."

No surprise there but the admission made Heather a bit uncomfortable. "From what I hear, Max was more than Tom's partner, he was Tom's best friend. Father Joe told me that for a while, the town didn't think Tom would get over the loss."

"But I did." Tom's words surprised both of them, Heather especially, as her hand hit her water glass, sending it tilting precariously.

Tom apologized. "Sorry, I didn't mean to sneak up on you, but I'm glad I did since I was the main topic of conversation."

Maureen looked stricken. Heather just wished she could back out gracefully.

"Coffee?" Maureen asked brightly.

"Sure."

"Chief," Heather said, raising her cup in a salute.

He settled in across from her at the table. "This is becoming a habit," he said.

"What?"

"Sharing meals."

"No." She shook her head. "I'm finished

with breakfast, and I'm about to head off for my first day of work."

"You're kidding. You got a job?"

"Admin assistant, not quite like back in Phoenix. I was a hygienist there."

"Well, your old boss did say he'd hire you back in a heartbeat. Did you interview with Dr. Goodman or his right-hand man, Maya?"

Maureen put a plate of pancakes in front of Chief Riley and gave Heather a tight smile.

"Dr. Goodman. But I got the idea that Maya runs the place. I'll be filling in for her while she visits family."

"She has a passel of grandkids spread throughout the United States. Goodman's the mayor's younger brother."

"I figured that out thanks to a photo he had on the wall."

"Small town," Tom said. "I had a visit from the mayor this morning. We've had a regular crime wave this past week. Two break-ins."

"Really? Where?"

"One was a house, and the other a business."

"Maybe," Heather said wryly, "I should re-think apartment hunting. I was going to go for a six-month lease. But if this is turning into Gotham…"

He grinned. "Don't worry. I'll keep you safe. What time do you get off? We should stop by and talk to Debbie Stilwater tonight. That was the plan, right?"

"Yes. And I've changed my mind. I'd like to try Little's again, too. The chief of police might make answers flow a little more freely."

"Six good?" he asked.

Heather dabbed at her lips with a napkin, put three one-dollar bills under the plate and then took hold of her purse as she scooted out of the booth. She was ready to start the day.

"It's a date."

She wanted the words back almost the moment she uttered them.

Because she almost meant them.

CHAPTER ELEVEN

Tom HAD BEEN heading for Sarasota Sweets when he'd spotted Heather in the Station Diner. That she was engaged in a serious conversation with Maureen had caused him to make a one-eighty. Good thing he had. He hadn't stopped to consider what Heather would be dealing with when it came to the good people of Sarasota.

No doubt she'd heard quite a bit from Bianca, too.

Heather seemed to be taking it quite well. She'd even joked a bit. He liked that. Enough so that he was glad pancakes warmed his belly instead of the blueberry muffin he'd been thinking about.

The bakery was doing a brisk business. Most likely, Shelley would make back more money than was stolen. Most of the people were there for a few sweets and a lot of details about the crime.

"Got a moment?" Tom asked.

Shelley snorted and waved a hand at the line that reached to the door. "Little busy here."

"I can see that. Maybe you can get someone to take over for a few minutes."

She nodded and one of her employees took her place behind the counter. The line moved to let her come out front.

"Let's go to my office," Shelley said.

A slight moan sounded, and someone even muttered, "Oh, just say it out here. You know we're gonna find out anyway."

Tom waved and said jokingly, "Keep in line. Settle down."

Shelley abruptly stopped, swinging around to stare at him, her mouth twitching. "Okay, who are you, and where is the real chief of police?"

"What do you mean?" He followed her into the kitchen, which smelled like chocolate chip cookies. Her office was little bigger than a closet.

"Tom Riley, I've known you forever, and since my husband works for you, and you stop by the house two or three times a month, I probably know you better than most. You're supposed to be upset because you arrested the wrong woman and—"

"And I'm here about your robbery, not my questioning the wrong woman. What happened?"

"You were actually funny out there—"

"Shelley, what happened?"

"Okay. I came in this morning and the back door was open. I'm sure I locked it, but Oscar looked and he said it would only take a credit card to open, the door's so old. He's going to—"

"Shelley!"

"I always keep a bit of cash in the register. Not much, but enough for change in case something happens last-minute. I had about sixty dollars in there. The register was open. The money gone."

"Anything else?"

"No, not really. A couple of cookies probably left with the guy."

"Guy?"

"Could have been a female."

"Your husband take a report?"

"I'm sure he did. He searched the back alley but didn't find anything. He checked some of the neighbors to see if their security cameras were on. So far he's come up empty."

"Anything else?"

"Oscar mentioned it's weird how nothing was out of place. It's like whoever came in went right for the register, took the money and left. If they'd gone in my office, they'd have found my company credit cards in the drawer as well as a bucket where my staff and I have been throwing change. We're going to use it for an end-of-the-year party. Granted, it weighs a ton, but there must be a couple hundred dollars in there."

Tom thought it weird, too, how two crimes committed the same evening had similarities.

"And," Shelley continued, "my wedding ring is in the top drawer of my desk."

"What?" He looked down, saw her bare finger with the pink indent and lines evidencing a recent removal.

"I meant to take it home but forgot. My fingers are a bit swollen from…" She suddenly looked shy.

He looked at her, really looked at her, and saw that even while she was talking to him about how she'd been robbed, she was smiling. People who'd just been robbed didn't smile.

"Swollen from…" he prompted. Even as the words left his lips, he figured it out. "Are you…"

"We, ah, we don't want anyone to know, but, well, Oscar's going to be a father again. We're pregnant."

"That's great. Really." Tom meant every word. Oscar and Shelley had been married just over a year. His friend had adopted Shelley's son from her first disastrous marriage. No chance the kid would ever feel neglected. He was named after Oscar.

If Tom knew Oscar, soon Shelley'd be sporting a brand-new temporary ring. No way would his deputy let his wife go around with a bare finger.

His ex-wife had left her ring in the soap dish by the kitchen sink. It was still there, Tom was pretty sure.

Maybe it was time to move it and move on.

"FORMS ARE HERE," Maya Gillespic said. "We ask our clients to go online prior to their appointments, print them and fill them out at home, but maybe two percent do. First thing, make sure you have plenty of copies. You don't want to leave a mom with a scared grade-schooler standing beside her while you run to the copy machine. A terrified first-grader can turn into a screaming mass of nerves in a heartbeat."

Heather already knew this.

"I arrive first," Maya said. "I turn everything on. I sterilize what the dentist and hygienist use, and I also wipe down the toys and video machines. We have a cleaning crew for the last two, but I don't trust them."

Heather nodded, thinking her old dental office could use a few Mayas. She appeared to do the work of three.

"I listen to messages. You'd be amazed how many times we get calls in the middle of the night, mothers wanting to know what to do about their child's toothache. What's funny is, come morning, only a few come in. From eight to nine, we have an open-door policy. No appointments but we will see anyone who brings a child through those doors."

"What a great idea," Heather said.

"Doctor Goodman had a toothache when he was twelve, on Christmas Eve. He had to wait three days before seeing the dentist. He says he never wants one of his patients to go through that much pain."

"Nice guy, huh?" Heather queried.

Maya nodded. "The best." She pulled out a file, then in a more serious voice said, "These three families get their dental work for free. Two of them are single mothers." Maya pulled a coupon book from the same drawer. "These are gift certificates to the Station Diner. When they visit, we give them one of these also. I always tell them the restaurant is doing a promotion and I need to get rid of them."

Dr. Goodman came in ten minutes before Maya unlocked the front door. There was no stampede of emergency patients. He greeted Heather as if they were the best of friends and then disappeared into his office.

"He usually doesn't come out until the first patient's been here twenty minutes. He has a routine. We all do. Today we're pretty busy. Back-to-back appointments." Together, the two women sat at the front desk and Maya introduced Heather to the list of today's patients.

At ten minutes before nine, the hygienist, Marcie Rickard, showed up. Nothing quiet about her. She brought attitude and music. Maya tsk-tsked but smiled.

"Hey," Marcie said, sticking her purse in a cupboard under the second computer. "Good to have you here. Maya's been talking about visiting her sister for years. Knock me over with a feather that she's finally doing it. Did you convince your sister-in-law, Trina, to go along?"

Trina? An unusual name and one Heather'd heard recently.

"No, she can't afford to take time off work," Maya said.

"Where does she work?" Heather asked.

"Little's Grocery."

Heather nodded, finally seeing the resemblance and remembering that the cashier at Little's had the last name Gillespie on her badge. She'd spoken with Trina and had even shown Trina a cellphone photo of her dad, but before Trina could more than "um," the security guard had interfered.

"You're a hygienist, too, right?" Marcie asked.

"Yes."

"Should be interesting." Marcie raised an eyebrow.

Heather scooted her chair back, away from the computer screen she'd been going over with Maya, and turned to face Marcie. "If you're thinking that the practice doesn't need two, you don't have to worry. Dr. Goodman made it clear that I'm only filling in for Maya, nothing else. Plus, I'm only temporary."

"Why?"

Whereas Maya had been all business, Marcie was all social interaction.

"I haven't decided if I'm going to stay in Sarasota Falls or not." Heather used the same explanation she'd given the dentist during her interview. "I've friends in the area, and I'm thinking about downsizing. I've never enjoyed big-city living, but…"

"My sister said you were looking for information about Raymond Tillsbury." Maya joined in the conversation, gazing directly at Heather.

Instead of answering the question, she decided to ask one of her own. "Did *you* know him?"

"I went out with him once, thirty-odd years ago, before I married and had my own children."

Heather's breath caught. Her first real connection to her dad. "Really? What was he like? Why—"

The front door banged open and a woman

herded in two small children, both of them protesting that they didn't need to visit the dentist.

Maya stood, all business again, and said, "Hello, Evie, you're right on time." To Heather, Maya said, "Go ahead and get the forms ready, attach them to a clipboard, give them to her and let's get started."

Heather did as she was told, having Evie sign in first. Handing over the clipboard, Evie said, "Nice to meet you, Heather. My mom said she had a wonderful visit with you the other day. Said she had you and Chief Riley over for supper."

Marcie whistled. "Chief Riley. I practically threw myself at him when I moved back to town. No luck at all. And you—" she gave Heather a once-over "—have been in town, what, a week?"

"A week," Heather agreed. "And it wasn't like that."

"I'm sure it wasn't." Evie's tone was half jest, half apology.

The door opened again and another mother, this time with one child, came in. Heather manned the sign-in sheet, Maya returned to the computer and Marcie disappeared into the back room.

Maya certainly had her routine down. She'd greet a patient, get preliminaries done and lead them into one of two rooms, each with a dental chair accompanied by a rolling stool, various equipment and necessary supplies for either the dentist or hygienist. After getting patient and parent comfortable—patient on bed, parent on bench—she'd go back up front to start the pattern all over again.

Marcie took over then, updating the chart with the parent, explaining what would be done. Usually she did this so the child could hear everything and even ask questions. Heather knew this because she used to do the same back in Phoenix. Sometimes an X-ray was necessary, most often not. Dr. Goodman appeared, almost magically, after Marcie had cleaned and polished the teeth.

"Let's take a look." Dr. Goodman's opening didn't change patient by patient, but his conversation did. While discussing gums, he'd also ask about scores on video games or what worked and what didn't with the latest *Star Wars* movie. Switching to the "bite" conversation, he'd brag about Nerf gun wars and camping. It was Dr. Goodman himself who handed out the toy boxes. There were four, and Dr.

Goodman seemed to know which box to grab for which kid.

Everyone received a bag with toothbrush, toothpaste, floss and a timer.

Before leaving, parents dealt with payments and some scheduled the next visit.

Heather kept busy shadowing Maya, checking in patients, calling patients to remind them about future appointments and sometimes just sitting next to a young patient making small talk in order to calm nerves.

In the end, she decided that children were pretty much the same as adults. They were scared of the dentist, whined a bit, wanted lots of breaks and were generally good-natured and entertaining.

Lunch was at eleven. Maya locked the door, and the women headed to the small break room. "Dr. Goodman goes home," Maya said. "He likes his wife's cooking."

"And he's addicted to one of the soap operas," Marcie added. "Unless we're overly busy, he takes two hours. I go back on the clock at noon and just do cleaning."

Heather hadn't thought to pack a lunch. She blamed it on first-day jitters, combined with not having her own place. She made a few noises about running to the store, but Maya, acting a lot like Bianca, simply got a second bowl out of a cupboard and spooned half her soup into it. "It's Mexican black bean with sausage. Made a big batch for the Founder's Day potluck. I'll be eating it for months. Glad to get rid of it."

Truth was, Heather didn't want to go to the store. She had an hour with Maya and wanted to know about the long-ago date with Raymond Tillsbury.

Marcie didn't give her time to start the conversation. Instead, the hygienist said, "So, first Chief Riley accidentally took you in, and then you wound up having a meal with him at the Turner place? How did that happen?"

Heather shared just a few details, most of which the two women already knew as Marcie kept interrupting trying to find out information Heather either didn't know or didn't want to give out.

"So you're probably related to Rachel Ramsey?" Marcie asked.

"I'd never heard of her until moving here."

Luckily, Marcie took that as a "no" because Heather was half-afraid she was related to Rachel.

When Marcie finally got all she was going to get, Maya took over. "So, why were you asking my sister-in-law about Raymond Tillsbury?"

Because their last name was different, Heather couldn't answer "He's my father." Instead, she said, "I could be related to him."

"He didn't have family."

"I've never heard of him," Marcie said. "But I only moved to town six months ago. I'd not heard of Rachel Ramsey until Sunday morning at church."

"He was an only child and mostly raised by his father," Heather said. "Then he wound up in foster care."

"That's Raymond," Maya agreed. "So, how are you related?"

"Not sure, but my parents recently died, and I came across his name while going through their stuff." Before any other questions came her way, Heather quickly asked, "You only went on one date. How come?"

Maya laughed. "He didn't like taking orders, and I live to give orders."

"Got that right," Marcie said.

"He'd just come out of the military," Maya added. "I think he was stressed. He just wanted to go to work and then go home,"

"Where did he live?"

"He had an apartment above one of the businesses downtown. Back then, they were dirt-cheap. Now," she added, "they've become a yuppie trend and cost a lot. Dr. Goodman owns a few of the businesses. I do the accounting, so I know having rentals downtown is lucrative. When I think that years ago my family owned a few of them…"

"Learn something every day." Marcie took a final spoonful before washing her bowl, putting it away and heading out front.

"She likes a little downtime," Maya remarked.

"What else do you remember about B… Raymond?"

Maya studied Heather. "You don't look much like him. He was a dark man, handsome. All the girls in town thought he was cute."

"Who else did he go out with?"

"I don't recall anyone. He wasn't here that long. Maybe a year or two. Then, he just took off."

Maya finished her soup, gathered the dishes and quickly washed them in the sink, brushing aside Heather's offer to help.

"Did he have any friends?"

"Father Joe."

CHAPTER TWELVE

TOM MADE IT BACK to the police station a full hour after he expected. He'd been nonstop busy all day, and it seemed the station had, too. There were three people in the waiting room. Leann had barely greeted him, she'd been so preoccupied collecting fines and arranging for a fingerprinting. Just down from her, Lucas Stilwater dealt with a weeping woman who seemed to have a lot to say but difficulty saying it.

She had to be a leftover visitor from the Founder's Day celebration because he didn't recognize her.

He shook a finger at Oscar as he passed his desk.

"I was going to tell you," his deputy defended, shaking a piece of paper in the air, "but I took a call and got busy."

"No excuse."

"Me-ow."

Peeking in his office, he sighed in relief. No mayor, no stack of new papers that needed his attention, not even the light on his phone shining red, signifying missed calls. He had paperwork to do and needed time to do it. He wanted to give Heather all his attention tonight when they visited Debbie Stilwater.

No, his mind backpedaled. He didn't want to give Heather his undivided attention; he wanted to give figuring out what caused her mother and father to change their names his undivided attention.

He logged on to his computer and started making his reports. He'd gone to the Duponts after talking to Shelley, a visit that resulted in an inflated missing list from the husband and a secretive here's-what's-really-missing list from the wife. After he left there, he'd given a speeding ticket to the town's oldest resident, who definitely should not be driving. Tom had stopped by the man's son's house on the way back to the station and mentioned the consequences of an accident.

Before he'd made it to the station, the Alzheimer's care center on the outskirts of town had called. Carson Brubaker, Shelley's dad, had gone wandering again. Tom had turned the SUV around, heading in that direction, and made it partway to the care center when he got the second call saying Carson had been found.

"Me-ow."

Tom misspelled a word. The sound definitely hadn't come from his deputy. Pushing back from his desk, he followed the sound to the waiting room. Lucas, still dealing with the weeping woman, gave a funny smile. Not good. Leann suddenly got very intense about pleasing the woman standing in front of her.

"I can't believe a dog license costs this much—"

"I agree," Leann said, "but I don't set the price and—"

"Me-ow."

The dog-license woman frowned. "Where's the cat? Does *it* have a license? Did you pay it? Or, is it just us common citizens who—"

"Yes," Tom interrupted. "Let me see the cat."

The whole waiting room grew quiet. Leann glanced at Lucas, who shrugged and quickly looked away. The dog-license lady backed up, clearly not wanting to be in Tom's scope. Leann said, "I found her under a car this morning and took her to the vet. She's undernourished, has a broken leg and needs a home."

"Then," Tom said slowly and carefully, "take it home."

"I can't," Leann wailed. "Peaches will eat it."

Even the weeping woman had quieted. Lucas leaned toward her and loudly whispered, "Big dog. Huge, in fact. Good with kids. Eats everything."

Tom immediately honed in on Lucas. "You like cats."

"I told my wife three was the limit. No way am I adding to our number. Ain't happening."

"Why don't you take it?" a voice asked from the entryway. Tom hadn't even heard the door swoosh open.

"I don't do cats," Tom told Heather. "But every bed-and-breakfast should have—"

"Can't," Oscar bellowed from his office down the hallway. "Aunt Bianca is allergic. She can do dogs but not cats."

Tom took a deep breath. "Does anyone want a kitten?"

The dog-license woman handed over a five-dollar bill and told Leann, "Keep the change," before scurrying out the door, bumping into Heather on her way out.

The weeping woman said, "I live in New York. Pets aren't allowed in my apartment building." The other three people sitting on chairs in the waiting room were teenage boys. The first one addressed Tom. "Dude, I—"

"Never mind," Tom said, watching as Heather stepped over to Leann and took possession of a mostly black but partially white kitten.

Lucas, suddenly all smiles, said, "Wife said to come to supper at seven." He checked the time on his cell phone. "She, by the way, is making your favorite." Looking at Heather, he added, "Spaghetti. Hope you like it. Oh, and you can bring the cat for that short a visit."

"She's only like four weeks old. The veterinarian is amazed she's alive." Leann walked around the counter and with one finger stroked the tiny kitten's head while explaining the food and the medicine. "I've been feeding her every few hours. It's easy. She's already eating gruel, and you can give her kitten food. She just needs you to rub her throat a little."

"Not me." Heather smiled up at Tom, who'd come over to stare down at the kitten.

"I'm not rubbing a kitten's neck every time I feed h—" Tom stopped. He didn't care that everyone in the waiting room was looking at him. He cared that Heather was looking at him. Those eyes, they were doing something to him, making him feel emotions he'd long locked away. For the second time in an hour, both times because of her, he backpedaled. "I can't believe I'll be rubbing a kitten's neck every time she needs to eat."

Heather smiled and handed him the kitten.

The people in the waiting room applauded.

Yup, he was toast.

"I'M FINISHED. SORRY IT took me so long." Tom walked along the police station's hallway and shrugged into his jacket, while frowning at her.

Make that frowning down at the kitten.

"You might," Heather said, "find that having a cat is fun. They're good company, and unlike a dog, they can handle being left alone for a few hours." She took his hand when he offered it, letting him help her to her feet, and handed him the box with the kitten in it.

She figured he took the box because she'd surprised him, rather than him wanting it. His expression as he gazed at the sleeping feline looked very much like someone who'd just received a Christmas present they weren't sure what to do with. She half expected him to hand it back. Instead, he took a few steps toward the door and said, "I'm not a cat person."

"How do you know? Have you ever had one?" This came from the female officer who'd rescued the cat earlier. Leann, Officer Leann Bailey, Heather remembered.

"No animals, not since I was a kid."

"Not true," Officer Stilwater objected. "You had Trigger."

Tom stopped so quickly that Heather ran into his back. "That was a long time ago, Lucas."

"Yes, boss."

Heather noted the tension in his shoulders. It hadn't been there until Lucas mentioned Trigger. Why? Could the chief of police have owned a horse? Surely a kitten was easier. Definitely less expensive.

Outside the Sarasota Falls police station, a gentle swish of cool air messed up Heather's hair. She didn't care. She had too many other things on her mind and was grateful that a tiny kitten had managed to distract her for a short while. She'd left work with a few questions and even more concerns. Worse, she had a feeling the answers wouldn't be the you've-won-the-lottery kind.

More the you-should-have-left-this-buried kind.

"We have an hour before we're due at the Stilwaters," Tom pointed out. "Why don't we go to Little's Grocery Store first and see if I can convince them to share what they have about Raymond Tillsbury."

"Good idea."

She climbed in the passenger side, slid the seat belt on and tried not to hurry him along. They were getting answers. Not always the kind she expected, but definitely answers.

"It's weird not to have a chain grocery store," she remarked.

"There are a few Littles around."

"Not like Safeway or Albertsons."

"That's true."

The store was fairly empty. She followed Tom through the aisles as he greeted people and stopped to answer a question about a barking dog.

"Can't you go anywhere without people wanting or expecting something from you?" she asked.

"No."

"It's gotta be hard to be you."

He didn't bother to answer.

Tom led her over to the manager. A small man who looked like he'd been inside all his life, he apologized and kept explaining that "I'm new, just two years." It took him almost an hour to find the information on her dad because it wasn't on the computer, but was in a faded brown file folder with about a dozen papers inside. One, Raymond Tillsbury's application. Two, his hiring contract and tax papers. There were three employee reviews, all stellar. Then there were letters of thanks from customers he'd assisted.

Tom went through the letters, took photos of them with his phone and passed them on to her.

She only recognized one name. Sarah Lewis. Her mom had written a letter thanking Bill for stopping someone who'd tried to snatch her purse. Heather nodded at the confirmation.

"The only thing I can see that's negative," the manager said, "is he quit without two weeks' notice. Whoever managed the store back then put a comment in the margins about how it surprised him.

"I wonder why he quit?" Tom mused.

Heather did, too.

They left the store and went right to the police station so she could retrieve her car. "I'm just stopping by my house to leave the kitten," Tom told her.

When she started to protest, he said, "We're not going to be out that long, and we'll feed her before we go."

We'll feed her.

Four days ago, he'd wanted to throw her in jail. Now, he expected her to help feed his kitten.

"I can do that." She got in her car and followed him a mere three blocks. She turned just past the courthouse, with its stone gargoyles, and pulled up behind him at an old but well-preserved small redbrick house. Parking in front of the house, she stepped out and noted how dark it was—only a porch light, and it didn't fit in with the surrounding homes. "You're not decorating for Halloween," she noted.

"Don't need to," he said. "All the neighbors have, so I figure no one will notice that I haven't."

"I noticed."

"Yes," he admitted, "but you're walking up to my front door. You have to notice."

"So will trick-or-treaters."

Tom laughed. "I guarantee no one will come here unless they want to toilet paper my tree, break a pumpkin on the porch, or leave fake body parts strewn across the lawn."

"Huh?"

"Halloween's always great fun in a small town."

The porch light overhead cast him in a soft yellow glow. He'd taken off his hat and his hair was mussed up and a little longer than she expected. His eyes were tired, but his smile was all for her. He looked vulnerable somehow.

"I love Halloween. My parents, Mom especially, went all-out decorating. Probably because it gave the children she took care of something special to do. They spent weeks painting boxes black, cutting black construction paper into long strips—all so they could crawl through the scary mazes we created in the backyard. Sometimes I'd put paper plates full of black Jell-O for them to crawl through. Freaked them out."

"Messy," he said.

"We had a hose."

"My parents weren't much for decorating, but when I was twelve, my mom made me a really cool Ninja Turtle costume. I still have it somewhere. Doesn't fit anymore."

"See, there's hope for you, and you still have that save-the-world mentality."

He laughed and unlocked the door. "I've been working it so long that Halloween is just an event that results in a long shift and a few extra reports to write."

"That's just wrong." Heather stepped back, put her hands on her hips and stared at his house. It wasn't big and it had good bones. That's what her dad would have said.

"Built in the fifties?"

"No, the end of the forties."

"Made to last."

He shook his head, and she knew she'd amused him. Her dad had loved old houses. Often after he'd picked her up from school or on the way home from church, they'd stop at an open house. He'd preferred the homes that had been lived in, not showy, but perfect for his family of three.

"We always rented," she said. "Dad dreamed of owning his own home, but we moved a lot. We finally stayed put when I was in high school."

He stepped inside, beckoning for her to follow. Once in his living room, he lay the kitten on the couch and plumped three pillows around it: two to imprison it and one in case the kitten rolled out of her box and fell to the floor.

He was such a faker, saying he didn't want a kitten but then going the extra mile. He left her kneeling next to the kitten and disappeared down a hall.

Clean, that was her first impression of his house, with very few photos and not a lot of color. An old, faded armchair was next to a fireplace that dominated the room. On the table next to it, a Jack Reacher book by Lee Child was facedown, half-finished. The television, of course, was huge. It and the fireplace dominated the room.

Above the fireplace was an empty space, a clear impression of where a picture used to hang.

Heather stared at the spot wondering why he hadn't replaced the picture. Surely every time he looked at the spot above the fireplace, which had to be every day, he noticed the absence.

Unless he wanted the spot to remind him of something. Something probably best forgotten.

He returned with a tiny bowl of water, which

he placed beside the sleeping kitten in her now too-full box.

"She'll roll over and make a mess," Heather advised.

"Oh, guess that makes sense." He moved the box to the floor, complete with two pillows. Leaning back against the wall and stretching his legs out in front of him, he relaxed a bit. She'd not realized how tall he was. He seemed to take up a lot of room, and she wondered what it would be like to curl up next to him.

She sat down on the couch, folding her hands in her lap, and watched him fuss over the kitten. "So, before we go to meet Debbie, I've a couple of things to tell you. First, I worked all day with Maya Gillespie."

He chuckled. "If Goodman ever stops being mayor, the town needs to put her in charge. She's a well-oiled machine."

"That's not a good description for someone. She's not a machine. She was very kind during my training today. She even shared her soup with me."

His eyes lit up. "Black bean and sausage?"

"Yes."

"Did you take home any leftovers?"

"No."

"If she's not mayor, she could cook for the Station Diner. Business would double."

"Do you want to hear what I have to say or not?"

He left the floor, coming over to sit next to her. He had to shove the coffee table away to accommodate his knees.

"What?"

It was only one word, but somehow the man's patient, kind tone, so very different than the one he'd used with her on Saturday, told her he would listen.

"She dated my dad, Raymond Tillsbury, when he lived here."

"That's good. You found out a few things," he said. "What else?"

"My dad rented an apartment above one of the businesses on Main Street, near where Sweet Sarasota is. Did you know it used to be a drugstore?"

He nodded.

"And," she continued, "the mayor's family owned it."

"Still do. The Goodmans probably own half the town." He was sitting so close to her she could feel the heat coming off of him. He was still in uniform—dark brown pants, light brown shirt and all kinds of gadgets attached to his belt. She'd never felt so safe. Maybe she could blame that on the handcuffs.

"Maya said something else."

A grandfather clock was in the corner of the room. She hadn't noticed it before. Had this been her house, she'd move the clock, make it a focal point. It tick-tocked, the only sound in the house except for the humming of a heater. Maybe that's where the warmth came from and not him. Surely not him.

"What did she say, Heather?"

"She said I didn't look like him." Pulling out her phone, she scrolled through photos and showed him photo after photo of her parents, neither blond nor blue-eyed like she was. She'd always thought her mother so beautiful, with silky light red hair that hadn't gone gray. Heather knew she'd go gray. She'd blamed it on her father, whose black mane sported silver threads, like the tinsel on a Christmas tree, back when Heather was in junior high.

Now she wasn't so sure.

"I don't know. I've been a cop long enough to know that families have so many branches that sometimes you can't tell they're from the same tree." He pulled out his phone and brought up a photo of his parents.

"They're short," she said.

"I know. I take after my uncle Danny. He's six-two."

"I never met any of my relatives."

"Well, you're going to meet Debbie tonight. So…"

"Do I look like her?"

He shook his head. "No, she's red-headed and so is her mother."

Heather grabbed her purse, pulled it into her lap and took out a brush from inside a Ziploc bag.

Tom raised an eyebrow.

"The day I met you, you asked for a swab of DNA as well as something that belonged to my mother. I don't want to start there. I want to start with my own mother, make sure she is my mother."

"Heather, I—"

"Tell me what I need to do. Do I need to find something that belonged to my father, too? I'm not sure that will lead anywhere since he was in foster care and wasn't from Sarasota Falls."

"You're jumping the gun a bit. But I'm not going to say it's a bad idea. What did you keep from your father?"

"Not much. I have his duffel bag from when he was in the army. I'll go through it."

"Okay. First, though, let's meet with Debbie Stilwater, see what she has to say and go from there."

"I have a bad feeling," Heather said. "I keep going over all I know and concluding that my parents left Sarasota Falls because of me. But that doesn't make sense. My father had a great job. My mother had family. You say that Debbie, her mom and her stepdad are great people. You don't run from great people unless you've got something to hide."

The clock struck seven. The sound was loud, dramatic, jarring. It was all Heather could do to not stand up, pace, run from his house.

He, of course, seemed to be feeling none of those things, and asked pragmatically, "Do you think they moved a lot because they were running, hiding, or both?"

"I wish I knew. That they were living under assumed names just floors me."

"We don't know why they ran yet. Give it time. Maybe they just wanted to be vagabonds. Some people are like that. Used to be, you had the West to settle in, make a cabin in the middle of nowhere all by yourself. Then, there were the hobos who rode the rails—"

"Oh, pahleeese. My dad wanted a home so badly that we went to every open house within miles of where we lived. He'd stand in somebody else's backyard and imagine where he could put a workshop."

"That's not unusual."

"It is when you actually own a home, a home with a backyard big enough for a dozen workshops."

"What are you trying to say?"

"It was the second thing I needed to bring up. When you picked me up because you thought I was Rachel, I was actually heading out to the farmhouse just past the Turner place. The one you and Albert talked about, saying the Ramseys had lived there, and the Welborn man you keep hoping to find."

"Why were you heading there?"

"Because I own it. My dad, who always dreamed of owning a home, owned it. I have the deed. It's in Raymond Tillbury's name. And, my lawyer said that my parents have been collecting rent on it for more than twenty-five years. I checked my bank statement when I got off work. I wanted to know how much I had because maybe I should be thinking about getting an apartment. I about fell over. I had an eight-hundred-dollar deposit. Took me a moment to recognize the description. It was the rent money from the farm."

"From Richard Welborn."

"I guess. And maybe from the Ramseys before that."

A shadow covered his face, but only for a moment. "That's great. If you're the owner, we can figure out a way to get in. Maybe I can figure out not only why he's paying rent for a place he's not living at, but where he is. And—" his eyes lit up "—maybe there's something there that could lead us to Rachel."

Heather stared for a moment, feeling somehow displaced, slightly affronted. He didn't understand. Her dad had owned a home, a dream home. Why hadn't they lived in Sarasota Falls?

To her chagrin, she expected Tom to understand—to care—because, well, because she trusted him. She was sharing with him how much and how fast her world kept changing. She'd made a huge mistake. She'd thought he was on *her* side.

And he was thinking about Rachel Ramsey.

Not Heather Graves.

CHAPTER THIRTEEN

HE'D DONE SOMETHING WRONG. He wasn't quite sure what, and unfortunately it had been a while since he'd cared about someone else's thoughts and feelings. He was rusty in the compassion department. And he'd lost her.

He remained on the couch, waiting for her to say something. Trying to think of something to say himself. Nothing came, so he said, "I need to change out of my uniform. Give me a minute."

She nodded, moving down to the floor to sit by the cat, her smile not quite reaching her eyes.

Funny, he'd never noticed how noisy the hum of his heater was. He thought about turning on the television, but by the time he found something she might be interested in, he could be changed. Heck, he'd only need five minutes, so why was he worrying about it?

He put on a pair of jeans and a gray T-shirt

before slipping into tennis shoes. When he finished, he headed back to her and asked, "You ready?"

"Didn't take you long."

"Never does."

It had gotten chillier and the wind had picked up. "I usually walk there," he said, "but if you're cold—"

"How far away do they live?"

"Four blocks."

"A walk sounds good." She dug her hands into her sweater pockets and fell in step beside him, hurrying a bit because his legs were so much longer. He offered to slow down, but she told him it was too cold for that.

Lieutenant Lucas Stilwater lived in a house almost identical to his except it was decorated for Halloween, and it had a lot more than a porch light blazing. The front door was open, never mind the cold, and laughter billowed out.

Beside him, Heather's steps faltered.

"You'll be fine," he told her. "Debbie's the easiest person in the world to get along with. Believe me. She puts up with Lucas. She's a saint."

He marched up the stairs, with her right behind him. Her steps might falter, but she wasn't the kind to give up. He liked that.

"Hey." Lucas welcomed them. "Come on in. Debbie's grumbling about the spaghetti noodles being mushy."

"I like mushy," Tom said. "That's how my spaghetti turns out every time."

"Yes, but you warm it up from a can."

"Got that right."

He let Heather go ahead of him. Her blond ponytail swung back and forth, just under his nose. She stopped in the middle of the living room, staring at a portrait of Lucas, Debbie and their three kids.

"Come in. Come in." Debbie came out of the kitchen, wiping her hands on a dish towel. "Lucas tells me that I might be able to help with a case you're working on."

"We hope so," Tom said.

Heather turned, looking at the portrait, then at Debbie, and then back at the portrait.

"It's time to replace that one. We've got two little grandchildren. They should be in the picture."

"You have a lovely family." Heather stepped closer to the portrait, almost touching it.

"The table's set in the kitchen. Come on, I've

salad and garlic bread and the works." Debbie rubbed her hands together. "We're all excited that Tom's bringing someone over."

"It's related to a case, honey," Lucas said. "I told you that."

Debbie smiled, disbelief in her eyes. "Sure."

Tom nudged Heather and together they both followed Debbie into the kitchen. Lucas got busy getting their drink orders and showing them where to sit. Once the food was on the table and their plates filled, Lucas said, "So, I told Debbie all about Tom arresting you. She laughed."

"Honest mistake," Tom said. "Look at her."

"I would have pulled her over, too, except she's shorter than Rachel."

"Debbie was Rachel's second-grade teacher. She used to bring her home for meals. Darn principal made her stop. It's a shame that the fear of being sued is stronger than the recognition that a child needs a friend."

"I've read up on Rachel Ramsey," Heather said. "She did have a hard life."

Soon the back-and-forth conversation was all about Rachel and her mother. There were a few things Tom didn't know, like Diane arriving in town driving an old Studebaker, but most he did know, like Rachel shoplifting just to have food to eat.

"So," Debbie said, motioning to Lucas to clear the plates, "how is it I can help you?"

Heather stood to lend a hand, but Tom said, "I'll do it."

The two men were quick. Good thing was they got to stay in the kitchen so they could hear every word.

Heather cleared her throat. "We had supper with the Turners on Monday evening."

"I already heard that, too. And you've been at the restaurant with Tom two times already. Some people are saying that you knew him before you moved here. But that doesn't make sense because then he would never have pulled you over."

"We just met, believe me. And us both being at the Turners at the same time was a fluke. A good one, it turns out. Because I learned quite a few things."

Tom watched Heather change seats so she was sitting next to Debbie. She pulled out her cell phone and brought up a picture. One he'd already seen. She stood with her parents, probably just a few years ago.

"Oh…" Debbie's voice grew soft, speculative. "The woman behind you looks familiar. Is that your mother?"

"Yes."

Lucas stood behind Debbie and frowned. "Looks a lot like you, dear."

Debbie reached for the glass of water in front of her and then took a long drink, looking at Heather instead of the cell phone.

Heather put her cellphone on the table, faceup so the picture was still visible. "My mom's name was Melanie Graves, but she and my dad passed away a little over a month ago. When I met with the lawyer and went through her and my dad's belongings and history, I found out that her real name was Sarah Lewis."

Debbie put down the now empty glass. "No, that couldn't be." Debbie looked at Lucas. "No, Sarah and her husband, Dale—Dale Walker— are at an air force base in Greenland. It's remote, and her husband's field is so specialized that…"

"Honey, you've always wondered." Lucas's voice was soft but firm.

Her fingers shaking, Debbie picked up Heather's phone and scrolled through the photos. "No, your mom is just someone who resembles my sister. I've got pictures, too." She pushed away from the table, still shaking a bit, and looked like she was fleeing Heather, rather than fetching photos.

"Lucas, I'm sorry—" Tom began.

"Don't," Lucas said, in a voice Tom had never heard. Lucas was the jovial officer. He always saw the glass half-full. He was the police officer who usually dealt with children. He was the one who best talked down a teenager, high on meth, who thought he was a superhero and the entire police force mere mortals.

"Don't," Lucas said again. "This is not something you should have sprung on us. You should have spoken to me first. Let me prepare Debbie. I don't believe the story, but you're here saying that Heather's mom might be Diane's little sister and she's dead."

"I wasn't sure there was anything to tell."

"Yes, Chief Riley," Lucas snarled, "you were sure. I've never seen you act unless you were sure—at least until this past week."

"It's my fault," Heather said. "I wanted to come here alone and talk to you and Debbie, and Chief Riley—"

"Tom."

"Volunteered to come along. I made him

promise not to do anything without me. He kept that promise."

Debbie returned, three albums in her arms. "Sarah rarely uses email. Their Wi-Fi is spotty on a good day. I just tried to call her. There's only one service carrier there. It rang and rang. She's sent things through the mail, and believe me sometimes it was months before we received them. They're blocked by ice nine months of the year and go about four months without daylight. I never thought my shy sister would wind up being the most adventurous of all."

She flipped open the first album. "This is Sarah standing next to her husband."

Even from a few steps away, Tom recognized that the two people were Heather's mom, Sarah Lewis, and Heather's dad, only he was in uniform, short-haired and wearing a hat that covered a good deal of his face. There were five pages of photos, all with the same background: a cold, white place.

In contrast, given what Heather had shared with him, Melanie and Bill Graves, in their roles as her parents, were at swim meets, on camping trips, at Disneyland.

"He should be ready to retire soon," Debbie said. "He's career air force. They've only been back for a visit a couple of times since they married. Never on Christmas. Maybe they'll come here first. Mom would sure like that. They were thinking about settling in Hawaii."

The first tears pooled in Heather's eyes. Tom saw them and wanted to take her hands in his, and tell her it would be all right. He'd make sure of it. But he couldn't make such a promise, and instead of being a hero, he felt helpless.

Heather reached for the purse she'd strung over the back of her chair and drew out an envelope. "My mom always wanted to go to Hawaii. She even had a big jug that she put all her change in saying it was for that special vacation." She withdrew ten photos and laid them on the table, separating them so they could be easily seen. The first one showed Melanie Graves holding Heather, just a toddler, with Bill behind her.

"That's Raymond Tillsbury," Debbie breathed.

Heather tapped one of the larger photos in the album still open on the kitchen table. "So is he."

NEVER IN HER LIFE had Heather been involved in an undertaking this emotional. Not even being arrested for something she didn't do.

Debbie's red hair curled under a bit, like

Heather's mother's had. And her hands were the same. It made Heather want to reach out and touch them, see if they felt the same, too.

"No," Debbie said.

Heather placed one of her photos right next to one of Debbie's. "Except for Sarah being bundled up in your photo, they're the same person. Look at the hair, the smile and even the way they hold their shoulders. And now that you've seen the photo of my dad, can you not see that Raymond Tillsbury is in both pictures?"

"What do you want?" Lucas asked. "Why are you here?"

"I'm trying to find out why my parents kept their true identity a secret and also if I have any family here."

"Sarah isn't Melanie, and Sarah didn't have any children. She couldn't."

Heather sat back. She wanted to be shocked, but she wasn't. She'd seen the photos of Debbie and Lucas's daughters. They were all red-headed, tall, like Debbie with a hint of Lucas in their faces. If Heather's hair had been reddish-blond, maybe she'd have a chance, but nothing made sense. "Why couldn't she have children?"

"She was diagnosed with endometriosis when she was twelve. By seventeen, she'd had two surgeries. It was a shame, too, because she loved children. Mom said that when it came to running a childcare, Sarah was a natural."

Lucas added, "She and Dale didn't want children. Said it would be too hard with his work. But they sent gifts to our kids."

Tom spoke up for the first time. "Heather's given me permission to check her mother's DNA. We wanted to right from the time I picked her up on Saturday. We were hoping to tie her mother to Rachel's mother."

"I remember," Lucas said.

Debbie slapped her hand on the table. "Then why are you here claiming that's my sister, Sarah—"

"Because of the ID that Heather found in the safe-deposit box. Heather, did you bring it with you?"

Reaching again in her purse, Heather brought out the two driver's licenses as well as the birth certificates. She handed them to Debbie, who looked at them for a few moments before handing them to Lucas.

"Look real," Lucas said.

"We showed the photos to Gloria Turner.

She thinks Melanie Graves and Sarah Lewis are the same person."

"Well," Debbie said, "her eyes are failing."

Even Lucas frowned, then asked, "You got any more proof?"

"My mom ran childcare in our home from as far back as I can remember. She was saving money for a trip to Hawaii, and she and my dad own the little farm just down from the Turners."

"The one Richard Welborn rents?" Lucas asked.

"Yes."

"Where the Ramseys used to live?" Debbie joined the conversation. "Sounds to me and—" She looked Heather up and down "Looks to me like the Ramseys are who you're related to. There's absolutely no reason for my sister to have a connection to that house. Also, she couldn't have children. And she's in Greenland."

Lucas was nodding.

"I'm getting a headache," Debbie announced. "If you could just…"

"We'll go." Heather stood, gathering the photos and other things and putting them back in her purse. "I'm so sorry that this upset you."

Debbie didn't move. Lucas ushered them to the door with a "We'll talk tomorrow" directed at Tom.

"Well," Tom said when the door closed behind them, "I was hoping that would go better."

"Me, too." Heather adjusted her sweater and stopped beside him on the sidewalk in front of the Stilwaters's house. The Halloween decorations added to her dark mood. "I don't blame Debbie, though."

"It is a lot," Tom agreed.

"If she believed me, then she'd have to admit her sister is dead. If she doesn't believe me, then to her, Sarah is still alive."

Tom put his hand on Heather's back and took a few steps. Heather faltered, looking over her shoulder at the neat, cozy house. She could only imagine what Debbie was feeling. She'd either gone to bed with a bad headache, the easy way out, or she'd gotten on the computer and emailed her sister and then tried the phone, either calling Sarah again or calling her mom.

Sarah wouldn't answer, ever.

"Coming?" Tom queried.

"Yes."

Before she could step up beside him, his phone sounded and he answered, "Riley."

Almost simultaneously the door to the Stilwater house flew open and Lucas hurried out. "Tom, did Leann just call you?"

Tom held up a hand, stopping Lucas in his tracks, and continued with his phone call. "Oscar, where are you and what time did the accident happen?"

"It's Richard Welborn," Lucas sputtered "Leann ran the license plate."

"What?" both Heather and Tom said.

"It happened at the end of the Turners' driveway about thirty minutes ago. Oscar caught the call," Lucas said.

Tom held his phone, not to his ear but in his hand, frozen as if he couldn't move.

Lucas continued, "Oscar gave her the plate and she ran it. Saw his name and called you, but you didn't pick up."

Tom went back and forth on his phone for a few minutes, confirming the driver's license was Welborn's, before finally turning his phone off, attaching it to his belt and again putting his hand on her back. "I'll walk you over to my place, see you off. Then I need to go. I need to go to the accident scene."

"Richard Welborn? He's who you were looking for the day you found me."

"Yes," Tom said. "And I'm not sure I believe in such a thing as coincidence. Lucille Calloway's funeral is tomorrow, and her killer's in critical condition today."

CHAPTER FOURTEEN

CHIEF TOM RILEY stood on the porch of the Welborn place at three in the morning, knocked on the door and tried to think about what he should say to Richard's elderly mother. He'd never had much luck talking with her. At most, she'd hold the door open an inch and murmur. She must have family somewhere because she was seldom home.

He hoped she had family as she'd need them by her side. Richard was in a coma and the prognosis wasn't good.

Officer Leann Bailey was at his side, ever the officer who might be able to offer a comforting word, be empathetic. He sure as heck wasn't certain he could be empathetic given the circumstances.

Not a single light flickered inside the Welborn place, and though they'd knocked and knocked, no one answered.

"You suppose she's long gone?" Leann asked. "No one's seen her in weeks."

"Heather saw a light here the other day."

"What was she doing out here?"

Tom had hesitated, which bothered him. Leann was a fellow police officer and one who deserved to know every detail. But Tom was starting to feel more protective of Heather than he was about the case at hand. He changed the subject. "The real question is what was Welborn doing in town. Probably visiting his mother, but then why was he leaving in the middle of the night? Why not stay until morning? Take the rural route away from town. We'd never have known he was here."

Leann fully engaged. "You're right. And another thing that doesn't make sense is why he would speed and drive recklessly. If he was trying to stay under the radar, no pun intended, he'd have been extra careful."

Standing there in complete darkness wasn't getting anything accomplished, so Tom drove back by the Turners' place. Bart's Auto Repair and Towing already had Welborn's wrecked car on the truck and was securing it.

Oscar was in the street, spotlights blazing, measuring the skid marks.

Tom waved, checked in at the hospital and went home to bed. He could do nothing else until tomorrow.

WEDNESDAY MORNING, when it came, started badly for Tom. He woke up at the first chirp of his alarm clock, and he'd only gotten three hours of sleep. He had a dozen things to do and limited time to do them. He really wanted to talk to Lucas about last night. And he needed to do it as an officer of the law, not as a good friend.

Tom knew without a doubt that the woman who'd raised Heather had been Sarah Lewis. And Debbie, her mother, stepfather and the two half-brothers needed to know the truth, deal with the truth and deal with Heather. Even if she might not be related to them. There was still a mystery to solve.

First though was Lucille Calloway's funeral, where he'd sit in a pew and hear remembrances of a woman who'd deserved more. He'd not been able to protect Lucille, but he could still honor her.

What really tore him up was he couldn't even tell her family that Richard Welborn had been brought to justice because losing control of a car, smashing headfirst into a ditch and becoming comatose wasn't justice no matter how you looked at it.

Tom had spent too many years thinking about getting justice, so focused on it that he'd lost track of what was important.

Lucille Calloway hadn't been that way. She'd told him more than once that she'd forgiven the man who'd run her car off the road. And because Tom had forgotten how to forgive, he'd be at the funeral alone. No wife by his side, no hand to hold and be reassured. The thought hadn't bothered him until he buttoned the last button of his uniform and looked at his reflection in the mirror.

And didn't like what he saw.

Someone who'd forgotten what it was like to be happy.

HER PHONE RANG at six thirty. Opening an eye, Heather glared at the clock by the bed and then at her phone lying beside her on the mattress. She'd set the phone's alarm to wake her up at seven. Dang, she wanted those thirty minutes. She checked the screen, noting the in-town area code. Okay, so probably not someone wanting to repair her auto glass or offer her a home surveillance system.

"Hello." Tom's voice, low and soft, erased all thoughts of sleep.

"Everything all right?" she asked.

"Right now, nothing feels right. There's a lot going on in my small town. I'm having trouble keeping up. Not sure I like it. But," he said slowly, "I do like you, so I wanted to call you first, see how you're doing. Last night was tough."

"I could have handled it better," Heather admitted, feeling something warm in the pit of her stomach. He liked her.

"How? You have Gloria Turner identifying your mother, you have ID—"

She interrupted him before he could continue. "I should have begun by saying who I was and what I was thinking. Sharing a meal probably made it seem like I was extending a hand of friendship. She felt tricked."

"If you'd started with the hardcore evidence, she'd have kicked you out or shut you down. What you managed to get were photos of your parents. Now you know they truly worked on having two lives. Debbie said they visited a few times. Do you remember your parents being gone for days at a time?"

"Yes. Dad said it had something to do with the military and that I'd be bored. They always left me with trusted friends. I actually thought their leaving was cool. They always left me with people who had kids. I'd pretend I had brothers and sisters. But I was always glad when they returned."

"If I know Debbie, she'll mull over this a day or two and then go visit her mother and talk it out. You'll be getting a phone call or visit."

"Fun." Heather didn't mean to sound snide, but she was neither convinced nor looking forward to it. She was just so darn tired and feeling uncertain. "Speaking of fun, what's going on with the accident from last night? Did you find out anything?"

"For Richard to lose control on the curve in front of the Turners' place makes no sense. What brought him back? I've a dozen questions. We've tried to get ahold of his mother, but she's not answering her door or the phone. That's the other reason why I called. We might ask you to let us in. I can't break in, and I'd rather not, anyway. Don't want to cause any unnecessary damage or concern if I can help it."

"Can I do that?" Even as she made the offer, some of the warm feeling ebbed away. He liked her. Yeah, right. He liked her because she might be able to help him solve more than one mystery.

"You're the homeowner. First of all," Tom said, "Richard is your tenant and he is now in the hospital, comatose. Second, his mother is old and not responding to enquiries—that constitutes a valid concern."

"I haven't got a key yet. The property management office didn't have any extras."

"Then after Lucille's funeral, I'll stop by the office and get it. Lucille was a friend of theirs, so I may see those folks before then. Please call them, giving me permission to get the key. Hey, I just pulled into the parking lot behind the station. I need to go. There's a lot to do. Most of my officers will be at the funeral. Sarasota Falls just might turn into a ghost town."

He ended their call and she left a message at the leasing office. Two hours later she realized how right Tom had been. The rental agency wasn't the only business to shut down for the day. Lucille had been a friend of the whole town judging by how absolutely empty it was, and by how boring the second day of work was for Heather. She was alone since Marcie, fairly new to town, had taken the day off due to the low caseload. Smart girl.

Maya had put Heather to work updating files and answering the phone. Looking out the window, Heather watched as car after car pulled into the parking lot of the big church across the street. Lucille Calloway's funeral had effectively halted every business on Main Street. A closed sign hung in the Station's window. Heather saw her favorite waitress dragging an ice chest, which also seemed to have a heated tray on top of it, down the street in her uniform no less, toward the church. Next to the restaurant, the owner of Rat's Nest—not the best name for a beauty parlor—turned her sign to Closed and three women, all with perfect hair, joined Maureen. They each carried a plate.

Heather could see Tom at the front door greeting people, ushering them inside the church and even handing out pamphlets. Closing her eyes, she thought about the double funeral for her parents. She'd been the one at the door, fluttering between the sign-in book and the memory brochures, and trying not to cry. Most of the attendees were either from the small church they attended or from her mother's childcare practice. Her father had been quieter, more to himself, but a few friends showed up, too.

Nothing like what Lucille had.

Not for the first time, Heather wondered what it must be like to stay in one place for a long time. Tom certainly seemed to prefer it. For that matter, so did Debbie Stilwater. She and Lucas exited a midsize white Ford. Lucas had his arm around her for comfort.

Heather quickly looked for Tom again. He stepped forward to shake Lucas's hand and even hugged Debbie, who seemed to hesitate for a minute before hugging him back. A lifetime of friendship there thanks to a small community.

The only surprise at her parents' funeral had been the daughter of the man who'd owned the helicopter. She'd shown up last, sat in the back and sniffled throughout the whole service. When it was over, she'd found Heather, took her hand and said, "I had to come. I'm so, so sorry." Then, they'd cried together, two twentysomethings who'd just lost beloved parents. Heather looked up the helicopter owner's funeral, but it had been the day before.

She should have gone. Dr. Goodman and a woman Heather assumed was his wife arrived next. Dr. Goodman let her out at the curb and Tom hurried down to carry the food she'd had in the back seat, enough to feed an army just by how many others had to join in to help carry. A man who looked a lot like Dr. Goodman arrived next. Heather recognized him from the photo in Dr. Goodman's office and from a talk he'd given at the Founder's Day celebration.

Like Tom, he'd come alone. He didn't bring any food nor did he offer to join the food chain that began at his brother's car. Dr. Goodman was two inches or so taller than his brother and about twenty pounds heavier. Heather remembered he was also the mayor. She stood and headed for the break room to make herself a cup of coffee. She'd spent thirty minutes staring at the church across the street instead of doing her work. Good thing Maya wasn't there looking over her shoulder. Heather doubted the strict office manager would have much patience for melancholy. Of course, Maya had been the first to arrive at the funeral, as far as Heather could tell.

The phone rang. Heather answered it, typed the woman's surname into the computer's search engine and waited.

"I've got your file. Is it Kevin or Beatrice?"

"Beatrice. She's been hurting since last night. She fell into the bathtub faucet and hit her two front teeth. I can already see discoloration, and they're both loose. I'd really like to get in today. They're not permanent teeth, but I want to make sure everything's all right."

"I'll see if we can make that happen, but I'll have to call you back. Dr. Goodman's not here. He's at the funeral."

"Oh, goodness, I forgot. Mrs. Calloway was my second-grade teacher. I should be there. No, it's too late. Yes, call me when everyone gets back. If need be, we can come tomorrow."

Heather made a note and then did some file updating. She'd seen enough people carrying food to know that the potluck would be after.

It was almost one when Maya and Dr. Goodman returned. "Sad, sad day," Dr. Goodman said as they walked in the door. "Seemed like half the people who were here for the Founder's Day celebration had to come back."

"She was loved," Maya agreed. "Did you see Cissy Tuttle sitting in the back? When Lucille held the Tuttle boy back a grade, Cissy took it personally, never forgave her. Yet, there she sat, crying. It would have been better if she'd cried for forgiveness while Lucille was alive."

Dr. Goodman shrugged. "Sometimes you have to ask for forgiveness at a funeral. It's the only place left."

Heather almost gasped. Thanks to Tom, she possibly knew a bit more about Richard Welborn than most of the inhabitants of Sarasota Falls. The idea forming in her head was wild, a long shot, but it wouldn't go away.

"I'm going to make a fresh pot of coffee," she told Maya.

"We're going to need it," Maya said. Heather retreated to the break room and made the coffee as promised. She also took out her phone and punched in Tom's number. He didn't answer, and she wasn't willing to leave a message, not one this important.

Heather knew why Richard Welborn had returned to town.

CHAPTER FIFTEEN

AFTER LUCILLE'S LAST bereaved family member drove away, Tom spent a few minutes with a most concerned funeral director wanting to discuss how the town was coping.

It was on the tip of Tom's tongue to say that people were upset, of course, but that life would go on, when it occurred to him that he really needed to get out to the Welborn place again. But first he'd check in at the station, see what was going on there.

It was a ten-minute drive back through town. Closed signs were being flipped to Open. The town was waking up. A few people waved. He couldn't shake the sadness.

After parking in front of the station, he exited his SUV and studied the building he'd worked in for more than a decade. It looked normal. Tom wished he felt normal. He walked up the path, pushed open the door and stepped in. For the first time he understood why the mayor had dropped by. Too much was happening in Sarasota Falls: break-ins, car accidents and even Rachel Ramsey look-alikes. If this kept up, Tom might have to hire another officer, and that certainly wasn't in the budget.

Leann, looking as tired as he felt, was at the counter. She stood and said, "I was just about to call you. I've got no known residence or place of employment for Welborn still."

"He was probably living under an assumed name."

"Sure is odd. Before he lived here, his record is spotless. We going back to his mother's place?"

Tom agreed. "I need to spend a few minutes in my office. Make a few phone calls. Then we'll go."

Sitting at his desk, he quickly checked his emails. The only one he found referring to Richard was the stolen-vehicle report. He really needed to catch up on paperwork, which he usually did while sitting in his SUV watching over his town. Lately, he'd not done much sitting.

He switched to his phone, saw he had a message from Heather and called her back. She didn't answer. He checked his watch.

She would still be at the dental office. Maybe he could stop by on his way out to the Welborn place. He signed off his computer and headed out front. Leann raised an eyebrow. She wanted away from the desk. On the other hand, Lucas was helping someone else and wasn't a bit bothered by desk duty—in fact, he loved it.

Leann opened her mouth, about to say something, when the front door pushed open and Shelley Guzman walked in, her husband right behind.

Oscar would have gone on patrol the minute Lucas returned to take over the desk, maybe forty minutes ago.

Shelley shook her head. "I feel silly, but Oscar insists that I need to come in and fill out a report. He says I should take the break-in more seriously."

"Every robbery is serious," Leann said.

"I just think the first time it was some kid looking for spare change and something to eat. If they knocked on the door, I'd give it to them. I'm even more sure of it now."

Tom had often heard such a declaration, but wondered if most folks meant it. Shelley might very well be the exception.

"We appreciate you coming in. Did you discover something else missing?" asked Tom.

"No." Oscar motioned for his wife to sit in one of the ugly orange chairs in the waiting room, which had emptied when Lucas's civilian left. "Someone broke in to Sweet Sarasota again last night."

Tom stifled the words he really wanted to say. "A break-in two nights in a row."

"Yes," Shelley interjected, giving Oscar a let's-calm-down look. "Someone got into the bakery by climbing through the bathroom window. The back door, thanks to Oscar, is now impenetrable."

"What was taken?" Tom could very well imagine the kind of door ex-military, ex-FBI agent Oscar Guzman would install to protect his pregnant wife.

"That's the strange part," Shelley said. "Nothing's gone. They put money in my cash register.

Oscar handed over a bag full of ones, fives and a few tens, plus change. "Sixty-four dollars and seventy-two cents."

"And they left me a store-bought bag of chocolate chip cookies. They must have felt guilty for stealing from me and were trying to return what they'd taken."

"Store-bought can't compare to your cookies," Leann chimed in.

"So true," Lucas added.

"I wish they'd taken something besides chocolate chip cookies," Leann mused. "If they'd taken something like a blueberry scone, we could narrow our list of suspects down to those people who like blueberry scones. Everyone likes chocolate chip cookies, only a few like blueberry scones."

"I don't eat scones," Lucas said.

Tom wasn't at all tempted to share that he didn't like blueberry scones, either. Instead, he asked, "You brush for fingerprints?"

"I did."

"Probably was a kid, then," Leann agreed with Shelley. "One who still has a conscience. Let's see, our biggest troublemakers are the oldest Gillespie boy, Mayor Goodman's grandson and—"

"Jason Bitmore," Lucas suggested.

"The Gillespie boy's in San Antonio, Texas," Shelley said. "He joined the air force and is going through basic training."

"I thought he'd changed his mind." Leann frowned.

"Grandma Trina threatened to cut him out of her will," Lucas said. "He believed her, but I hadn't realized he'd signed up and left."

"Timing is everything when it comes to the military," Oscar said.

Once again, Tom thought about the invisible Sarasota Falls hotline and remembered how he'd been a bit more in the know about the little things back when his wife cared about the town and him.

Now he was forced to rely on others, like Leann, who was pretty good about knowing what was going on. Lucas, however, was better.

Shelley stood, clearly ready to leave, and said, "Maybe Jason wanted money for car repairs?"

"Except your bakery was robbed the same night Jason had his wreck," Lucas pointed out. "Not only did he not have enough time to consider the cost of repairs, but he was occupied."

"I'm not sure that's true," Oscar said. "We don't know what time the bakery was broken in to. It could have been before Jason's car accident."

Lucas started typing on his computer keyboard. "Now that I think about it, Jason's broken in to a building nearby before."

"Stop!" Tom couldn't let this go on. It was speculation, and the reception area was not the best location for their back and forth. Also, Jason wasn't stupid. If he was going to break in to homes and businesses because he needed money, he wouldn't hit previous marks, not without a good reason. He'd go out of town. And Tom couldn't think of a good reason.

He straightened and headed for the door. "You find me proof that Jason did all this, and I'll get a warrant. In the meantime, we've got other issues to deal with."

"If you're going to see Mrs. Welborn, I can come with you," Leann offered.

"No, Leann, you head to Little's Grocery Store, see if you can't find out who's recently purchased that brand of cookies left at the bakery. Then head over to the Bitmore house and talk—"

"I can do that," Oscar interrupted.

"No, because it concerns your wife, I'd like to distance you from the investigation."

"But—"

"We're talking about sixty bucks and cookies, taken and returned. This is not something you need to pursue."

Oscar's lips went into a thin line, but he retreated. Shelley put her hand on his arm and soothed, "He's right, Oscar."

"I know what to do," Leann said, coming around the desk and readying herself. "I'll call you," she said to Oscar, "right after I report to the chief here."

Oscar nodded, the thin line disappearing.

"What do you want from me, Chief?" Lucas asked.

"Take Shelley's report, log in the money and call Jason's parents. See what he was doing last night."

"On it. Anything else?" Lucas asked.

"Yes." Tom stared hard at Lucas. Cops were family, and he realized he was stepping on Lucas's family, but it had to be done. "While you're building a time line for Jason, I also want you to look for Sarah."

"My sister-in-law is not—"

"Yes, she is. We have someone living in Sarasota Falls who claims that your sister-in-law was her mother. And those photos were pretty spot-on. I'd think you'd want to know more. All that aside, I want to know why

Sarah left and even more why she might have changed her name. Notice I said 'might.' If your sister-in-law is alive and well in Greenland, then you've nothing to worry about. But if she's dead, and if she happened to marry Raymond Tillsbury under an alias, I want to know how that all came to be. How they met, when they married, why they left and—"

"All this on the taxpayers' dime?" Lucas asked.

"There's a tie-in somehow to Rachel Ramsey." Even as Tom said the words, he felt a vague surprise. The tie-in to Rachel Ramsey felt like an afterthought, like old news, something brittle, forgotten.

He wanted to know all this information because of Heather.

Someone new, soft, who was quickly becoming impossible to forget.

THE AFTERNOON LOOKED to be ridiculously slow. Heather called back Ms. Gilmore, who promised to be there at straight-up two. Still, they had a cancellation and one patient came in with a runny nose. Maya promptly rescheduled him.

The few parents who did bring their children in were all talking about Lucille's funeral, who they'd seen, what their favorite memory of Lucille was and speculation about why Richard Welborn had been in town. Their words only convinced Heather more that she needed to find Tom and share her hypothesis.

At two, Ms. Gilmore showed up with Kevin and Beatrice. Maya ran around the front counter to give all three of them a hug.

"Connie worked here before Marcie."

"Years ago," Connie Gilmore said. "Before children."

Beatrice was a blonde while Kevin had light brown hair, like Connie. They both were well-behaved and quite comfortable with being at the dentist. Kevin followed Maya around the desk and sat in her lap. She promptly turned on her computer and found a learning game.

"Maya spoils him," Connie said.

"I think Maya spoils everyone," Heather agreed.

She asked Beatrice to sit down and open her mouth for a quick assessment of the child's teeth. Then she took Beatrice for an X-ray.

"We have the same red mark," Beatrice said, pointing to the tiny stain above Heather's lip.

"That we do." Over the years, Heather met

quite a few people with similar birthmarks. An hour later, with no other appointments booked for the day, Dr. Goodman said, "No sense in keeping everyone here. Heather, go ahead and take off early. We'll see you in the morning."

"I can do that." She quickly cleaned up, sterilized the equipment and grabbed her purse before stepping outside. She sat on the bench in front of the office and punched in the chief's number. He didn't answer. This time, she didn't leave a message.

She sat for a few moments, staring at the church and wondering if she should head over there and force Father Joe to speak with her.

He knew something.

Something that had him avoiding her.

Before she could act, her phone rang. Tom's voice came over the line. Funny, she'd not even known him a week, had had to overcome a horrible first impression, and now he was the person she most looked forward to talking to.

"Hey," she said. "I have a theory as to why Richard Welborn was here."

"I could use an idea or two," Tom said. "This morning, I visited the hospital and didn't pick up a single clue as to Richard's motivation for coming to town. The first phone call though, when I got back to the office, was a man in Roswell who said Welborn came here on a spaceship and was had been forced to return."

"My theory is a little tamer."

"Good, I want to hear it. Why don't you meet me at the Station. I could use a cup of coffee before I get the key and head out to talk to Richard's mother. The phone number we have just rings and rings. I know the hospital's tried a few times, too."

They picked up their conversation ten minutes later, sitting in a back booth and with Maureen waiting on them.

Heather couldn't hold off any longer. "I think he came to attend Lucille's funeral."

Tom's fingers faltered on his coffee cup handle. Brown liquid splashed on the table before Tom righted the mug. Shaking his head, he said, "No way."

"He wanted to make amends." Heather was sure of it.

Tom apparently hadn't gotten past her first missile. "You honestly believe he planned on attending her funeral this morning?" Amazement laced his words, but Heather didn't back down.

"Yes, I do. Maybe he'd intended to disguise

himself or maybe he planned on just showing up, turning himself in. He probably couldn't live with the guilt."

Tom took a sip of coffee, not looking convinced.

"He was desperate to get here." Heather had been so sure. Watching all those people going into the church this morning, listening to Maya's and Dr. Goodman's memories, and even Ms. Gilmore on the phone saying in a sad voice, "She was my second-grade teacher..." How could you not feel guilty about her death?

"No, he was invisible, except for the rent checks he sent the rental agency, and they weren't checks, but money orders. Hard to track." He finished his coffee, smiled at Maureen when she gave him more and then said, "People like that don't have guilt."

"You've been a cop too long."

This time his coffee cup didn't slip. "What?"

"Really. I've heard bits and pieces about the accident. He was driving drunk. It's wrong. He should have to face the consequences. I agree with all of that. I do. But what was he? Mid-twenties, like me?"

"Yes." Tom looked like he wanted to end the conversation.

"You know, Father Joe said he was surprised that Richard would be driving drunk. Of course, I'm surprised anyone would drive drunk. But why would Father Joe say that?"

"Richard was a truck driver. He was gone four, five, six days at a time. A DUI on his record would keep some companies from hiring him. Now, I'm thinking that he's still a trucker, but likely making less and getting paid under the table."

"What did he usually do when he drank? Have someone else drive him?" Heather asked.

"Far as I know, he didn't frequent any of the local bars, but again, he wasn't in town much."

"Did he have a previous record?"

Tom frowned at her. "You're asking a lot of questions."

"I feel involved. He's renting the house I apparently own. You arrested me as I was going out to see it. And when you talk about Richard, it's in the same tone of voice as when you talk about Rachel Ramsey."

"It is not," he protested.

Maureen filled his coffee cup again and said to Heather, "You're right about the tone of voice when he talks about the two of them. I can't believe I didn't notice it. I liked Richard. He was a good tipper. He was always in and out of here fast. I got the idea he had someplace to be rather than here."

"You never told me that," Tom said.

"You never asked."

"His mother must be worried," Heather mused. "You need to get out there and tell her."

Tom nodded, but added, "I'd prefer having another officer with me. It's always easier with a partner. Bailey was with me last night, but today everyone's already doing double duty."

"Why don't you take Father Joe?" Maureen asked.

"I tried calling him earlier. He didn't answer."

"He never answers my calls, either. Look, I should go with you," Heather offered. "It's my key that will open the door should she—"

His face contorted and the "no" came before he even bothered to think it through or let her finish.

"Why not? It's not like you're going to arrest anyone or walk into any danger. You're checking up on her and want to talk about Richard. What the next steps might be, if he recovers. I think it would be fine." She reached out and put a hand on his, noting how he didn't pull away and how for just a moment he relaxed.

"I doubt—"

"I remember when the cops showed up at my door. It was a Saturday, and I was cleaning, wearing old sweatpants and my favorite ripped T-shirt. I thought they had the wrong house. They were both young and stammering. It took me a full ten minutes to understand what they were telling me. I will say this, one of the officers was crying while the other gave me the news."

"Take her," Maureen said. "Then the news won't come from the man who was always looking to arrest her boy."

Tom muttered under his breath, "Why don't you change and—"

"No, I'll wear the scrubs. Why waste time? We need to give her time to call someone while it's a decent hour."

Maureen waved away their check. "I'll take care of it. You go on."

She nodded, but already her heart was telling her that she should rethink this. Being around when the police turned up at someone's home reminded her too much of her parents. Yet, her mind was saying it was the right thing to do.

He opened the door for her, ever the gentleman. This time he didn't put a hand on top of her head to make sure she didn't hit it as he was guiding her in. Instead, he touched her back and heat seared.

No, no, no. This was the man who suddenly brought up Rachel Ramsey every time she started to trust him. And, judging by his tone, his eyes, his profession even, his heart wasn't big enough for the three of them.

His touch, though, sent a different message.

CHAPTER SIXTEEN

THE LAST CIVILIAN Tom had in his front seat had been Debbie Stilwater. She'd needed a ride home from church because her car wouldn't start and Lucas was taking a report.

Heather was much cuter—smelled nicer, too.

"You like rock or country?" If she said classical, he'd forgive her, but he wasn't sure if he could listen to it for more than four minutes.

"Country."

His favorite, too. He pushed the radio button and Garth Brooks's voice came out.

"I like his wife, too," Heather said.

"I saw Trisha Yearwood in concert years ago," Tom said. "My parents took me. All my friends were into rock bands and going to concerts without parents. I enjoyed every minute and still listen to her CDs when I have a chance. That concert is one of my favorite memories."

"Where are your parents? I know you're living in the house you grew up in. Did they move to something smaller? That's what my parents planned to do when they retired. They'd been talking about Alaska of all places, buying a little store."

Tom laughed, trying to picture his mother, all four foot eight of her, trudging through the snow. She'd do it, but she'd hate every moment. "No, they moved to Florida, got a condo by the beach. I call them every week. Mom's having a blast. She's got Dad into so many clubs, he had to build a spreadsheet."

"They don't call you? When my mom was alive I probably called or texted daily."

"With my job, nine times out of ten, the phone pings with a personal call right when I'm in the middle of something I can't interrupt. It's hard to say, 'You have the right to remain silent…oh, can you just hold on while I take this call from my mom.'"

Heather laughed. "I guess that could be a problem. I'll keep that in mind next time I have to call you."

"If you have to call me, it will be about something I need to know."

He watched her nod, the smile fading from her face, resignation taking its place.

"Don't worry," he said. "We'll figure out what happened with your parents, why they changed their names and if you have a connection to Rachel Ramsey."

"When will you have the DNA report?"

"Sometimes it takes days, sometimes weeks."

"I don't like the waiting."

"Me, neither."

Heather stared out the window, not looking at him when she spoke. "I wish Father Joe would be more forthcoming."

Tom hesitated. He thought the same but knew Joe might be holding back because of his ethics, both personal and professional. That Heather's parents were deceased should have released him from feeling obligated to keep their secrets, unless he was hiding something else. Mentally, Tom moved Joe to the head of his list of people to see.

Right after Richard Welborn's mother.

Pulling into the long driveway that led to the white clapboard farmhouse, Tom could only wonder what sort of reception he and Heather were about to get.

"Place looks a little better. I wonder if Richard was doing the work or whether his mother feels up to it," Tom remarked. "Usually when

I'm out here, it's pretty overgrown and messy."
He parked, got out and hurried around to open
the door for Heather. She hopped out of the
vehicle.

"I've been trying to avoid thinking about the
place. If Richard's mother moves out eventually, what happens then? I'm wondering if I
could live here…"

"It's kind of in the middle of nowhere. You'd
have a ways to drive to work and then no close
neighbors."

She laughed. "When I was in Phoenix,
sometimes my commute to work was an hour
and sometimes it was three, depending on traffic. The drive is nothing. I haven't, however,
lived in the middle of nowhere by myself."

As she followed him to the house, he realized he didn't like the thought of her out here
by herself. He'd be doing for her what he now
did for Richard's mother: making special out-
of-the-way trips just to check in.

She stood at his elbow when he knocked
on the door and waited. He'd never even met
Richard Welborn's mother officially. In the
last year, he'd only been able to talk with her
through the closed screen door once, and that
was because he'd caught her outside and made

it up the driveway before she could run into the house and pretend she wasn't there. She'd made it clear he wasn't welcome.

She must still feel the same way. From the house came no sound, not even the fluttering of the front window curtain. No lights were on.

He pounded, with all his strength, and shouted, "It's about Richard."

"Shout that he's hurt," Heather suggested.

"He needs you! He's hurt!"

"Louder," Heather encouraged.

"He's in the hospital!"

Just inside the door, something thumped. Maybe Richard's mother had just fallen. Tom reached in his pocket, ready to use Heather's key. The door inched open and Tom saw exactly what he'd seen the last time he'd managed to catch her. Gray hair, a scarf, thick glasses and an old yellow sweater.

"What happened to Richard?" the voice asked, quivering. The thin hand holding the door frame trembled a bit.

"There's been an accident. We tried to notify you earlier but nobody answered the door."

"I wasn't worried yet," the woman murmured, but the door didn't open any wider.

Tom heard a brief intake of breath. "Now I'm worried."

"Richard's car hit a tree last night, just a mile down—"

"The Turner place," Richard's mother said, voice scratchy. "Is he... Is he..."

The door didn't move, but there were the beginnings of a keening noise, the sound of pain. Beside him, Heather stepped closer.

"He's in the hospital, critical condition. We can drive you there."

"Yes. No." A few curse words followed, surprising him. She ended with a half hiccup. "Please, God, no."

"Ma'am, is there anyone I can call for you? Someone else to drive you or stay with you for a while? I have phone numbers for you, the hospital as well as the doctor. I wrote them down this morning."

He expected her to open the door, take the piece of paper, but instead, she sharply ordered, "Tell me. I'll remember."

He looked down at the black scrawl in his record book and recited the numbers.

"Ma'am, I—"

The door slowly shut. The last time she'd slammed it, surprising him with her strength.

He didn't like the hollow feeling that resonated in his gut.

"What do you think?" he asked Heather.

"We can't leave. Does she drive?"

"Yes, the Turners have seen her a time or two."

"Do you know how old she is?"

"No clue."

Heather stayed on the porch, her lips pressed together, in deep thought. "Someone needs to be with her. She's got to be brokenhearted and scared."

"If you have any ideas..."

Heather knocked on the door, raised her voice and shouted, "Ma'am. I'm Heather Graves. I'm here with Tom. My parents own this house."

Another thump sounded.

"Richard's in a coma." Heather stood close to the door, kept her voice normal and continued, "There's a chance he won't make it. I know you want to be with him. It's hard. We'll drive you, stay with you and make sure Richard is taken care of."

The keening continued and from inside he heard a small voice say, "What's wrong? Don't cry. Please don't cry."

Tom stepped closer to the door, closer to Heather. If Richard's mother was talking to herself like this, then she might be in worse shape that he'd surmised. The best thing would be to go in, check on her, take care of the situation.

"It's okay." Richard's mother's voice got stronger.

"Please." Heather looked distressed, and Tom wished he hadn't brought her out here. She didn't need to deal with something like this. She leaned toward the front door, talking to the screen. "We just want to help. That's all we want."

"Right." This was Richard's mother again. Tom wanted to jump in, join Heather in dealing with the situation, but Heather had the woman talking. Something he'd never been able to do.

"We'll drive you to town. Take you to Richard."

The door opened again, still an inch, the same face peered out. The woman didn't say anything just stared at Tom.

Heather stepped away, and Tom opened the screen and then pushed gently at the door, which swung open revealing a tall, thin woman staring at him.

"You'll take me to him first, no other stops." This time the voice wasn't scratchy. Tom felt something tug at his memory. Then he noted the tiny red birthmark just above the left side of her lip.

"Rachel," he breathed.

The word was barely out of his mouth when a small blond head poked around the side of Rachel, looked up, and said, "Mommy, are we going to see Daddy now?"

HEATHER STARED AT the woman standing in the doorway.

"Take off the wig," Tom ordered.

The woman didn't move, just stared, longing and defeat in her expression. Then slowly, she nodded and both the wig and the glasses disappeared. Rachel Ramsey, now with loose blond hair, opened the door all the way and stepped outside.

"Mommy doesn't like the wig," the little girl said. "She says it makes her head hot. I wear it sometimes, and it doesn't make my head hot."

"Dang," Rachel said, staring at Heather. "Who are you?"

"Mommy, no bad words," the little girl scolded.

"I told you. I'm Heather Graves. I—I own this house."

Rachel gave a little shake of the head, as if trying to quit whatever she was thinking.

"My parents were Bill and Melanie Graves."

Rachel's expression didn't change.

"Sarah Lewis and Raymond Tillsbury."

"Those names mean nothing to me," Rachel said. "Why are you here? Are you a relative he called or something? But—" she turned to look at Tom "—you didn't know I was here until just now. You wouldn't know to bring a family member."

"I don't think I'm a family member." Heather wished her words sounded more convincing. Truth was, she'd already felt the doubt, thanks to the dozens of people who'd said, "You look just like…" *the woman standing in front of her*.

"I'll be your landlord now that my parents have passed away. We just happen to look alike. I'll tell you more later, after you see Richard." She didn't want to think past that, not now that there was a child involved, a very small child.

Rachel blinked, tears slipping past her

lashes. "Chief Riley, is there a chance, will he make it?"

"We don't know yet. He has a head injury and we're not sure what damage has been done to the brain. The doctor's put him in the coma so his brain could rest. At least, that's my understanding from talking to them this morning. This—this is your daughter?"

Rachel bit her bottom lip, looked at the sky, then down, and then at Tom. "Yes, this is Abigail Welborn."

Tom nodded. "Welborn?"

"Look," she said, "Richard feels horrible about Lucille's death. But you have to understand he had nothing to do with what happened five years ago with your partner. Please don't take that out on him."

It took a heartbeat or two for Tom to answer, and Heather knew the man was falling apart inside. Outside, however, he kept it together. She'd give him that.

"Right now," Tom said, "the only thing we're concentrating on is getting him stable. You need to come with us."

He hadn't asked Rachel about having weapons or told her to get on the ground or drawn his own weapon. His eyes weren't hard, either.

Heather closed hers. In the past few days, she'd almost lost sight of the cop that had given her nightmares. That cop had been replaced by the one who now owned a kitten and who'd put his hand against her back and caused her to lose her breath.

The only evidence of just how affected Tom was, was the slight tremor in his hands. Heather doubted anyone else would have noticed it.

"I need to get my purse and some things for Abby."

Tom nodded. Unasked, Heather followed Rachel into the farmhouse. It looked smaller on the inside, maybe because every curtain was drawn and all the furniture dark. The only colors came from the children's toys scattered throughout the room.

"I'll bring her iPad," Rachel said. "It's fully charged. And a coloring book, crayons and her doll. Maybe—"

"I'd keep it simple. Right now, you're heading for the hospital."

"But she might need…" Rachel's voice broke, and she put a hand out to steady herself on the back of an old rocking chair. "What if she goes to foster care. I couldn't bear that. Oh,

God, do you think Chief Riley could just for-get he found me. At least for the next fourteen years, just until I get her out of high school and into college." Now her voice rose, her words tumbling faster and faster. "I need her to be raised by someone who loves her, who will never abuse her. I need her to be able to take care of herself when I'm gone."

"I…" Heather felt out of breath, almost dizzy. She'd never worried growing up. She'd always known she was loved. Once, in second grade, when a boy during recess had taken her lunch box, her dad had been at the school the next morning. The boy had apologized, and her dad had taught her that you didn't let others take your lunch box. You opened your mouth and screamed until an adult came.

Years later, her dad had insisted on teach-ing her how to defend herself in case the day ever came when he wasn't around.

No one messed with Heather Graves, so said her daddy. And her mom, for that matter.

The memory struck deep inside Heather's heart.

Tears dripped down both women's cheeks. Rachel kneeled on the floor and gathered loose crayons into a large bag that said Abigail's

Backpack. Heather stood in the dark room, her own tears salty on her lips, and missed her dad, her mom, her old life.

She'd come here asking questions. Watching Rachel, Heather understood without a doubt why Tom had pulled her over last week. If she wasn't related to this woman, she'd eat her hat.

It was a saying her mother had always used.

Each new piece of the puzzle made Heather appreciate her parents more. And now she got why her parents had never brought her here. They didn't want her to have anything to do with the dysfunctional Ramseys.

But discovering her heritage had become a train wreck she couldn't walk away from.

She needed to research Rachel's father more, but she had a feeling that, like everything else she'd come to believe, it would only return an answer that made no sense.

CHAPTER SEVENTEEN

HEATHER DIDN'T LOOK happy about Tom's returning her to Bianca's Bed-and-Breakfast. He'd seen it before. Some civilians, once involved in police work, wanted to see the case through to the end. He didn't think that was Heather's issue, though. No, she probably wanted to find out what her real connection to Rachel was.

In his mind, and probably Heather's, there was no doubt.

Somehow, Heather and Rachel had to be related. Since Heather's mother couldn't have children, it went back to Diane Ramsey. Unfortunately, every time Tom tried to get close to solving their kinship, something got in the way: car accidents, deaths and even cookie robberies.

"I can meet you at the hospital," Heather offered. "It's no problem. I can help with Abigail. I'm good with children."

"I don't think so," Rachel said, her face pale in the moonlight. Tom couldn't get over the resemblance now that he had them together, but while Heather looked tired and apprehensive, Rachel looked slightly ill and wholly shell-shocked. In truth, the two women couldn't be more different, not just with respect to actions, either, but to goals. Heather was looking for family ties; Rachel had always been tied to a family best left alone. Rachel probably thought Heather was one more problem.

"But—" Heather began.

Rachel simply shook her head.

"I've already called social services," Tom mentioned. He'd also radioed for backup. Both Oscar and Leann were on the way. He strayed from procedure so that Rachel could visit Richard in the hospital.

It was a humane consideration.

"Call me," Heather pleaded. "I don't care what time." For a moment, he thought she might argue further, but in the end, she'd simply given him a tight smile and exited the SUV. Good. He was getting too used to her help and her company, and with Rachel Ramsey in custody he needed to focus on her—only her.

The Sarasota Falls Hospital used to be the

size of a large Victorian home. Then, a little over ten years ago, the old munitions factory had been turned into a tristate Alzheimer's care center and the town suddenly needed a bigger hospital, not just for the Alzheimer's patients, but for the families that moved here because they'd placed loved ones in the center. And new jobs had been created, so another wave of people poured in.

Tom remembered that the police force had added a new man about that time—him.

He pulled into a parking space near the emergency room entrance. An empty spot was reserved for the police. He flung open the driver's door before the key was out of the SUV's ignition and quickly opened the back door. Abigail jumped down, clearly intrigued by being out so late. Rachel exited from her side of the vehicle.

She'd changed in the five years since she'd been so instrumental in Max's death. Gone was the high school kid. In front of him was a thin woman, too pale, who looked older than she should have.

Grimly, he guided her to the hospital's front doors, led her inside and nodded to the admissions nurse. "Chief," the woman said. She barely looked up, no expression on her face, not even a raised eyebrow. His officers had been told to stop by and check up on Welborn often. She probably thought Rachel was Heather.

After all, he'd been escorting Heather all around town. How could anyone mistake the two? Rachel was definitely taller, and Heather was definitely softer, kinder, engaging.

"What is that smell?" Abigail stopped, tugged on Rachel's hand and stood on tiptoes looking at the nurse as if she were to blame. Rachel caressed the top of Abigail's head and said, "It's just the way a hospital smells. Nothing bad. Nothing wrong."

Startled, the nurse looked from Abigail, to Rachel, to Tom, and then regained her professionalism and composure, and declared, "No children after nine."

"This is a special case," Tom returned, getting Rachel and Abigail past the first patient rooms before the nurse could protest further.

He heard the hospital doors opening behind him and the nurse greeted Leann by her first name, then asked, "Who's with Chief Riley?" Sometimes his only female officer had a hard time putting forth her cop persona because she was related to half the town.

"Just one more day in the life of a police officer," Leann replied glibly. A moment later, she caught up with him, a half smile on her face. It twitched just a bit when she saw Rachel and Abigail. "Hey, Chief."

"Glad you could come." Tom kept it professional, guiding the whole troop to Richard's room. A few times, Rachel slowed, looking like she might collapse. All it took was Tom clearing his throat for her to step up. She was probably half-afraid he'd change his mind and take her directly to the station.

Abigail didn't falter even as they passed an elderly woman in a wheelchair with a doll clasped in her arms. Abigail wrinkled her nose but had better manners than some adults and didn't complain, just tucked closer to her mother.

Richard's room, in ICU, was the last one on the left. A chair was in the hall. Tom had sat on it for more than an hour this morning. Rachel, acting more like the girl he remembered, uttered an "oh" at the sight of Richard hooked up to so many machines. She said "oh" again and pushed past Tom to enter the room, immediately taking a seat and grasping Richard's hand.

"I'm so, so sorry," she whispered. "I didn't know. This is all my fault. All my fault."

Tom swallowed, trying not to think about Max, who'd died on the scene, no hospital stay for him, no chance to say goodbye, no opportunity for Rachel to say "I'm so sorry." He tried not to think about Lucille Calloway.

"Chief, I can stay with them," Leann said, "if you have other matters to attend to."

"No, I'm fine," he answered.

Abigail stood silently beside her mother. After a moment, she climbed into Rachel's lap and patted Richard on the arm. Then she started spewing grown-up platitudes in a child's voice. "He'll be okay. I talked to God on the way over here. Papa will be just fine. Okay, Mommy?"

"Five more minutes," Tom said. "Then we need to head to the station."

"Thank you," Rachel responded. Not what he expected. He felt his cheeks going red as the ire rose in his body. He didn't want Rachel to be nice or polite. He wanted her to feel the hurt that she'd caused. She'd been partly responsible for Max's death and—

"Chief, go down to the waiting room. I can handle the situation here." Leann actually nudged him toward the door, a look on her face he'd not seen before.

"I need to talk to Rachel." Tom took two steps and then stood just outside the hospital room's doorway, where he could still see in at the scene unfolding.

"You need to have the right frame of mind to do it." Leann said what Tom already knew. He knew he'd been waiting five years to talk to Rachel.

"We all know how much you loved Max," Leann said softly. "Now is not the time, and probably you shouldn't be the one to oversee the talking."

"Who else have you called?"

"Lucas."

"When will he be here?"

Leann stepped farther into the hallway, still speaking softly. "Lucas's on his way. Oscar's dealing with a fight between a couple of neighbors. Did you call social services about Abigail? Far as I'm aware, since Diane Ramsey's death, there's no relative nearby, unless you know something I don't."

"I did, but I'll check with them. Right now

there's no tie between Heather and Rachel except for looks."

"That's a mighty powerful tie," Leann said.

Tom didn't want to respond. If the two weren't related, good. If they were, his biggest problem would be personal and not professional. He liked Heather, genuinely liked her.

Leann raised an eyebrow—she was getting awfully good at that—and went back into the room. He headed for the waiting room, luckily empty, and started making calls. By the time he finished the final conversation ten minutes later, he was feeling more in control.

Leann met him in the hallway. "What about Abigail?"

"Social services will have someone here in the morning."

"And what about tonight?"

"Abigail can sleep in the cell with her mother."

Leann nodded. It wouldn't be the first time a kid had stayed with a parent overnight in the Sarasota Falls jail, but it had been a long time.

"It's what we'd do for anyone in this situation. Safest place." Tom wasn't sure if he was trying to convince Leann or himself.

"Bianca's registered with social services," Leann reminded him.

"Heather's staying there. Until we know if there's a connection between Heather and Rachel, it's not prudent to put them together."

"There's no connection," Rachel said, coming up to them, making Tom wish he'd closed the door and also wonder just how much she'd heard. "Until tonight, I'd never even known her name."

"I stay with Mommy," Abigail insisted, joining her mother. Then, she asked, "What's a cell?"

Tom closed his eyes, exhaustion threatening to make its presence known. There was no perfect outcome for tonight's scenario.

"Rachel," Tom asked, "can I call one of your mother's sisters?"

"No. They hated me." She glanced at Abigail and her expression softened. "They didn't get along with my mother. If you remember." She looked Tom square in the face. "You tried to place me with them years ago. They didn't want me. I'm not putting my daughter someplace she's not wanted."

"What's a cell?" Abigail asked again.

"Let me call Bianca," Leann suggested.

"We can put Heather up in the Sarasota Grand Hotel. Now that Founder's Day is over, they have rooms."

"No, and Rachel, it's been more than five minutes. It's time to go."

Rachel took Abigail's hand. "Can we ask the nurse for an update?"

Leann's cousin, Tom found out, was one of the night nurses and would be more than willing to give an update. She couldn't seem to take her eyes off Rachel. "The doctor will be here in the morning, and he can tell you a lot more about Richard then."

Though not uttered, the words *if he makes it* were clearly implied.

"The head wound is our biggest concern," the nurse continued. "He had a CAT scan last night and unfortunately the swelling means the doctors cannot perform surgery yet."

"That's bad," Rachel said.

"Usually." The nurse smiled a little. "The good news is we see brain activity. So, the doctor's hoping the swelling not only didn't press near the brain stem but also stopped. Richard is scheduled for another CAT scan in the morning."

Rachel blinked, hard, and then thanked the

nurse. She walked toward the door, her shoulders stiff and determined. Abigail was at her side. "We'll be back in the morning, right, Mommy?"

Rachel looked back at Tom.

"I'll make it happen," he promised.

It was almost midnight when they got to the police station, but judging by the cars in the parking lot, his officers were all here. This time, he really had Rachel Ramsey.

Tom walked through the entrance, Rachel in front of him, almost the same scenario as last week when he'd walked through the doors with Heather. He couldn't help but compare the two. Heather with her freshness, her quest for answers and her outlook on life. Rachel was a pale copy of the girl she'd been. Quiet didn't become her.

Shoot. This is what he'd waited for. The chance to bring Rachel Ramsey to her knees, hold her accountable for Max's death, bring about justice. The little girl that clung to her mother's hand made Tom feel sick at heart. So many lives affected by one stupid decision.

"Chief, you want me to take her into the interrogation room?" Lucas asked. He should be off duty, but he was here. A week ago, Tom would have been certain that Lucas was staying because of Max, but now Tom wasn't so sure. Maybe his lieutenant was staying for Tom.

"No…yes, please do that. And read her her rights. I need to make a phone call."

"Ma'am," Lucas said to Rachel, "Officer Bailey will take…"

"Abigail," Rachel answered.

"…Abigail to the break room. We've toys and some ice cream."

"Ice cream!" Abigail's eyes lit up. "I love ice cream."

Every kid said the exact same thing. The only difference in today's scenario was that most of the criminals Tom escorted into the jail protested their arrest, proclaimed their innocence. Rachel wasn't doing that. She was eerily silent.

Lucas turned Abigail over to Leann while Tom went into his office and closed the door. The glass didn't get him privacy. He wasn't quite sure what he'd have done if he could have secluded himself. Put his head down, scream, cry. Instead, he turned on his computer and brought up the file on Rachel—no new entries except for a note about Heather's arrest. Even though he knew the details by heart, Tom skimmed them again. The time line hadn't changed: a convenience store was robbed, the cops were called, Max happened to be nearby. Jeremy Salinas apparently lost control of his vehicle and witnesses said that Max was close behind. Max got out of his cruiser. Rachel fell out of the passenger-side door, writhing on the ground, acting hurt. Max, Tom knew, only saw that a young person was in trouble, hurt, and he'd hurried to Rachel's side. Jeremy shot him point-blank. Then, both Jeremy and Rachel ran off, stealing another car, and another, until they'd disappeared off the face of the earth.

Five years. It was a long time to hide.

Tom's hand went to his phone, and he punched three numbers before he realized that he shouldn't call Heather this late and until they knew more, he could not involve her. He hung up, still holding his phone and feeling a sense of emptiness.

A knock took Tom away from the memories, the truths, of that day.

"You ready?" Oscar queried. "I can do it if you don't want to."

No doubt Lucas could, Leann could, any cop Tom had worked with could.

"I'm ready." On the way to the interrogation

room, Tom stopped to check in on Leann and Abigail. They sat at one of the round tables. Leann was coloring in a book and telling the kid about all the different shades of red. Abigail had a half-eaten ice-cream cone in hand and was nodding off to sleep. It was going to be a long night and Tom didn't know when he'd get the same opportunity—nodding off to sleep, not the ice cream.

When he got to the interrogation room, Rachel sat ramrod-straight, her hands on the table, her fingers twisting in nervousness. Her body had the classic get-me-out-of-here posture. Her eyes, however, told another story, one of defeat and hurt. Tom looked away for a moment. Then he sat down in a chair across from her, switched on the tape recorder and said, "You were made aware of your legal rights and chose to waive them?"

Rachel nodded.

"Please answer out loud." Tom's voice remained steady.

"I was. I do."

"If you want a lawyer, we can call for one now."

"I will want a lawyer, but not right this minute." Her voice was strong, determined. Tom felt a tiny bit of respect. She was going to do the right thing.

He turned to Lucas. "Did you offer Ms. Ramsey some water?"

"I did," Lucas replied. "She said she wasn't thirsty."

"Okay," Tom said. "Rachel, just a minute ago, I checked on your daughter. Cute kid. Abigail's happy with her ice cream and is almost asleep. How old is she?"

"Just turned five." Rachel's words were a little above a whisper.

"Kindergarten next year," Lucas said. "Lots of fun."

Rachel nodded. It made Tom think about all the fun Rachel would miss because she'd be serving a jail sentence instead of joining the parent–teacher organization.

"You realize," Tom said, "that your guilt is not in question. We know that you were with Salinas that day and that you pretended to be hurt. We not only have it on tape thanks to a surveillance camera but we have an eyewitness."

Rachel stopped fidgeting. Laid her hands flat on the table, rigid. She leaned forward, looking at Tom. "I'm so, so sorry about what happened to Officer Stockard. So, so sorry."

For a moment, Tom thought she might reach across the table and take him by the hands. It required all his willpower not to move those hands, but to keep them steady on the table. Just another day, just another interrogation.

Her apology, though, got to him, not just the words but how much he wanted to forgive her. He cleared his throat and asked the details that had to start every interrogation: state your full legal name, date of birth. Ascertain the date and time of the altercation before finally asking the questions that might have important, terrible answers.

"Did you and Jeremy Salinas plan the robbery of the convenience store on Fifth and Main or was it spur-of-the-moment?"

"I didn't plan anything. I just went along."

"Were you aware of a plan by Jeremy Salinas to rob the convenience store on Fifth and Main or was it spur-of-the-moment?"

"I don't think he planned it, no, not for that day at least. But I'm pretty sure the possibility of robbing it was something he'd considered."

"Why do you think that?"

"Because once it started to happen, he seemed to have every step planned."

"You mean he had the weapon?"

"He always carried a weapon. We went into the convenience store often. He'd remarked a time or two that the afternoon clerk was a little lax."

"Go ahead and tell us the events leading up to the robbery."

Rachel tensed. "It was a Thursday. I'd not been to school all week. I woke up that morning about eleven. My mother was in bed, sound asleep. She usually woke up around three or four."

That didn't surprise Tom. Diane partied late into the night usually.

"Jeremy came by about noon."

"Why weren't you going to school?" Lucas asked.

Tom had almost forgotten Lucas was leaning against the wall to his left.

"I…I wasn't feeling good."

"Go on," Tom urged.

"There was no food in the house. Not even bread. Usually we had bread. I knew I needed to eat. Jeremy said we'd go get some Twinkies or something at Little's."

"You never made it there," Tom said. "I traced your whereabouts that day. You're not on their camera."

"That's right. We didn't make it there. I got sick. Jeremy had to pull over. Pissed him off."

"So," Lucas said, almost sounding relieved, "you really were sick, and that's why you missed school."

A bit of the old Rachel returned. She shot Lucas a look that suggested "be real" before continuing. "I threw up. He managed to pull over, so it wasn't in the car or anything. That would have caused a problem."

Unbidden, Tom wondered if something so simple as Jeremy Salinas driving off and leaving his girlfriend behind because she'd thrown up on his car would have changed how Max's life ended.

"I didn't want him mad at me." Rachel couldn't seem to keep her fingers still. "I told him I needed bread or crackers or something."

"Crackers?" Lucas sounded incredulous.

Tom got the idea there was something Lucas had figured out that he hadn't. Not as quickly, at least.

"I'd taken a home pregnancy test on Monday morning. I already knew what it would say. I was probably two months along. He was going to know sooner or later."

"Abigail?" Lucas asked.

Rachel nodded. "I wish I hadn't told him. He didn't take it well. He got in the car and drove off. Leaving me on the side of the road. But he immediately came back. I jumped in before he could change his mind. He drove to that convenience store and we went in. I was only thinking crackers."

Ten years. Tom Riley had been a cop ten years. And he'd never sat at an interrogation table unable to ask the questions. At the moment, all he could do was stare at her.

"I remember," Rachel said, "that when we first walked in it was odd Jeremy headed for the checkout counter, instead of where crackers would be. I even started to pass him. Then I saw the gun."

"Where was it?" Lucas asked.

"Pointing at the cashier, who immediately opened his register and started handing Jeremy money."

"What did you do?"

"I was in shock." She looked at Tom. "I'd done some stupid things. Heck, I'd shoplifted from that store, right in front of that clerk, too. I'm sure he'd seen me. But a gun? Never."

Tom could only stare back at her, feeling a little shocked himself.

"Everything happened so fast. I was still reeling from telling him I was pregnant. I watched him rob that store and didn't do or say anything. Almost every day, I wonder why I just didn't hit the floor, cower, let him go off without me."

Lucas gently nudged Rachel forward. "What happened next?"

"I actually grabbed a candy bar on our way out. Jeremy was running. I was behind him. We jumped into the car. I remember how hot I felt, and I stumbled. Then I was buckling in. Yes, putting on my seat belt, as if it was just another day, and he floored it. Wasn't but two minutes and there was that cop car behind me." Again, she looked at Tom. "I was relieved. I thought good, now this madness will stop."

The interrogation room's door opened, and Oscar came inside. He set down a glass of water in front of Rachel. "Just in case." She took the glass, drained it in three long gulps and then put it down.

Oscar didn't leave. Tom couldn't muster the

energy to ask him to. It didn't matter. Rachel started again.

"Jeremy was in his Camaro. He'd souped it up, had a V-8. We could have left Officer Stockard in the dust." Silence, heavy with interrupted dreams, hung in the room.

"The witnesses said it looked like Jeremy lost control of the car."

"He did. He did lose control. We were at the last light before city limits. He wanted me to count the money, and I was crying. He asked me…he asked me if I thought there was enough money for an abortion."

The story behind the crime. Never had Tom expected to feel sorry for Rachel. No, her actions had resulted in Max's death.

"Then what?" Lucas asked.

"I couldn't count. I was crying so hard the tears were choking me, running into my mouth and down my throat. Jeremy cussed at me, demanded I count the money, and I told him I wouldn't have an abortion. His right hand flung out, hard, got me in the stomach. I was surprised more than hurt. Then he said I'd get an abortion. He'd see to it, and I got angry. He thought he could hit me! I hit him back, and he lost control of the car. We crashed into that pole and the cop was right behind us. Jeremy aimed the gun at me and told me to get out. I couldn't move fast enough. I opened the door, fell out. That's when Jeremy shot Max Stockard. Just a few feet from where I lay. And all I could think about was the baby.

"About Abigail."

CHAPTER EIGHTEEN

THE ALARM SOUNDED at six. Heather sat up and grabbed her cell phone. She wanted to call Tom right away, find out what had happened after he'd dropped her off.

Last night, she'd tried to sneak into the bed-and-breakfast unnoticed, but Bianca had been awake, sitting on the sofa in the living room, waiting. Not sure what she should share with the proprietor, she'd hurried in and mumbled something about being tired and needing to get up early for work.

It was true. A full day of appointments had been scheduled at the dental office.

Her sleep hadn't been sound. All night, she'd tossed and turned, gray dreams of hallways and that dark, dark living room. At about three in the morning, she'd slid out of bed and grabbed a photo album. She found the pages she wanted.

As an only child, she hadn't lacked in the

photo-opportunity department. Her parents had taken pictures of her eating, sleeping, playing, sleeping, eating. She'd always found it a bit embarrassing.

Now she stared at the photos from right before she'd started kindergarten. Preschool hadn't been necessary. As her mother did home childcare, Heather'd had a dozen friends and her mother had schooltime built into the day.

It only took a few minutes before Heather found the one she wanted. She'd been in someone's living room, just a little girl with long blondish white hair, wearing a white T-shirt and pink stretch pants. Her mother was hunkered down next to her, a smile on her face.

She thought about the little girl she'd seen last night, the one who'd ridden in the SUV and chattered about Scooby-Doo and ABC-mouse. That little girl had been in pink stretch pants. Abigail also had white, white hair. And there was the red birthmark right above the left lip.

Tom had said birthmarks usually weren't hereditary. He'd been wrong.

Heather fell asleep holding the album and dreaming about her parents, wondering why her father wasn't in any of the photos before she'd been three.

Later, in the morning, she dressed for work and hurried down to breakfast to sit across from Bianca, thinking of a dozen questions to ask about the people and places in Sarasota Falls. Even if Bianca could only answer one, that would be one answer closer to finding out the truth.

"I guess you heard about the robbery?" Bianca said, placing a blueberry muffin on a plate and putting it in front of Heather.

"I did. Tom says he's confident they'll catch whoever did it."

"Especially since the robber returned items to Shelley. Pretty amazing. Makes the chief's job easier looking for a crook with a conscience."

Heather nodded, thinking that finding the cookie bandit was not even a thought in Tom's mind. "I'm kinda glad no one else is here," she said. "I was hoping to ask you a few questions."

Bianca smiled, and Heather half expected her to rub her hands together and say, "Good."

The proprietor didn't; instead, she said, "I was hoping you'd ask. But first, you're going to need to tell me exactly who you are and what you're looking for."

A year ago, before her parents died, Heather had known exactly who she was. A week or so ago, when she'd arrived in Sarasota Falls, she'd known that there was something more to know. Today, she felt a bit lost.

"I'm Heather Graves, daughter of Bill and Melanie Graves." Heather set her photograph album in front of Bianca. "They apparently used to be Raymond Tillsbury and Sarah Lewis."

"Oh, my."

In the end, Bianca had related the same scenario that the Turners had, but she had one piece of information that made a huge difference.

"I know this living room." She pointed to the one where Heather had been wearing the pink sweatpants and was all of two or three. "See all those Precious Moments collectables on the shelves. Well, that was Renate Penny's place. She did childcare. Sarah Lewis, your mother, worked there."

"Does Renate still live here?"

"No. She moved quite a few years ago to be near one of her daughters."

"Can you find out her address for me, maybe a phone number?"

"I can do that. Sarah Lewis was always a favorite of mine. She and her sister, Debbie, were Girl Scouts. I must have bought enough cookies to feed an army, or at least enough cookies to feed my nephews."

"What about the little girl? I mean, it's me. And surely you'd know if Sarah Lewis had a baby. Plus, if I understand the time line correctly, she married my dad after she left Sarasota Falls. Add to that, Debbie says that Sarah couldn't have children."

"Oh, my." It seemed to be Bianca's favorite utterance. "I don't have all the answers. I don't recognize the little girl. I mean, I realize you say it's you, but I didn't have children, so I wasn't always around the children in town. You'd want to ask a few of the kids near your age."

"Probably not. If I left Sarasota Falls when I was two-ish, then the kids my age would have been two-ish, and they won't remember anything."

"Which takes us back to Renate," Bianca agreed.

Ten minutes later, Heather had an address

and was on her way to the dental office. She tried calling Tom, but he didn't answer. Shouldn't cops always answer?

Bianca would probably be a bit annoyed when she found out about Rachel being arrested and Heather not sharing. Maybe Tom was still dealing with Rachel.

Who looked so much like Heather.

Whose daughter looked even more like Heather, at least at age two, wearing pink sweatpants.

IT WAS ALMOST noon when Tom finally woke up. He checked his phone: dead. After plugging it in, he took a shower and then shaved because the features staring back at him from the mirror looked scraggly and tired.

Not an unusual look for a cop, but he didn't feel scraggly and tired. He felt scraggly and somewhat rejuvenated.

He had Rachel Ramsey in a cell.

That wasn't why he'd slept so good.

Having answers, having a new direction to take and, yes, having Heather Graves to work alongside added a dimension to his life that had been missing.

He doubted very much that Heather would appreciate being considered a dimension.

After he dressed, he checked the charged phone and smiled. Three messages from her, all with Call Me.

For the last five years, every "call me" had to do with a police situation or a civic duty.

His smile faded. Alongside Heather's messages were six from the owner of the local Sarasota Falls newspaper. Tom deleted them.

He tapped Heather's highlighted number and waited. She didn't answer, so he called Bianca's Bed-and-Breakfast, another number he had stored because Oscar Guzman used to live there.

"Hey, Bianca. Is Heather there?"

"She's at work."

He debated all of twenty seconds before finding Sarasota Dental and calling. Maybe he should have taken the full minute. Maya answered and Tom said, "May I speak with Heather, please."

"Chief Tom Riley, is this you?" Maya quickly replied. "What's this I hear that Rachel Ramsey was arrested last night? Really? She was living in the house she pretty much grew up in? How'd you miss that, Tom?"

"I'm not at liberty to give any details."

"It's all anyone is talking about."

"Great. Is Heather available?"

"You mean is the new town celebrity available? I can't tell you how many people have come in just to introduce themselves to her. We finally took her off the front desk."

"Why would people think to do that?" Tom sputtered.

"Ah," Maya said, "you've not watched the news this morning."

Tom grimaced. Great, more publicity they didn't need. Things were still complicated enough. And Tom knew, just knew, that the Rachel Ramsey–Heather Graves connection would mean a sequel to that TV movie about the case. If the same guy played him, Tom would dye his hair gray. Distinguished was better than doofus.

"I'll get her."

A moment later, Heather came on the line. "Hey."

"Have you seen the news? Because I haven't."

"I have. Someone got footage of all of us entering the hospital. There's a great shot of Rachel and I, standing next to each other. I've been trying to deny it, but...hold on."

Tom look a deep breath. He didn't need to see the footage to acknowledge the similarity. He'd recognized it while glancing out of his SUV at a tiny car traveling just a bit beside him. It hadn't just been a visual thing, either. It had been an electric current of connection.

Heather came back on the line. "Dr. Goodman says for me to take the rest of the day off. He's being pretty good about it. Seems worried even."

"You want to get something to eat?"

She hesitated. "No, I just ate a few hours ago. I do have something I'd like us to do. Are you on duty?"

"No, the mayor made an appearance late last night. He doesn't want me to be lead on this case. Says I'm, as well as anyone who worked alongside Max, too close to it. Oscar's in charge. I have today off."

Personally, Tom was glad. After listening to Rachel last night, his heart and his sense of justice were at war. There would be no perfect ending to this case. He still planned on stopping by the department, overseeing a few things, getting the most recent updates.

"Then I need to talk to you, in person."

He heard Maya sputtering in the distance, "I can keep a secret."

"Nothing's going to be secret for long," Heather predicted softly.

"I'll come pick you up."

"No, I want to change clothes. Come get me at the bed-and-breakfast. I need about thirty minutes."

It didn't take him thirty minutes. It only took him ten, and that was because he called Leann to tell her about a storm to their east. Nothing to worry about, just to be aware. Visiting the bed-and-breakfast was becoming a habit. He sat in the living room with Bianca and ate a blueberry scone from Sarasota Sweets. He hadn't even swallowed the first bite when he realized that Bianca had missed her calling and should really be a counselor.

"You going to be able to live with her being related to Rachel?" she asked.

"We haven't proven that connection," Tom said.

"Yet," Bianca said.

"We're all related to each other if we go back far enough."

Bianca laughed. "Not going to stand up in a

court of law, Officer, and you haven't answered my question."

He finished the pastry, chewing with gusto so she'd not expect him to answer. He was frustrated, curious and scared. Usually during an investigation, he wasn't scared.

Bianca handed him a glass of milk. He wanted coffee, but drinking the milk saved him from having to answer her. Truth was, he wished more than anything that Heather wasn't related to Rachel. Bigger truth was, he'd fallen in love with her anyway.

She came hurrying down the stairs, wearing jeans and a red T-shirt and red tennis shoes. Her hair was in its usual ponytail, and her face was half serious and half smiling.

"Bianca and I figured something out," Heather said.

His gaze swung to Bianca. Apparently, she knew more than he did about the connection between Heather and Rachel—no wonder the question.

"Look at this," Heather insisted.

She sat down beside him and dropped an open photograph album into his lap. She leaned in, showing him picture after picture, clearly wanting him to notice what she was noticing.

He wasn't. He didn't.

He only had eyes for her. At the moment, he didn't care what she looked like at age two. He cared that she was so close to him that he could reach out his hand and stroke her soft blond locks. If he wanted, he could tilt her face toward him and run a finger down her cheek. It would be silky smooth, warm, tender.

Yes, he could completely ignore, forget, her connection to Rachel because the connection she had with him obliterated it. He cleared his throat, hoping that he'd managed to hide his feelings, and looked back down at the album.

The photo was of a little girl smiling at the camera the way the fully grown woman was smiling at him.

Beautiful.

"You said you had something you wanted to do."

"Bianca gave me Renate Penny's address. It's in Springer, a town—"

"I know where Springer is."

Heather's smile widened. "Of course you do. I want to drive over there, visit her and get some answers to questions I'm beginning to wish I'd never asked."

"I could do it. Alone. That way—"

"That way you could tell me just what I need to know when I most need to know it," she said, seeming to read this mind. "No, thanks. I need to hear all this myself." Immediately, to Tom's consternation, she switched gears. "What's wrong with me? I've had a great life. Why didn't I just leave it like that?"

This time, Bianca answered. Tom had almost forgotten she was in the room.

"Because humans, by nature, are curious. And it's too late to turn back the clock. You won't rest until you know the truth."

"I can't believe that I never noticed that my dad wasn't in a single picture until I was two." Heather claimed the photograph album from Tom. "Yes, I know he claimed to be the one taking the photos. Then, note that every single picture of me is in the same house, nowhere else."

Tom agreed. All Heather's baby photos seemed to be in one house, a house that, according to Bianca, belonged to Renate Penny. After age two, Heather had her picture taken at Disneyland, camping at the Coconino National Forest in Arizona, on a steamboat even.

"Come on," Heather ordered, reaching out a hand to help him up. "Let's go to Springer."

"I'll pack some scones for you to take. Renate always loved them. She's a baker, you know, and…" The words dropped off as Bianca left the room.

"You sure you want to do this? You don't have to."

"We've already gone over this. Besides," she said, her hand still in his from helping him up, "I'll have you right beside me." She slipped her fingers between his and squeezed.

"Okay." Helpless, he felt helpless.

"We'll take my car," she added. "I don't want to pull up in her driveway in a police vehicle. That always puts people on the defensive."

"Not always," Tom argued.

"Always."

Tom wasn't sure about her car. It was a tiny old two-door compact. It was clean and had a small cross hanging from the rearview mirror.

"How fast does it go?" he queried.

"Fast enough."

He didn't bother to tell her how fast his SUV went, or that he liked both speed and reliability in his vehicle. Neither of which hers appeared to have. "This isn't a car. It's more like a toy. In a pinch, I could pick it up, tuck it under my arm and chase down a mugger."

Heather huffed. "It gets me where I need to go and has great gas mileage." She frowned in the direction of his SUV. "Unlike yours."

"Yes, well, I did say a mugger, one mugger, because if there were two and I was driving your vehicle, I'd have to handcuff one to the side mirror and bungee-cord him to the top, and that would only work if he was a small guy." Tom opened her door for her, adding a gallant swoop of his arm before stepping back as she slid behind the wheel. He closed her door, jogged to the passenger side and made a great production of maneuvering in. "If any of my officers see me in this, I'll lose my cop card."

"You have a cop card?"

"Have you ever heard of a man card?"

"It's not that bad," she scolded.

She started the car just as a zap of thunder rumbled overhead. The white clouds shifted to gray.

"Bianca," Heather said, thankfully changing the subject, "called Renate. She's home and willing to talk to us."

"Good."

"Bianca suggested I ask all my questions over the phone, but I wanted to do it in person.

Renate remembers my mother and has nothing but good things to say."

"I've found," Tom said, "that talking face-to-face, laying a few photos or details on the table, often jogs a person's memory."

"I'm hoping she'll have more photos of my mom, and maybe, maybe of me." Heather pulled out her phone and found Renate's address.

"We won't need directions," Tom reminded her. "I know how to get there."

"You've been before?"

"To Springer, yes. To Renate Penny's house, no, but Springer is smaller than Sarasota Falls. It's basically four blocks of downtown and twelve blocks of residential. They've pretty much got one industry."

"Which is?"

"The prison."

The first tiny drop of rain hit the windshield. Heather hit the wipers and didn't so much as flinch. He liked the way she drove, both hands on the steering wheel, a tiny wrinkle of concentration in the middle of her forehead. It hadn't been there before the rain. Or before he mentioned the prison.

"Will Rachel be sent to Springer?"

"No, Springer is a men's penitentiary." He didn't offer to tell her where Rachel would probably be sent and she didn't ask. Instead, for the next hour she queried him about how he felt with Oscar taking lead on the case, and about his parents. She sure knew how to jump around.

Maybe she talked that much so she could pretend the thick, dark clouds weren't rolling in. The car's headlights were almost useless.

"Maybe I should pull over?" she suggested.

He was of two minds.

"Can you make out the yellow stripe?" he asked.

"Yes."

"Other cars?"

"Yes."

"Then let's keep driving. You're doing fine and the other drivers are just as nervous as you are."

"I'm not nervous."

"Of course not."

"It almost feels like evening but—" she checked the time on her dashboard "—it's only two."

"A New Mexico storm. Nothing like them."

"They happen often?"

"No, not in October, but they have a way of knowing the worst time to hit."

"Like now."

He nodded. "Chances are in Sarasota Falls, Leann is getting a dozen calls, everything from downed tree limbs to strange noises being heard."

"You want to turn around?"

"No, my team can handle it."

"Maybe you should call in or something?"

He shook his head. "No service. Storm's the best interrupter Mother Nature could manage."

The smell of rain entered through the vents. Heather switched on the heat mostly to help defog the windshield. Then she turned on the radio, some light rock, and leaned forward as if it helped her to drive.

"You don't seem affected at all. If anything, you look even more relaxed than when we left.

"You don't worry me a bit," he lied before switching to the truth. "Springer is about twenty minutes ahead. They have a two-man police force. I've sent officers to help them a time or two."

"You didn't say much when Bianca brought up Renate Penny. What do you know about her?"

"Well, I can tell you she babysat me a time

or two. Usually my aunt watched me while my mom worked, but once or twice she went on vacation. I remember that Renate has three kids, all older than me and scattered. When her husband retired, she and her husband moved nearer his folks."

The car hit a slippery patch. Heather's fingers gripped the steering wheel, and she asked, "Where did your mom work?"

"She was a librarian," Tom quickly continued, "and my dad was a plumber. Freaked them out a bit when I decided to go into law enforcement."

"They worried."

"Still do, even though they're safe in Florida and tell me how glad they are that I'm here, where there's so little crime compared to their town, where there's a lot more."

"I loved the library. My mom, if she only had six or seven kids under her care, would take us there. We'd go for story hour. Sometimes they'd have puppet shows."

"Sounds like your mom was the best kind of childcare provider."

"She was. Most of the time we had a waiting list. I can remember parents coming to the door and begging her to take on one more kid.

Their kid. She always said that eight was her limit. Which, of course, was why they wanted her. She made the kids her family, spent time not only teaching them, but also loving them."

"She sounds like a wonderful woman."

"A wonderful woman and an even better mom." Heather's voice broke a little. "It makes sense that she ran a childcare business at home. She must have learned from Renate. She continued doing what she'd always done, only under a different name."

"And we have to find out why the different name," Tom said.

He couldn't miss Heather's smile when he'd said *we*.

CHAPTER NINETEEN

SPRINGER HADN'T CHANGED since the last time Tom visited. The clouds lifted a bit as Heather drove down the center of town. Only a few cars were parked in front of businesses. No one walked the sidewalks.

"Where to now?" Heather asked.

Tom had to wait until she was right up to the streets in order to read their names. Renate lived on the third crossroad. Hers was the fifth house in. Heather pulled into a driveway that had seen better days, but the lawn was lush and someone had a green thumb.

"Wish I had an umbrella," Heather muttered.

"I can go knock and see if Renate has one," Tom offered.

"No, a little rain never hurt anything." She followed him out of the car, hurrying up the three steps that led to the porch. He moved her so she was in front of him, his body shielding hers from the rain, and he knocked. The motion sent her leaning into him, and when she tried to move away, there wasn't room.

She felt good. Too good. The top of her head brushed against his chin. He had to force himself not to wrap his arms around her, circle her with his body and keep her safe.

Serve and protect.

Never had he enjoyed his job more.

Bianca had asked if he could forget that she was related to Rachel. Yes, he could. No doubt.

The door opened, and a woman with wild red hair and a bright purple outfit beckoned them in. "I wasn't sure you'd still come," she said, handing them both towels.

"We were partway here when the heavy rain started," Tom told her.

Ten minutes later, Tom and Heather sipped tea and politely ate cookies. Tom sat alone on an armchair, observing. The living room was mostly brown and orange, full of knick-knacks, mostly cats, which had given them a few minutes of small talk while Heather described Tom's cat. The environment was tense, more on Renate's part than Heather's, which was somewhat surprising. To lighten the mood, Tom compared Renate's cookies to the ones sold at Sarasota Sweets.

"My husband always did say I should have started a bakery," Renate said before sitting down next to Heather on the couch. "It might have made things easier."

Tom noted how the woman reached over to pat Heather on the knee and how she couldn't seem to look away, even when he tried to join the conversation. Slowly, she put on her glasses and started looking at Heather's childhood photograph album.

"Oh," she said, with a sad smile. "That's the Gillespie girl. I remember this photo. She's in the military now. And, that's..." She went on for a few minutes identifying people.

"I think," Heather interrupted, "that you watched me when I was really young."

"Heather..." Renate said slowly, but there were no questions in her eyes, no denial on her lips.

"My parents died recently. They were Sarah Lewis and Raymond Tillsbury."

"I'm so sorry," Renate said. "That's terrible. Terrible. Sarah was—was an awesome girl who grew into an incredible woman."

"All these photos," Heather said, laying five on the coffee table, "are from when I was under two. Bianca recognized your living room. What happened? How did I go from here—" she pointed to a photo of a little girl sitting on the floor holding a stuffed animal in her lap, a smudge of something on her sad face "—to this?" she asked, opening the album to a random page with a photo taken at an outdoor carnival. The smudge had turned into full ice-cream face and a big smile."

"I can only answer the first question," Renate confessed. "It is my living room. Are you sure you're the little girl?" She hid her emotions well, but he thought he saw her blink a few times and not the I'm-about-to-cry kind of blink.

Oh, yeah, she knew something and it was tearing her apart.

"Yes." Heather tapped the two pictures. "I'm sure both of them are me."

"Could you possibly be related to—" Renate began.

"No, all of them are me, age two and above. We—" she shot a look at Tom "—want to know how I wound up with Sarah and Raymond. What my real name is. No one seems to know. I'm sure it's me. One hundred percent."

"You'll need to excuse me." Renate closed the album as if she didn't want it open and accusing. Then she disappeared into the kitchen and a moment later, it was obvious she was on the phone arguing with someone.

Tom stood, went to the door and tried to hear her words, but outside a storm was raging and thunder overshadowed everything else. Annoyed, he returned to Heather. "I can make out a few words, but none that I can put together into anything that makes sense."

"Who do you think she's called?"

"Well, she said her husband was at the church at a meeting. She probably called him."

"I'm a little scared," Heather confessed. "What if I don't like what I find out."

Tom put his hand on hers. "At the very least, from Renate we should get more verification that Diane was your mother. No surprise there. Maybe, if we're really lucky, she'll know that Raymond Tillsbury was your biological father."

"I can live with that. I can."

"Me, too." When she looked at him sharply, he added, "It's the best scenario."

To Tom's amazement, Renate returned with a banker's box. Before he could do more than gape, she explained, "I learned early on to keep good records."

"Why don't you use a computer?" Heather asked.

"When I started, I didn't own a computer. It wasn't until my youngest daughter hit high school that we bought one. By the time I got comfortable with it, I was done doing child-care."

Renate started going through files.

"You know where to start?" Tom queried.

"Sure, the Gillespie girl is about five there. She went to kindergarten with my sister's boy. That gives me a good idea of the age. My files are organized by years. Here are the files I'm looking for, and here are the kids who were in my care."

She pulled out what seemed like an application. Paper-clipped to that was a sheet of notes. Attached to each one was a photo. Renate started with the first, even supplying a few comments.

"Maria Gillespie, well-behaved, helper, hates green peas. She," Renate said, pointing to a photo that included a very young Heather, "is holding the mirror that Heidi is staring into."

"My kind of girl," Tom remarked. Heidi?

Renate read a few more names, identifying one of the other children, and then she paused for a moment. "I can't tell you how many times I moved this file, sometimes putting it in the safe, sometimes in the trash can. I always put it back. I'm not dishonest. I've never done anything that made me ashamed to own up to it."

She put some papers on the coffee table in front of Heather. Tom moved over, nudged Heather aside and took a seat beside her. He peered over her shoulder as she read. It was Diane Ramsey's agreement with Renate, probably, most definitely, written in Diane's loopy scrawl. Tom took out his phone and asked, "May I take a photo of this?"

Renate nodded.

Tom knew he'd probably have the original within twenty-four hours, but he didn't want to wait that long to compare handwriting.

The one-page document gave Renate permission to watch Heidi Ramsey, age twenty-two months. It listed no allergies or special needs. Diane had agreed to Renate's childcare hours and the cost of childcare.

Renate traced her finger over the photo of Heidi. "I didn't babysit her—you—for long. It was hard watching you, so hard."

"Why do you say that?" Tom looked at Heather. Her face was scrunched, her hands clenched. She had to be feeling what he felt. No doubt, no doubt at all now.

"Look here at what I wrote. Heidi Ramsey, not potty-trained, few words, always hungry, loves pancakes, comes dirty, picked up late." Renate looked up. "I called social services twice. They didn't investigate because there were no sure signs of abuse."

"But you were concerned?" Heather asked.

Tom was impressed. It had to be uncomfortable, hearing someone talk about her, under a different name and under dire circumstances.

"I was very concerned. I knew the markers for a two-year-old. You didn't meet any of them. And, oh, did you love being hugged. It was like you knew that my house was the only place you'd be hugged, so you were going to get it while you could."

Tom made up his mind right then to hug Heather often, every chance he got, just as soon as she'd let him.

Renate continued. "I figured out quickly that you were smart. If I remember, after just two months with me, you were talking up a storm, at least a two-year-old storm. Sarah would give you a bath almost every day. Sometimes I'd find her crying because she'd found a bruise, and we couldn't quite tell if it was a I-bumped-into-a-table kind of bruise or a some-one-pinched-me kind of bruise. Diane never seemed to notice that she brought us a little girl who was dirty and smelled of urine, and we returned a little girl who was clean and smelled like pancakes."

"Diane Ramsey really was my mother?" Heather's words sounded like a statement more than a question.

"You did say you were one hundred percent sure that you were the little girl in the photo all grown up."

"One hundred percent sure."

"Did you meet the father?" Tom asked.

"No, but I do remember thinking you sure didn't look like any Ramsey. Diane, either, for that matter."

Renate Penny remembered quite a lot, Tom noted. She probably hadn't needed the files to nudge her memories. In some ways, it was like she'd been waiting for them.

"If Kyle Ramsey wasn't really Heidi's father, why was she going under the last name of Ramsey?" Tom asked.

"Guess it was easier that way."

"But you'd have to file the names of who was under your care with the state, right?"

Renate looked a little guilty. "I didn't become a licensed childcare provider until a few years later. At first, I only watched family and friends. Then the business grew. You know, Heidi was only the second kid I took on who basically belonged to a stranger."

"How did you wind up with her?"

"Joe asked me to do it. How do you say no to him?"

"Father Joe?" Tom asked.

"Yes. He had tried to counsel Diane a few times. Nothing took. He was concerned. He even offered to pay me for watching Heidi. Not that I'd let him."

"Was Diane working?"

"She did something with cars. Not fixing them, but delivering them for her family. I remember she'd take long road trips. Once she showed me a photo of her in an old Model T Ford."

Tom made a note.

"When did you stop watching me and when did my mother quit?" Heather asked, looking down at the photo of Sarah sitting behind her on that long-ago living room floor. "Because

Diane Ramsey certainly didn't qualify as one, not the way Sarah Lewis had."

"I can tell you." Renate reached for another file in the box and quickly ran her finger down the last page inside. "She quit on May ninth. Gave two weeks notice, right after we lost Heidi. I always thought it was because she couldn't bear getting close to the little ones and then having them go home to their families, especially when the family wasn't nurturing."

"You lost Heidi?"

"Diane stopped bringing her. I assumed she realized she couldn't afford it. Later, someone told me the father, the real father, took custody."

"Any chance Raymond Tillsbury was the father?" Tom asked. "It would explain how Heather came to be with them."

"I don't know. He never came around when I had her. I never saw him with Diane. One time, I know, he chased Kyle Ramsey out of Little's Grocery Store. He'd been shoplifting."

"My dad didn't suffer fools well," Heather said.

"Was Sarah a good employee?" Tom had his notebook out and was quickly writing down the dates Renate had shared.

"The best. She never missed work and wasn't squeamish about getting her hands dirty."

"Where did she go to work afterward?"

"She went off to school out of state. Then I heard she'd gotten married to some guy she met and followed him overseas since he was in the military."

"That's the story," Heather whispered.

"What?" Renate looked confused.

"Did you know that Sarah couldn't have children?" Heather asked, rather than answering Renate.

"She shared that. I believe that's why she worked here and maybe that's why she couldn't take falling in love with the little ones and then having to say goodbye to them each day when they returned to their parents. She'd have made an awesome mom."

"She was an awesome mom," Heather said.

"So," Tom said, "Sarah worked for you. You knew she couldn't have children. You also knew that Diane's husband, Kyle Ramsey, wasn't the father, and you're pretty sure that Raymond wasn't the father, either."

"Pretty sure," Renate agreed, looking anything but.

"This means," Heather said, "that Rachel is my half sister. Did you ever care for her?"

"No," Renate said, "and I've always felt guilty about that. See, one of my policies is—was—if you don't pay, you don't stay. Diane owed me two weeks when Heidi stopped attending. She never paid."

"Renate, this first photo you've identified as Heidi. Let me show you a few more photos." Tom slid the photo of Heidi over in front of Heather. He then put a few new photos next to the baby photo of Rachel. "This is Rachel her junior year and Rachel today." He tapped the photo of the last child. "Rachel's daughter, Abigail."

"Oh, goodness. I didn't know Rachel had a child. They do all look alike." She stared at Heather and said, "So, Heidi. It's good to see you after all these years. And I know you had a good life."

"How do you know?" Heather asked.

"Sarah Lewis was your mother."

"I need to know who the father is," Heather said.

"Why?" Renate asked. "Why do you need to know?"

"Because I need to know who I am, all of me."

"Can't you just leave it alone?"

"No."

"Who told you that Sarah and Raymond had gotten married?" Tom asked.

"My brother." She turned to Heather. "He's also the one who brought you to me as a toddler. And he's also the one who confided in me that Sarah and Raymond were raising you. I've always known who was taking care of you. When I'd heard you were back, and asking questions, I was so afraid."

"Afraid of what?" Tom asked.

"Afraid that you'd find out that I helped kidnap that baby." The voice came from the kitchen doorway.

Father Joe.

CHAPTER TWENTY

WHEN THEY LEFT Renate and Father Joe, it was dark with a fine mist of rain peppering the windshield. The thunder had retreated into heavy gray clouds, which were already disappearing, leaving a blue hue of sky exposed. The weather, like the mystery of Heather's life, was experiencing a calm after the storm.

"They kidnapped me," Heather said. "I'm having a hard time wrapping my mind around it."

"I'm not sure it falls under the true category of kidnapping. If Diane had reported you missing, then yes, but…"

"What are you saying?"

"I'm saying that while Father Joe and your parents did something illegal by taking you, they didn't take you by force or endanger you. They did move you interstate, which ups the severity. And, there might be a bit of fraud, but the question of who they defrauded—"

"Who will press charges against them? I certainly won't." Heather felt fiercely protective of her parents. She also felt somewhat grateful to Father Joe for having the guts to make a change where a change needed to be made.

"Who doesn't report their own child missing?" Tom's voice was a combination of amazement and anger. He didn't wait but answered the question himself. "Someone who either gains from the child's disappearance or someone who is afraid to report the disappearance."

"What?" Heather sputtered. She'd been half-afraid he'd say someone who didn't want the child.

"Well," Tom mused, "we talked about the birth father being in Sarasota Falls, someone who Father Joe knew, someone paying Diane's bills."

"Wasn't Kyle Ramsey paying Diane's bills?"

"Hah." Tom almost laughed. "The only time Kyle had money is after he cheated or robbed somebody."

"That, at least, explains why Rachel stayed with Diane for all her childhood. My birth father paid for me to disappear. Her birth father didn't."

"We're still hypothesizing," Tom reminded her. "I haven't given up on the idea of Raymond being your father. It just makes too much sense."

"He was too good a person to do—" she began.

"He was also in the military and gone a lot. There's the chance he didn't know you existed until after you were born, and then he came and found you."

"That only makes a tiny bit of sense. Very tiny. My dad wasn't the kind to put off for tomorrow what could be done today. If he were truly my birth father, he'd have gone the legal route. He'd have gotten custody—"

"And had to share you and deal with Diane for the rest of your life."

"Not the prettiest picture," Heather agreed. "But not an unusual one, either."

All serious and with his notebook out again, writing in the gloom of the rainy night, Tom said, "We still can't completely eliminate him as a possibility."

Heather nodded. She sincerely hoped that Raymond Tillsbury was her true father. He was a good man. "I know it's wrong, but I wish my parents would have kidnapped Rachel, too," she said. "Talked Father Joe into it. Met him somewhere. Raised her with me. We'll never know why they didn't."

"They were probably terrified that if they tried to take her, too, they'd put you and everyone in danger, so they helped in the only way they knew how."

"How?"

"They somehow arranged to buy that house and for Diane to live in it at a ridiculously low rent."

Her parents had done that?

Tom frowned. "Maybe that was Diane's price. A free place to live. I need to find out when she moved in. And any other details… Who's left that would know?"

"At least now I have an idea why they had a rental here in Sarasota Falls," Heather said softly. "I need to go out there, make sure everything is all right. Rachel might have milk in the fridge or the mail could be stacking up."

"I can send a deputy."

"No, I want to do it. Would that be legal? I am the landlord, right?"

"Yes."

Heather gripped the steering wheel and continued driving through the dusky darkness.

She almost wished she'd let Tom drive. Then she could lean back, close her eyes and think all of this through.

She'd think a bit about him, too. His jean-clad legs. His wide shoulders made it so every time she adjusted the radio or reached for her purse, she brushed against him.

"You all right?" Tom asked.

"Fine." No way was she going to tell him that she wasn't all right and that even in the midst of this chaos, she was still affected by him. She slowed down as a truck overtook them, spraying an extra shower over her little car.

They were almost home.

Home?

Sarasota Falls.

"I know I have to be patient," Heather said after a few minutes. "But it's hard. I mean, I gave you everything you needed for DNA, so we should know eventually, but if my father isn't Raymond Tillsbury, then I bet Father Joe does know who my father is, despite what he told us, and we do need to pressure him," Heather said, speeding up a bit.

"Pressure a priest?" Tom couldn't keep the skepticism out of his voice. "He could claim

that his position as a member of the clergy requires him to refrain from supplying the name,
but maybe enough time has passed that he'd
reconsider telling us."

She nodded. Father Joe had looked as if he
had more to say to them.

"I'm wondering if someone powerful has
Father Joe spooked."

"So, my birth father might still live in Sarasota Falls?"

"It's a possibility. Or, it could be Father Joe's
protecting a family who'd be destroyed or hurt
by discovering an indiscretion."

"If I thought my existence would hurt someone, I'd keep it private."

"Too late for that," Tom pointed out. "Bianca knows, my whole staff knows, and while
none of them are what I'd call gossips…" He
paused and Heather knew he was reconsider-
ing Bianca. "It's still too many to be safe. Plus,
Rachel's been arrested and reporters will be
digging. You're her dead ringer. It's an obvious
connection they'll be diving into, for sure. At
this point, we need to know the truth before
our lives spiral out of control."

Our lives.

Heather had nothing left to say. She felt overwhelmed. What she'd give to sit down with her mother and just hear the truth. It wouldn't change a thing about the way she felt about her parents. They, according to Father Joe, had come to him with their idea. They were in love, intended to get married, and Sarah couldn't sleep knowing that a little girl was going hungry and showing up at childcare with bruises.

Her father had seen war up close and personal. He, much like Tom, was a protect-and-serve kind of guy, and he'd certainly protected Heather her whole life.

Father Joe, although he hadn't shared what he'd learned from Diane during their counseling sessions, was concerned enough that he helped.

Tom put his hand on her leg and squeezed just a bit, enough so she knew he was along for the ride not because he was a cop, but because he was her cop.

TOM DREW LONG shifts over the next few days. Who knew that a small town could be so busy? His absence made Heather realize just how much time she'd been spending with him.

To her chagrin, she also realized just how much she missed his company. How had he managed to become such an established part of her life? So much so that she was often checking her phone to see if he'd called.

He was busy; she knew that. Had to accept it, too. Rachel was talking to lawyers. Richard was still in a coma. Tom and Heather had visited him twice, both times just sitting in his room and telling him what was going on, leaving out any mention of Abigail.

On Monday, Tom found time to phone. The case was at a standstill while he waited on the DNA results. To Heather's annoyance, while he was willing to talk about her case, and her circumstances in general, he wasn't willing to talk about Rachel. All he'd say was the wheels of justice turned slow.

At the coffee shop on Wednesday, she'd met Leann and during their conversation the officer had quoted the chief's words about the wheels of justice, adding, "And sometimes you have a blowout at the worst possible time."

Heather left with her coffee and the feeling that she was a part of something, not just the quest to find her identity, but as a member of the Sarasota Falls family. And they were family at the police station. Oh, Lucas was still a bit put off, but Tom must have said something because Lucas had extended an open invitation to lunch, and to just talk and share stories.

The next night, Bianca's nephew, Deputy Oscar Guzman, and his wife and baby son came to the B and B for supper.

Heather liked Shelley. This particular night, Heather liked her even more after hearing about what Shelley called "the great mistake," referring to her ex-husband. "I'd do it all again," Shelley said, "if it was the only way to meet Oscar."

"She's only saying that so next week she can dress little Oscar up in a police costume for Halloween," Oscar teased. He waved a full spoon in front of his son, refusing to let the one-year-old dictate.

"You could swing by the party for a short while," Bianca said. "It's little Oscar's first Halloween. And it's a school night so no one's going to stay late or be too rowdy."

"Halloween's always busy. Come on, little one, you need to eat. We're all working." He smiled at Heather. "Even the chief."

"Why are you telling me that?" Heather tried for nonchalance, but didn't fool anyone because Shelley rolled her eyes, and Oscar just grinned.

"We've never seen the chief in such a mood before. Half the time, he's easy to get along with."

"That's because he arrested Rachel Ramsey," Heather pointed out.

"No, it's because of you," Shelley said. "Oscar tells me about his day, what he can share. And lately a lot of it has been about Tom. It's good to see him so happy. Like his old self."

"You knew his old self? What about his ex-wife?" Heather asked. "I am a bit curious."

"Yes, I knew Cathy. What I remember most," Shelley said, "is how vibrant she was."

"She always wanted more," Bianca said, taking the now sleeping baby from Oscar and slowly pacing back and forth. "I knew she wouldn't stay in Sarasota Falls. She wanted bigger and better."

"Nothing better than here," Oscar noted. "I've been a lot of places, stateside and overseas. I found paradise here." The way he looked at Shelley made Heather long for the same. Her father had looked at her mother that way, as if amazed at her.

Bianca left the room and came back a few moments later without little Oscar. "Sometimes people, like Tom, go through high school and you're with the same person the whole time, and you assume your life will never change."

While Bianca took dessert plates from a cabinet and set them on the table, Shelley headed for the kitchen. Heather knew what this meant—another inch on her waist. If Shelley wasn't bringing over apple pie, she was dropping off brownies. Being pregnant seemed to make her bake more, more than she needed at Sarasota Sweets, even. And poor Bianca only had two guests staying in the bed-and-breakfast tonight, and they had gone out to eat.

Bianca was handing desserts out to the mailman in order to get rid of them.

"Tom was the football player," Bianca said after swallowing her first bite of apple pie, "who made all the touchdowns and then settled down and was happy. That happiness was shaken to its core when Max died."

Heather nodded. She could see that.

"And Cathy was the cheerleader who, when Tom got so very dedicated to his job after his partner's death, suddenly didn't have a team to cheer for."

Shelley looked at Oscar, and Heather saw

the worry there. Being a cop's spouse had to be hard.

Not that she and Tom were a couple. They weren't. They were just spending a lot of time together because of her mystery.

And when the mystery was solved? For a long time, Heather thought that meant she'd return to Phoenix, her old job, her old life.

Now she wasn't so sure. Back there, she didn't have a team to cheer for.

CHAPTER TWENTY-ONE

FRIDAY MORNING, Tom had breakfast with the Sarasota Falls Chamber of Commerce at the Station Diner. Mayor Goodman was there talking about tourism and how successful the Founder's Day celebration had been and how they needed to figure out the next best thing

Some of the business folks attending were as focused as the mayor; others had questions for Tom. Most wanted to know what was happening with Rachel. A few queried about Heather. Tom wasn't sure if he was grateful or annoyed that the questions had to do with his relationship with her and not if she were related to Rachel.

The mayor, looking tired, bullied everyone into following the agenda. "Our population is down," the mayor said. "We've got three empty storefronts."

"Meaning," Bianca whispered to Tom, "that he's not receiving rent on them."

Tom nodded. The mayor and his family had always been a force.

When the meeting ended, midmorning, the mayor followed Tom to his SUV. "I hope you're not upset with my suggestion that Oscar take the lead on the Rachel Ramsey case."

"I'm not. It was a good suggestion."

The mayor looked surprised. Typically, such a call would have met with resistance.

"I'm too close to the case. You were right."

"What's happening? Do you know?"

"She has a lawyer, a fairly good one, and what looks to be in her favor is that Jeremy Salinas threatened to kill her and her unborn baby if she didn't get out of the car. She's claiming that she didn't know Jeremy planned to kill Max."

"Do you believe her?" Mayor Goodman asked.

"Not for me to decide," Tom said. "We'll let the courts do that."

"Oh, don't use that line on me, Thomas Riley. I knew you when you couldn't keep a diaper on. What do you think?"

"I think she's telling the truth."

"Then, when you testify, you'll stick up for

her?" Mayor Goodman raised an eyebrow, disbelief all over his face.

"I'll state the facts. And truthfully, right now, we're hoping having her will draw Salinas in."

"He's still in the picture? Do we need to put extra patrol to keep the area safe?"

"We're being diligent. I wouldn't worry just yet."

"Sometimes," the mayor said, "I think I was born to worry. What about Heather Graves? You figure out a connection?"

"We're working on that right now. I should have a DNA report soon."

"What about the robberies?"

"We're looking into them."

"Word around town is you're looking after Miss Graves a bit more than the job requires."

With that the mayor walked to the parking lot next to the Station Diner. He stepped into his beloved burgundy-and-black Studebaker. Tom watched a moment and then hurried down the sidewalk to fall into step beside Heather.

"You on break?" he asked.

"No. We only had two appointments. They didn't need four staff for two children. I'm low man on the totem pole so got the rest of the day off." She looked him up and down. "Why aren't you in uniform?"

"Chamber-of-commerce meeting. Just broke up, so I'm free. I'm thinking spur-of-the-moment here. How about you?"

"Spur-of-the-moment what?"

"Step into my carriage." He opened the passenger door to his SUV.

"You're kidding. I'm in my scrubs."

"And you look great, Scrubby."

"Scrubby? Don't go there."

He smiled, reached for her and whispered loudly, "The mayor just accused me of wooing you. I like to be guilty of what I'm charged with. Come with me today. Let's have some fun."

It had been a while since Chief Tom Riley had asked a woman for a date. Heather Graves, though, was worth the wait.

"I'm game if you are." She swung into the passenger seat, buckled up and said, "Let's go."

He stopped at a corner market, ran in and got snacks and bottled water, and then headed to the outskirts of town. It wasn't until they'd passed both the Turner place and her house that she asked, "What are we doing?"

Tom paused. What was he doing? Back in

Sarasota Falls, his desk had never been so cluttered in all his years as chief. It was almost the weekend and he needed to be on top of things. Yet, here he was, in the wildest area just outside his jurisdiction, pulling into the scenic overlook, opening his door and then hers, and it seemed like the best idea in the world.

"There's something I want to show you."

"Here, in the middle of nowhere?"

"It's not the middle of nowhere. This is Jicarilla Apache land. I've been exploring it since I was a Boy Scout."

"I should have known you were a Boy Scout."

"All the way to Eagle," he proclaimed proudly.

Tom noted that she was smiling.

"Most of this is government land, but there's the Blackgoat Ranch, a homestead of over a hundred and fifty years."

"Is that where we're going?"

"Yes, about a quarter of a mile in." He glanced at her shoes. "Think you can walk that far?"

"These are my work shoes. They're built for comfort and endurance."

He thought about taking her hand, wished he could, but though they'd been together just about every day for almost two weeks, it had always been on police business.

"Where exactly are you taking me?"

"A surprise."

"I'm guessing it's not the upscale-restaurant or movie-night kind of surprise."

"You got that right."

Within a few minutes, they were on the trail. He knew the way even though he'd not hiked back here in almost ten years.

His ex-wife didn't like the outdoors much. She preferred air-conditioning to fresh air and hardwood floors to dirt. She'd wanted to sell his family home and move into one of the cute new condos built toward the lake. No backyard at all, just a square area big enough for a table and two chairs.

He'd put his foot down, and they'd stayed in the house his parents had sold to them.

"You've got that look on your face," Heather said.

"What look?"

"The look that means you're weighing a problem and how you can solve it to suit your expectations."

"I don't have a look like that."

"Yes, you do. The first time I saw it was

when you arrested me and everyone around you said I wasn't Rachel, that I was too short. You started talking about my height."

"No, I didn't."

"You did, too. I could hear you yelling from across the station. And then when we were sitting in the Turners' living room and Gloria mentioned that Sarah Lewis's picture would be in an old yearbook. You were still trying to figure out a way to get the yearbook and we were already onto another subject."

"You can't possibly know that."

"It's all in your face."

"That's not good. If you can read my expression, that means…"

"Well, it wouldn't have been hard for your officers to read your expression the day you brought me in. You were all words. As for the Turners, both of them were preoccupied and paying no attention to you."

"You were paying attention to me," Tom said slowly.

"I was."

"I like that." Tom veered off a worn path about four inches wide. Dirt no longer showed but the grass was shorter.

She stopped beside him, studying the landscape, and then stepped in front of him. She walked to the Native American ruins just ahead and ran her hand across the broken rock wall.

"It's a kiva?"

"It's what's left of a kiva, for religious rites, and over a thousand years old."

Heather quickly removed her hand. "I shouldn't be touching it."

For the next ten minutes, Tom led her around, pointing out symmetrical patterns as well as talking about items that had been excavated. She nodded and followed right at his heels, so close that when he stopped, she walked right into him.

He righted her, his hands clasping her arms. She looked up, expectantly, and before he could stop himself, not that he wanted to, his lips were on hers.

He'd forgotten.

No, he'd never known.

Her lips were soft and warm under his, pliant and giving at the same time. He wanted her closer but that wasn't possible. Her arms went up and around his neck. In the car, she'd smelled like strawberries. Right now, though, she smelled like strawberries mixed with the crisp October air and with maybe a hint of rain.

Yes, rain had a scent, and it made him more alive than he had felt in years, six to be exact.

The kiss ended way too soon, and Heather pushed out of his arms, looking at him with swollen lips and inquisitive eyes. "I'm sorry," she whispered, not sounding a bit apologetic.

"For what?"

"Er, for tripping."

He grinned. "You should trip again, and again, and again."

Her neck went red first and then her cheeks flamed. "This is probably not a good idea."

"Why not? We're both adults."

"Yes, but you're about to indict a woman who we're fairly sure is one of my relatives. You also have to accept that when my parentage is discovered, a whole new can of worms will be opened."

"I don't care who you're related to."

"Easy to say right now when you're not sure."

He looked past her, at the tree limbs swaying in the wind, at the white wisps of clouds wafting by, and the blue sky stretching across the forest.

"When you're a cop, every day offers a new surprise. Like you." She hadn't stepped that far away, so he reached out his hand and tilted her chin up with his pointer finger.

"Why am I a surprise?"

"Because, since the first time I set eyes on you, you've been leading me up one road and down another until we landed here." He stepped back, sat on an old stump and motioned her to follow, happy when she did.

He put one arm around her and then pointed to the top of the distant Jemez Mountains. "One day, I'll take you there by an old road no one knows about but us locals. There's the remnants of a ghost town."

"So, for you a hot date is either sitting on a stump at some old ruins or exploring a ghost town?" she queried.

He thought a moment, then answered, "It's not the locale that makes a date hot, it's who you're with."

She laughed, a sweet melodious sound that made him wish he could put his other arm around her and turn her to face him. But she still sat a bit stiffly, just enough so he knew she wasn't quite comfortable with how fast he was moving.

He tried to decide what to say next, but she had questions of her own. "Who else have you brought here?"

"Everyone from my graduating class."

"That's not what I meant. I'm talking hot dates."

He wished he could tell her she was the first, but he was a thirty-six-year-old male and there wasn't that much to do in the town of Sarasota Falls. If he'd been bright enough, he would have used his date's reaction to the ruins to gauge compatibility.

"Did you bring your ex-wife?" Heather asked.

Good thing he was in shape or he'd have spilled her off his knee. He'd been expecting her to ask about Maureen the waitress.

"The grapevine's been keeping you up to date."

"Well, when you started popping up in my life every day, the townsfolk wanted me to know your story. To be honest, I wanted to know."

"I can understand that. Cathy Cardano was a year behind me in school, but she liked hanging around with upperclassmen. She had wild red hair and a laugh you could hear for miles."

"She was your first." Heather's words weren't a question but a statement.

"She was. And I loved her, I really did, still do, in a way."

Heather nodded.

"I still love who she was, how we were together at the beginning."

Heather nodded again, and Tom felt himself faltering. He was having a hard time explaining that he still loved his ex-wife but wasn't in love with her.

Heather started to wriggle out of his grasp, and he tightened his grip. "Hear me out. Cathy and I didn't divorce because either of us cheated, or even argued a lot…" He paused, took a deep breath and let it out. "We divorced because I didn't put her first. I put the job first."

"My dad always said that he was glad he'd gotten married after he exited the military because while he was in, he'd been married to the job," Heather said.

Tom looked past her, at the clouds that were turning smoky gray, signaling an upcoming storm. They'd have to leave soon, but he wanted to make sure she understood.

"Every cop's wife knows she has to share her husband with the town he serves, and

Cathy was good with that until—until Max was killed, and I spent the next six months doing everything I could to find Rachel and Jeremy Salinas. When I failed at doing that, I filled the empty space in my life with work. I should have filled it with her, but I didn't know any better."

"You were what?" Heather asked, "Late twenties?"

"Early thirties."

"How long after Max died did Cathy leave you?"

"A little over five months. I even know the date, July third. See, we'd gotten married in June. She'd wanted a June wedding, like a lot of brides. The year Max died, I'd forgotten our anniversary, see. She sent flowers to me, right to the police station. Boy, did I get teased. I remember thinking that day that I should do something big to make it up to her. Then, I took a call and forgot a second time. I took her to supper and a movie that weekend."

"That's nice."

"No, it wasn't special at all. Because I was gone so much, she went to a lot of movies with her girlfriends. I should have done something super."

"Like bring her up here for a picnic?"

"No, remember she doesn't like the outdoors all that much. I should have booked a room at some resort in Santa Fe. We could have sat by the pool and gone to a really nice place for supper. She'd have loved that. I chose supper and a movie here because I was afraid that something might happen in town while I was gone."

"She knew how close you were to Max. She could have been a little patient."

"She was a lot patient. I realize that now. About two months after Max died, our house got quiet. No more loud and laughing. She started taking online classes, in fashion and design to start with, which she followed with a course in cosmetology."

"Sounds like a very diverse personality."

"Good way to put it. She was very happy when I was her cop. Being a police officer usually means you're part of a family. We'd gone to Max's for barbecues most weekends. Sometimes we'd go out to Leann's family's place. They live in a minimansion with an indoor pool. When Max died, though, I felt like I'd lost my family and didn't want to do anything fun. It felt wrong without him."

"It's okay to grieve, and there's no real

time limit. Everyone's different. My parents have been gone months now, and sometimes I feel guilty because maybe I haven't grieved enough. I only took a week off work."

"I didn't take any time. If I had, maybe I'd have noticed her on the computer for hours. I came home from work one Friday night and found an advertisement on the kitchen counter for student teachers needed overseas. I almost threw it away. I thought it was junk mail."

Heather settled back into his arms. Her hand touched his knee and she squeezed, not saying anything, just being there. For him.

"If I'd been around, paid attention, I'd have seen what she was doing. But I was so involved in work that my home was just a place to sleep. My wife was just a person I was living with."

"So you found the advertisement... What happened next?"

"I called her cell phone, but she'd disconnected it. Come to find out, she'd purchased another phone and had another number for months."

"She put some planning into this."

"Yes, but she'd been giving me time, time to redeem myself. I didn't."

When he'd first started talking, he'd wanted

Heather to know the truth. However, the more he talked, the more he realized just how bitter the truth was. He'd allowed the situation with Jeremy and Rachel to take away everything in his life that mattered.

Except his job.

Because he didn't know how to let go.

He cleared his throat and continued, "It took only about five minutes to figure out her new number. She was gone for good, though."

"Have you talked to her since?"

"I have. She's been back to visit her family. She's seeing somebody and is perfectly happy. I'm glad for her."

"If Max hadn't died, would the two of you be together still?"

Tom looked into Heather's blue eyes, so deep, honest and now inquiring. Until the kiss, he'd always thought the answer was "yes." But kissing Cathy hadn't taken his breath away, hadn't made him think he could sit on a stump forever with her on his lap and have her in his arms. No, Cathy had been bumper cars and cotton candy. Great fun to be with, but too easy to say goodbye to.

Tom didn't think he'd like having a day go by without Heather in it.

"No," he replied. "I don't think we'd still be together. We both wanted different things, and in the end, our dreams pulled us apart."

She'd asked a simple question...he'd given her a simple answer. But in truth, there was no simple to it.

Yet.

CHAPTER TWENTY-TWO

HALLOWEEN BEGAN WITH a clear sky and no hint of rain. Tom wished the day would hurry and end. The weekend had featured many pre-Halloween parties, and now that the real holiday was here, he'd already put in nine hours. There was no chance he would get to see Heather. Halloween was not routine for cops. People partied, even if Halloween fell on a Monday night. Then some of them, unwisely, drove.

Every one of his officers was on duty.

"Hey," Leann said, walking into his office, carrying a stack of papers. "You said you wanted to look through these for when you tackle the budget."

Before he could respond, his landline rang. He motioned for Leann to set the papers on his desk, then he answered.

It was a good five minutes before he hung up.

"About two weeks. That's how long it took."

It had been a solid fourteen days since he'd sent the DNA samples to the lab in Albuquerque. Not the longest a result had taken, not the shortest, either.

"Was that the...?"

Tom nodded. "The forensics lab."

Leann didn't move. Just stared at him, eyes full of compassion. "They're full sisters?"

Tom nodded again. "It's official even though we knew that, thanks to Father Joe. Kyle Ramsey is not Heather's father, but it seems unlikely that Raymond Tillsbury is her dad, which we'd hoped."

Leann uttered a word Tom seldom heard her say.

Tom shook his head. Both Father Joe and Renate had said Raymond wasn't the father, but Tom hadn't been able to get past that the man had showed up to town after Diane had. It would have made so much sense for him to have done that just so he could watch over Heather, or back then, Heidi. Then...

Funny how this was the second time Tom was so closely tied to a case that the outcome felt so personal. The last time had been Max; this time it was Heather.

Leann whistled. "You going to tell her? Or you want me to?"

"I'll tell her," Tom said, thinking that just a few minutes ago, he'd been annoyed because he'd not be seeing her. Now he wished for a different reason.

"I'm good here for another hour," Leann offered.

"Thanks. I'll be back soon." At the door, Tom bypassed Oscar, who didn't really know the Ramseys, and Lucas, who knew too much. Walking down the station's steps, he stopped to let two witches and one pumpkin walk by. It was, after all, Halloween. The clear sky from the morning had segued into a soft gray, offering a perfect atmosphere for the evening. The town was buzzing with excitement.

Driving down the streets, Tom thought about those happy little kids, giggling and laughing. More than anything, Tom prayed that Heather's story had a happy ending, too. Possibly here in Sarasota Falls…

Bianca's Bed-and-Breakfast was fully decorated. Based on the noise coming out the open door, she was hosting a party. After he parked, he didn't bother knocking. The door was open and someone was exiting.

"Tom," Bianca called, when he made it just a few feet in. "I'd have invited you, but you always seem to be working."

"I'm still working. Heather around?"

"No, she took off early this afternoon. The dental office closed early, and she said she wanted to go out to the house and look around."

Tom closed his eyes. She'd mentioned doing this on their way back from talking to Renate and Father Joe. He'd known she was more than curious, not only about the place her parents had owned for over twenty years, but also about the woman who lived there.

He should have carved out time to go with her. Well, at least he had a good excuse for seeking her out. She'd be even more curious when he told her the DNA findings.

"Quite honestly," Bianca said, "between you and me, she knew everyone was coming tonight, and she's tired of people asking her so many questions. I don't blame her. Wish I hadn't asked so many."

"At least you answered a few, too."

"I did, didn't I?"

He was stuck for a few minutes, chatting with Bianca's guests, but he didn't stay long.

Outside, twilight touched the air. Around him, some small goblins were holding hands with a parent or sibling and door-knocking. He hit the siren, a short blast, and earned a few smiles.

Oscar had been carrying candy around all week. For the first time in a long time, Tom wished he'd thought to do the same. And he remembered a time, long ago, when he'd imagined walking around with his own son, maybe dressed like a junior chief of police.

He called Leann, told her he'd take a little extra time and headed for the town limits, thinking that gray skies weren't so bad. They were perfect for the type of night it was. Any other time he'd have been driving down this road, he'd have been feeling the gloom.

But he was on his way to be with Heather.

The Turners' place looked empty. They must be in town. Last year, Gloria had decorated her wheelchair so it looked like something a superhero would drive around town in. Albert had refused to dress like a sidekick—it probably was too much of a stretch for the older man.

There were no streetlights on the dirt road leading to Heather's house, but even from a distance, he could see a light was on in the living room. Pulling into the driveway, he noted that she needed air in her car's rear tire. Then he got out and headed up the walk.

The door opened before he could knock.

"I saw you coming down the road. I'm glad your SUV is so clearly cop-issue."

"You a little spooked?"

"Just a little. It's true, this is the middle of nowhere. And I'm wondering why I chose Halloween of all nights."

He followed her into a living room with a comfortable couch, two armchairs, a coffee table and a television. A clock on the wall had stalled at nine o'clock. "Anything amiss?" he asked, sinking into the sofa's cushions.

"Far as I can see," Heather said, "the place is neat and clean—very clean, actually. Abigail's room is full of well-loved toys and books. Rachel's room is fairly empty." She moved a *Frozen* video case off of the armchair next to the couch, and sat. She didn't appear to be sinking and she looked fairly comfortable as she snagged the DVD off the side table and placed it safely back into its case.

"Anything that might lead to Jeremy Salinas?"

"You think she knows where he is?"

"She says no, but she might have a clue she's not aware of."

"She's terrified of him and hiding in the most obvious place."

"What?"

"Well, think about it. She's hiding from him, and she came back here. She thinks this is the last place he'd come. Oh, and no way has she kept anything tying her to him. She wouldn't want anything that tainted in the same house as Abigail."

"You're comparing her to you. You wouldn't keep anything of his near a child of yours. She's Rachel. You're Heather."

"Glad you noticed," Heather said.

He looked around the living room. A lone light, center of the ceiling, long cord hanging down, lit the room. The walls boasted the clock, still pointing to nine, and one photograph. Abigail. Rachel probably didn't want her photo anywhere, not when he, the chief of police, kept pounding on her door asking about Richard.

"I turned off the water for the washer and dryer," Heather said. "I brought what little mail there was in. The milk in the fridge is good for another week."

PAMELA TRACY   341

"She won't be home that soon," Tom predicted.

Heather nodded.

"Neither will Richard. And that's if he ever recovers. Stopped by this morning. No change."

"Who will care for Abigail? Surely there must be someone…"

Tom shook his head. "Abigail will stay in temporary foster care. Then she'll be placed into either a group home or long-term until Richard gets better and is released."

"How long will he be in jail?"

"That's not something I can answer."

"You probably have an idea."

"Years. And his fine will be substantial. Lucille died as a result of her injuries."

"What if the family doesn't want to press charges? Lucille had already forgiven him, and she'd told her family to do the same."

"But—"

"Have you asked them?"

He felt somewhat indignant that she'd question him. "Look. Richard drove away. If he'd stayed and administered—"

"Why did he drive away?"

"We don't know for sure. However—"

"Just like you didn't know why Rachel got

out of the car. You didn't know that Jeremy Salinas threatened to shoot her and her unborn baby just moments before he shot Max."

The living room was tiny, and getting tinier by the word.

She was right. Partly. He needed to rethink a few things.

Tom cleared his throat. "Speaking of Rachel, that's why I drove out here."

"Oh…" Heather leaned forward. "You learn something new?"

"We got the results back from the DNA testing."

"Mom's hairbrush, dad's ancient toothbrush."

"It was enough."

She clasped her hands in her lap and waited, not quite looking at him and definitely not waiting for him. "Rachel's my half sister. I was expecting this."

Tom leaned forward, wishing he hadn't sat down. "Hear me out. The forensic scientist I spoke with in Albuquerque said that half siblings share twenty-five percent of their genes."

"Okay."

"Full siblings share fifty percent."

"Okay." This time her answer came a bit slower.

"You and Rachel are full siblings."

She stood, looked very much like she wanted to go somewhere, but then frowned and sat down. "You mean that Kyle Ramsey is my biological father?"

"Not a chance. We'd sent a summary of the case to the forensic lab. They had access to Kyle's DNA as he's in prison now. No match, not for you or Rachel."

"Then, who is ?"

"We don't know yet. We're back to it being someone in town."

"Maybe we'll never know."

"That could be."

"I need to talk to Rachel. Have you told her yet?"

"No, I'll do it tonight or tomorrow morning."

"My full sister. Wow."

He tried to smile. He wanted to. But in his book, being related to Rachel Ramsey wasn't something to celebrate. Even as he helped her gather her belongings and lock up the place, he thought about the future. Because he knew

Heather would make a place for Rachel in her life. They'd visit, send care packages and more.

Only for Heather could he make this exception.

CHAPTER TWENTY-THREE

LATE THE NEXT AFTERNOON, Heather walked into the police station. Leann was at the front desk. "Hey," she said, looking up. "Chief's not around."

"I'm not here to see him. I'd like to visit with Rachel."

Leann's smile slipped. "I'm not sure the chief would okay that."

"Rachel's allowed visitors, isn't she?"

"Yes."

"Then it really doesn't matter what the chief would okay." Heather had spent the morning with social services. She'd explained who she was, asked to take over Abigail's care from the approved foster parents, and started filling out the forms. She had made some decisions. She was staying in Sarasota Falls, and while Rachel was incarcerated, Heather intended to watch over Abigail.

"Hold on. Let me call him."

Heather waited, not patiently. She'd mulled this over all night and again this morning. Full sisters. Everything clicked into place.

"Chief says he can be here in twenty minutes."

"I took today off work. I can meet whenever he can."

"Heather, this isn't a good idea," Leann began.

"Do I need to fill out any paperwork?" Heather asked.

Leann looked around. Heather knew she was hoping that Oscar or Lucas would suddenly show up, offer a second opinion, possibly talk some sense into Heather.

Soon Heather was filling out the visitor-information card and then following Leann down a hall to the same room and same table where Tom had interrogated her.

"I still don't think this is a good idea," Leann said, heading out the door, only to return with Rachel. "I'll be right here in the hallway. Shout if you need anything."

Rachel looked tired.

"You doing okay?" Heather asked. It seemed like a lame question.

"No."

"Can I get you anything?"

Rachel gave a half smirk; it looked half-hearted. "No."

"Did Tom talk to you already?"

"You mean about us being sisters and all? Yes, he did. I'm not surprised. My mom said that my dad wasn't exactly faithful. Bit of a surprise, though, finding out about you. Bigger, and better, surprise finding out my dad isn't Kyle."

"You have any idea who our father is?"

"Look—" Rachel leaned forward, giving Heather pause, scaring her a bit "—I've got more to worry about than who the sperm donor is. I realize you're on a quest to discover your past, but I—"

"I saw Abigail this morning."

Rachel's posture changed. The toughness softened. She sat up. "How is she? Did she ask about me? How come you saw her?"

"She's in foster care and with a really good family. I've been asked not to share their name, some kind of legality. But, Rachel, listen to me. I've already set up another meeting with social services. If it's okay with you, I'm willing to take Abigail until you're out. I—I guess I'm her aunt. I'll even bring her to visit you."

"I don't want her to visit me in jail."

"Okay, then I'll make sure there's lots of letters and videos and—"

"I—I don't like this. I don't know you. And you're dating the chief of police. He'd never take on Abigail. He hates me more than life."

"No, he doesn't. He'd take on Abigail. I know he would."

"No."

"Rachel, think about it. Right now, Abigail's in a temporary foster home. When you're sentenced, she could go to a family—"

"Richard will watch her. He'll wake up. He has to."

"He'll be serving time, too. A lot, maybe. I'm willing to watch her as long as it takes."

"Are you willing to stop seeing the chief of police?"

"No, because you're wrong about him.

"I'm not."

"Okay." Heather pushed herself up. "I've made an offer. I really want to watch Abigail for you. Get to know the only niece I have. But I respect your wishes." She took two steps toward the door and raised her hand to knock, letting Leann know she was ready to leave.

"Why would you do that?" Rachel said softly.

Heather rested her forehead against the door, feeling the smooth, hard wood. "I don't know. Two people took me in when my situation was worse than Abigail's. Apparently, I had bruises. I keep thinking about it. I, well, I was lucky. Someone took me out of a bad situation, even if they had to do it in an unusual way. I had the best childhood a kid could hope for. I wish you'd have followed, been with me. Taking Abigail, getting close to you, might be a mistake, but who knows, maybe some day we'll be family, there for each other."

"You'll watch over Abigail, so she's not in the system, switched from place to place, maybe hurt? And that Jeremy won't find out? You'll see that the chief is good to her?"

"I will. You already know that I own the house you live in. I'll move in there, put her in school, make as much of a home as I can. I helped my mom with her childcare business. I like kids. I'll be Aunt Heather. When you get out, Abigail will be waiting for you. I will, too. We, uh, share the same blood."

Rachel's jaw clenched. Heather could see the

battle raging in her eyes. It had to hurt, having no control.

"For Abigail, I'll do anything. Unfortunately, I don't know who *our* father is. I remember Kyle. I was glad he left. There were a few townies who hung around. I'll give you their names, but I don't hold out much hope. They were brief and partiers. And, if you dig, you'll find an angry wife glaring at you. I know I opened the door to that house a time or two to a woman looking for her husband. Not fun."

"Bianca said that Diane arrived in town with me. I was almost two."

"So, someone she knew before she moved here, but someone she was with while she was with Kyle."

It was a slightly different Rachel now. One who was sitting straight, still looking tired but not as wounded. "Maybe you should ask Bianca some more questions."

Heather paused, took a breath, tried to remember the conversation and then let out the breath. "Bianca did say something else. She said that Diane arrived in town in an old burgundy-and-black Studebaker. I just saw one the other day. Who…?"

"The mayor drives a Studebaker," Rachel responded. "He loves old cars. Buys them and fixes them up. Diane told me she'd purchased it from her family."

"Oh, wow. The mayor. I work for his brother." Heather's mind was going in all directions, remembering other things, like the little girl with the chipped tooth and the... birthmark.

Heather didn't like the ideas forming in her mind. The mayor collected old cars, which meant he might have known Diane before she moved to town.

Puzzle pieces were falling into place. Did they fit? Or was she forcing them? Days ago, she'd considered that little girl sitting in the dental chair, Beatrice, a distant relation. Now she figured not-so-distant.

"Ew," Rachel said, after Heather shared her concerns, "the mayor might be our father. Ew."

Heather felt the same way.

"I DON'T BELIEVE IT." Tom felt like he'd been kicked in the gut and stepped on. The mayor? No way. Yet, everything both Heather and Rachel said made perfect sense.

"I'm not even sure what crime I can charge

the mayor with unless he had something to do with your kidnapping. Even then, if he gave permission for Sarah and Ray to take you, and Diane didn't protest, his lawyers will have a field day."

"He won't want his name plastered all over the newspaper," Heather said.

"He won't want his story turned into a TV movie like Shelley Guzman's story was," Rachel added.

Right now, the two of them even sounded alike. He sucked in a breath so quickly it whistled. Just last night, when he'd returned to work, Lucas had asked some hard questions. Questions that Tom thought he'd dealt with.

"You've been with Heather?" Lucas had asked.

"I told her about the DNA."

"Had to do it on Halloween this late at night?" Lucas had queried.

"Had to," Tom admitted.

Lucas had waited a moment, then asked, "Can you get past how much Heather looks like Rachel?"

"Not a problem," Tom had said. "Those two are nothing alike."

But looking at them now, listening to them, he realized what he already knew.

They were very much alike.

Tom wouldn't let it be a problem.

But it was, because they'd been having a discussion and he'd been distracted by his thoughts about Heather.

"What? What did you just say?"

"I just," Rachel said, "pointed out that the only person in town who has one of the mayor's antique cars is Jason Bitmore."

"What made you think of that?" Tom asked.

"Because I remember being surprised when he sold it to Jason," Rachel said. "He never sold his cars. They're in a big shed in the back of his property."

"You've been there."

She blushed. "With Jeremy. He, um—"

"Stole the wheels off three classic cars," Tom said, finishing her sentence. "Six years ago. On a Halloween night."

"He did," Rachel admitted.

"It seems my job just got harder." Tom motioned for Leann. She took Rachel back to her cell while Heather followed Tom to his office. He motioned for her to sit while he called Oscar and asked his deputy to bring in Jason

Bitmore. A little back-and-forth followed with Tom instructing Oscar to find out how and why Jason managed to convince Mayor Goodman to part with an antique car.

Tom already knew what Oscar would find out. It hadn't been a coincidence that Jason had a car accident the night the Duponts and Sarasota Sweets had been broken in to. Jason had been busy that night and had gotten careless.

"Oh," Tom added, "and find out why he broke in to your wife's shop."

Next, Tom called the sheriff in Ritter, Texas, and gave the man the mayor's name and asked him to visit a man named Owen Tanner.

"He locates old cars and sells them to those who want to—"

"We know him," the sheriff said.

"I need you to fax me copies of any dealings he had with Mayor Rick Goodman. And, no, I don't have a subpoena. If he asks for one, tell him you'll have it in twenty-four hours."

"Doubt he keeps records," the sheriff informed him.

"You figured it all out," he mused after he'd gotten off the phone. "Of course, the only ones who might be able to put the mayor and Diane together nine months before your birth would possibly be her father. Owen Tanner. He finds old cars and sells them for profit. Maybe he keeps records."

"I heard you," she said.

"You find out anything else from Rachel?"

"No, not really."

He stood, reached out a hand to help her up and pulled Heather to him. "You all right?"

"I am. I really am. What are you going to do next?"

"Head out and talk to the mayor."

"Can I go with you?"

"Why?"

"I want to see him. Maybe—"

"No, not a good idea. It looks like he did all he could to convince you to get out of town."

"Wimp," she said.

"Yes, and he has a lot to own up to. I've worked with him for a long time, since I earned this badge. And, yes, he's flawed…" He paused, then added, "Misguided."

"Like Rachel used to be."

"There's a big difference between being party to a murder and—"

"Cheating on your wife, having children you don't take care of and, if you consider Jason, we can probably add contributing to the delinquency of a minor."

"Who taught you all this cop-think?" The corner of his mouth turned up.

"You did."

He stepped around his desk and gathered her in his arms. "I'm glad it's over. Now things can settle down, and we can really get to know each other. You are staying?"

It was a question, but it also sounded like a gentle command.

"Yes, today I told Rachel that I'll take care of Abigail until she's out of jail or Richard is well enough."

"You're talking Jeremy Salinas's child?"

"Yes, Rachel's child. My niece." Her voice was raised, and her brow furrowed in frustration. "I can't believe you're surprised by my offer."

"And I can't believe you'd make such an offer without talking to me."

"Why—why would I talk to you first? I'm doing the right thing, the only thing."

"I'm not sure I could take on Jeremy Salinas's child."

"You don't have to. I am."

"Yes, but I intend to take on you. I was even thinking forever."

"Abigail had nothing to do with your partner's death."

His throat tightened. A rational part of him told him to deal with it. But his heart was torn.

When Heather walked out of the room, his heart was broken. Her steps sounded down the hall. She was hurrying. She wanted away from him.

Like his ex-wife had wanted away from him.

He had a code. Putting on his hat, he headed down the hall, nodded to Leann and told her where he was going before he beckoned Lucas to join him. He needed backup for dealing with the mayor.

And what he needed for dealing with Heather was to be able to talk to his best friend. But Max couldn't give advice, thanks to Rachel and Jeremy.

No, he couldn't look at Abigail every day knowing her parentage.

It was wrong. He knew it. He just couldn't let his heart change his mind.

Not about this.

CHAPTER TWENTY-FOUR

"RICHARD WOKE UP! This morning!" Bianca yelled up the stairs. Then, she added, "And it looks like he'll be all right. I mean they can't tell about everything yet, but he's talking cohesively."

Tom, Heather thought, would probably add "and he should be able to stand trial."

"Tom's allowing Rachel a compassionate visit," Bianca continued.

Okay, Heather gave Tom a point for that small mercy.

"They're on their way over. I mean Oscar and Tom. Apparently, they have some things to tell us. Er, you," Bianca amended.

It had been four days since Heather'd seen Tom. Her heart danced a little, but she knew how to turn off the music of her soul. Tom didn't deserve such a reception.

Almost every day, after work, Heather had driven to the foster parents' home in a nearby community north of Sarasota Falls to sec Abigail. Rachel and Richard had done a great job of raising a happy, healthy little girl, who felt a whole lot better knowing she had an aunt who looked "exactly like Mama."

Tom was wrong to put the sins of the father on Abigail.

"They must have called from the squad car," Bianca said when the front door opened. Oscar came in first, bypassed the doughnuts and grabbed an apple before giving Bianca a peck on the cheek.

"You don't want a doughnut?" she asked.

"Shelley can't seem to stop baking. If we have a dozen kids, I'll be bigger than a house."

Tom apparently didn't have the same worry. He took a doughnut and settled in one of Bianca's living room chairs. Bianca herded Oscar into the room and gestured for Heather.

"It was my memory that solved this case, so I get to hear everything. It's only fair."

A few seconds of silence followed before Oscar leaned forward and said, "Chief says the mayor's house was practically empty. He couldn't get over the change because he remembered it when it used to practically burst at its seams with a wife and four children."

Tom nodded. "His family used to host an Easter egg hunt in their backyard. We kids looked forward to it all year."

Heather almost felt sorry for the mayor. Almost.

"He couldn't stop talking," Tom said. "He must have had all the guilt bottled up. The mayor knew he'd messed up, almost continuously for twenty-eight years, from when he'd purchased an old car from Owen Tanner and started an affair with Tanner's youngest daughter."

"Diane," Bianca breathed.

"Some of this we got from her father, who is still alive but doesn't want anything to do with—" Oscar sent Heather an apologetic glance "—with any of this. Apparently, Diane Tanner considered the mayor quite a catch. It apparently hadn't occurred to her that, since he was married, he was already caught."

"How old was she?"

"Eighteen."

"And he a man of forty-something," Bianca muttered.

"After Heather's birth and Diane's family's annoyance with her, she drove the car Mayor

Goodman purchased to Sarasota Falls and stayed."

"How did she hook up with Kyle Ramsey?"

"She got mad at the mayor and did it to spite him. At least that's what he says."

"Ew," Heather said, thinking about Rachel. "But she didn't stay mad forever." Again, thinking about Rachel.

"That must have given Mayor Goodman quite an ulcer," Bianca said.

Tom agreed. "In Goodman's mind, Diane was a mistake that dominoed. He says he watched Diane with you and didn't like what he saw. Heather, your parents didn't exactly kidnap you. Goodman was your dad's landlord, knew he was a good guy and saw that a romance was brewing between him and Sarah. He also knew your dad was pretty much broke and that your mom couldn't have children. He made them an offer they couldn't refuse."

"To kidnap me."

"No, Goodman is your father. It's not kidnapping if the parties willingly go into an adoption. They used an out-of-state lawyer and Sarah and Ray took custody of you."

"Why didn't I find any of that paperwork?"

"Goodman says he burned it, too afraid

someone would find it. Maybe Sarah and Ray thought the same."

"Then the mayor got Diane pregnant again. And this time, she wasn't eighteen and somewhat naïve. She made him pay. He was terrified she'd expose him."

"I never trusted the mayor." Bianca frowned. "I didn't vote for him. But why, if he was paying, why didn't they live better?"

"The mayor says Diane didn't hold on to the money. Much of it disappeared into Kyle's pocket or she used it for partying."

Heather flinched, again thinking about Rachel.

"The mayor contacted your parents," Oscar continued. "They came here but realized that Diane was out of control. You and Tom were right. They were afraid that taking on Rachel might mean losing you."

"So, they bought the house and rented it to Diane."

"With the mayor paying the rent most of the time."

"What a tangled web of secrets," Bianca said, standing and stretching. "Glad this story has a happy ending."

Tom didn't look Heather's way. Fine. Sometimes happy endings took time. Sometimes, a happy ending wasn't the one you expected.

Both Bianca and Heather followed Tom and Oscar out to the SUV.

"We're glad you stopped by," Bianca said. "We were wondering…"

"You still want my truck on Saturday?" Oscar asked.

"Yes," Heather said, "I don't have much. If I take your truck instead of my—"

"Toy car," Tom interrupted.

"Then I'll only need to make one trip."

"She's moving to her house this weekend," Bianca explained. "She wants to clean it real good, get it ready for Abigail."

"You hear anything?" Oscar asked.

"They said after I get a permanent address, they'll do a home visit. Then, most likely I can take over her care."

"It can take weeks, months even," Oscar advised.

"Not this time," Heather said. "I'll call social services every day if I have to."

Oscar climbed into the passenger seat. Tom walked around to the driver's side. Heather saw him open his mouth, like he wanted to say something, but he didn't.

Instead, he tipped his hat and then hopped in his SUV and drove away.

Stubborn man.

Stubborn man that she loved.

Couldn't have.

Didn't need.

"HI, TOM." JIMMY WALKER, old, bent and a member of the chamber of commerce, as well as owner of the Station Diner, entered Tom's office. Lately, time seemed to crawl and the cases handed to Tom were mundane.

"Jimmy, what can I do for you?"

"Well, you know I'm on the town council." Tom did know this. And he could guess what was coming next.

"You're stepping into the role of mayor."

"No." Jimmy coughed and sat down. Tom couldn't remember a time the man had been healthy. Heck, he couldn't remember a time Jimmy had been young.

"I'm not taking over as mayor. Health won't allow it, and besides, we've got a better candidate in mind."

Tom turned away from his computer screen, folded his hands in front of him and gave the man his full attention. "What's up, Jimmy?"

"We're not a big town," Jimmy began. "We don't have a deputy mayor, and so, yes, according to bylaws, with my seniority, I'm next in line."

"Then, you can just appoint an acting mayor until..." Tom's words tapered off. "No, you're not here to ask me to be mayor."

"I am. We had a special meeting tonight. It was unanimous."

"Sure it was. No one was there to talk any sense about why I'm not the one for the job."

"It would only be temporary."

"No, it wouldn't. Once you got me in place, I'd be there forever. I'm happy as the chief of police."

"You're not happy," Leann called from the front-desk area.

"You want me to close the door?" Jimmy offered.

"No. We're good."

"I'm sorry you're not happy. You want to talk about it?"

Tom cocked his head. "Are you serious?"

"I am. I know you and Heather are having problems. I never married, but over at the diner I hear quite a bit. I've given advice to quite a few couples—"

Tom held up his hand, effectively halting Jimmy.

"Okay." Jimmy, making a big production of it, stood. "I'm not done talking to you. You'd be a great mayor. You're what this town needs. Plus, there's at least two of your staff who could be acting chief. We don't have anyone—"

"Willing to be mayor. I get it. The answer is still no."

Tom heard the front-desk phone ring as he handed Jimmy his hat. "Bianca will be here tomorrow," Jimmy said. "We'll take turns bugging you until you accept."

"Great."

"If you'd just—"

"Not interested."

Leann skidded to a stop in front of him. "Chief, that was social services. Abigail Ramsey's missing."

Life, as Tom knew it, had just stopped being mundane. "Have you called Heather?"

"No, but she was there earlier this morning, in Springer. Social services thinks maybe Heather took Abigail."

"Pfftt, not a chance. Keep trying Heather. She gets spotty reception out at her place. I'm going to make her get a landline. First thing I do after finding Abigail."

"You going to the foster family's place?" Leann asked.

"Right after I find Heather. You stay here. Call Oscar and Lucas, find out where they are and tell them they'll hear from me"

"Should I tell Rachel?"

"Get Bianca over here. You can tell Rachel with Bianca in the room and then Bianca can stay with her while you man things out front. We'll tell Richard in a few hours. He's still weak and I don't want to worry him if we find the little girl quickly."

"Got it." Leann flew out to the front.

Photos. Tom wanted photos of Abigail. He hated that the foster family's place and Heather's property, in Sarasota Falls, were in opposite directions. And he was mad at himself. He should have been out there with Heather, giving her advice and helping.

The SUV started easily and Tom headed for the farmhouse. It had been second nature back when he was trying to trip up Richard, but now when it should have felt right, it felt wrong. He called Oscar and told him to gather as many able-bodied men and women as he could and get to the foster family's address as fast as they could.

Social services would have photos, he told himself, but maybe he'd find a few at Heather's place. He figured it still had Rachel and Abigail's belongings.

But her car wasn't in the driveway.

He turned around, headed for the Turners'. Not seeing her car there, either, he immediately left, and his phone pinged. Quickly, he filled in Albert Turner on what was happening. The past chief of police had spotted his SUV through the window. He said he was already in his truck before Tom was able to say goodbye. His job: find Heather.

Tom tried Heather's phone again as his SUV skidded onto the highway. No answer.

Where was she?

He called Lucas, who answered, "They're gathering forces. Wouldn't surprise me if the ladies' bible-study group beats you there."

"What are you doing?" Tom asked, not surprised that his lieutenant had already heard the news and was acting.

"Halfway there. I'll bet you, too."

Instead, Tom beat Lucas. Siren on, pedal to the metal, he passed every car in front of him.

He recognized all of them as friends heading a good hour away to help look for the missing five-year-old girl. For a town with a small population, Springer, with Sarasota Falls's aid, lit up the sky.

Tom's phone pinged again. Leann. "I just got off the phone with Heather. She's on her way."

"Tell her to drive carefully," Tom barked.

"Call her yourself," Leann barked back.

The forces had commandeered the nearby grade school for their headquarters. At Tom's direction, Oscar began organizing the volunteers. Tom, meanwhile, couldn't let go of his phone, making call after call, desperate for any new news. Oscar approached him. "We've divided into four teams. Everyone's double-timing it out there. I've got people in every direction and branched all the way to the national forest. The temperature is dropping. We really don't want that little girl outside when it gets cold. They don't think she's wearing a coat."

"Do you know why or when she wandered away?"

"Probably an hour ago, after her aunt left. The foster mom put on *Frozen* and went in to do the dishes. When she came back, the little girl was gone. Door wide open. She ran around the neighborhood, but no luck. That was when she called social services to let them know."

"Does the mom think she was taken or wandered away?"

"Unsure."

Tom's phone buzzed. He pressed the screen and slapped the cell to his ear. "Riley."

"State police here. We've just heard that the aunt's been found and is on her way to your location. I'm looking forward to you questioning her."

"She had nothing to do with it."

"How do you know?"

"Because I'm going to marry the aunt. She's about to become a cop's wife, and she's smart enough to do the right thing." He hung up.

Oscar smiled. "Good enough. All the rural routes are covered. Why don't you go back over the neighborhood closest to the house?"

Tom's phone pinged. This time it was Lucas. "I'm at Route Two at the junction. I found a shoe."

"A little girl's shoe?"

"Would I have called about any other kind? I'm near the pocket of trees where the road swerves sharply to the left."

"Abigail made it that far?" Tom was amazed.

"I'm hoping that if her shoe made it this far, Abigail did."

Tom quickly filled in the deputy and then jogged out to his SUV. Ten minutes later, he joined Lucas in shining a flashlight left and right.

"Kids do the strangest things," Lucas said. "My middle daughter ran away when she was eleven. Wrote us a note that she was going to live in a Dumpster. Instead, she went to her best friend's house. That mom served only green peas for supper that night and said that was the only thing they ever ate. I had my daughter back the same evening. To this day, she hates green peas."

"Here's another shoe." Tom bent down, running his flashlight over dry remnants of grass and dead leaves. He reached out to tug the red tennis shoe toward him and saw the sock and the bare leg and the sleeping child.

"Thank God," he breathed, bending down to pick her up.

"Cold," she murmured in his ear. "Want Mommy."

"We'll see what we can do," he promised. "First, are you hurt?"

"No."

"Did somebody bring you here?"

"No, I walked. I want to find Auntie. But I got lost."

Lucas quickly left and soon returned with a blanket to wrap Abigail in.

"She's okay," Tom said. "Really okay. She wanted to be with Heather. I don't blame her. I want the same thing myself."

"If you'd figured that out sooner, we'd not be out here," Lucas muttered.

They'd no more than loaded Abigail in Tom's back seat when a tiny compact sent dirt flying as it swung behind Tom's SUV. Heather opened its door, fell out and then hurried to Tom's side. "You found her. Is she okay? What happened?"

"Lucas and I found her. She's all right. A bit shaken up and searching for you."

"Oh, sweetie."

"I looked for you. You drove way too fast."

"Can I get in with her?"

"Sure."

Crawling into the SUV's backseat, Heather gathered Abigail into her lap and stroked her hair. "Could we find another blanket?" she called.

"I've got one in the trunk." Tom fetched it, tucked it around Abigail.

"You did a great job organizing the search. Thank you," Heather said.

"It's my job, but thanks. Right now, we should get Abigail to the doctor."

"Yes, let's hurry."

Tom asked Lucas to make sure everyone had gotten word of Abigail's safe return.

Tom locked and shut Heather's driver-side door before returning to his SUV. When he climbed in, Heather asked, "Which doctor?"

"There's one at the school where they set up a base during the search. We'll go there. Have him check Abigail out, just to be sure. By the way, where were you?"

"I was at the library. I wanted to use its Wi-Fi so I could read about social services. I want Abigail with me, and everything seems to take forever."

"How did you find out what was going on?"

"Maureen saw my car in the parking lot and came in, wondering why I was there and not here. I almost fainted. I was so-o-o scared."

"I wasn't scared," Abigail insisted. "I was lost."

"You were, sweetie. And don't get lost ever again."

It only took ten minutes for the doctor to assess the few scratches Abigail obtained during her "wilderness adventure" as he called it. Then Tom found himself looking into Heather's eyes as she put an arm around Abigail.

"Would you mind waiting in the car," he said to Heather. "I need to make a quick phone call."

"I want to stay with Abigail."

"She's almost done. Trust me, I won't let her out of my sight," Tom said.

She nodded and left through the school's main doors, thanking the searchers who were returning. Most made their way over to Tom in order to tousle Abigail's hair. A few took photos; all sighed in relief.

His first call went to Jimmy Walker. His first question was "How much good can a mayor do?" He liked the answer. Didn't need any more convincing.

Then he picked up Abigail, holding her tightly in his arms, and walked out to tell the woman he loved that he'd been an idiot and that he'd be willing to raise a dozen Abigails with her.

First, though, he opened the back door of the SUV and handed Abigail to Heather. "She's about to fall asleep standing up," he said.

"Poor baby." Heather tucked the two blankets around Abigail and rubbed the child's arm. "Thank you, again, for all you did. You... you were amazing."

"You're the one who's amazing."

He scooched into the back with them.

"Heather Graves, let me introduce myself. I'm chief of police and acting mayor, Tom Riley," he whispered. Abigail's eyes were still shut tight.

"Mayor?"

"I'd wager that a letter from the mayor to social services about temporary custody of a certain five-year-old may be a swaying factor in my taking on the role. And there are plenty of other great things I'd like to see happen for the town. Seems social services is under my jurisdiction. So, if all goes well, even as soon as tomorrow, we'll be able to pick up Abigail."

"Custody."

"I approve of one-word responses. Sometimes, one word is all that is necessary. By the way, will you marry me? I don't think I can do this custody thing alone. I don't know much about children, and quite frankly—"

Heather firmly took his chin, pulled it her way and kissed him hard and long.

She didn't need words, truly—not a single one, it appeared. Sometimes actions were the best indicator.

"Good," he murmured against her lips, "because I don't ever want to go four days without seeing you ever again."

"I trust that it will never happen," she said, through the many kisses that did not stop.

"Are you kissing for real?" The question came from a tired voice in the back seat.

Tom thought about answering. Instead he chuckled as Abigail summed up what she was witnessing with a single word.

"Ew."

* * * * *

If you enjoyed this heart-stopping and heartfelt romance from Pamela Tracy, check out her other Harlequin Heartwarming titles:

KATIE'S RESCUE
WHAT JANIE SAW
HOLIDAY HOMECOMING
SMALL-TOWN SECRETS
THE MISSING TWIN
A HEARTWARMING THANKSGIVING
HOLDING OUT FOR A HERO

Get 2 Free Books,
Plus 2 Free Gifts—
just for trying the Reader Service!

Love Inspired®

LI17R2

Get 2 Free Books,
<u>Plus</u> 2 Free Gifts—
just for trying the Reader Service!

LIS17R2

Get 2 Free Books,
Plus 2 Free Gifts—
just for trying the Reader Service!

HARLEQUIN *super romance*

Get 2 Free Books,
Plus 2 Free Gifts -
just for trying the *Reader Service!*

STRS17R